salt and saffron

salt and saffron

Kamila Shamsie

B L O O M S B U R Y
LONDON · BERLIN · NEW YORK · SYDNEY

First published in Great Britain in 2000

Copyright © 2000 by Kamila Shamsie

The moral right of the author has been asserted

Bloomsbury Publishing Plc,
50 Bedford Square, London, WC1B 3DP

A CIP catalogue record for this book
is available from the British Library

ISBN 978 0 7475 5395 3

10 9 8 7 6 5 4

Typeset by Hewer Text Ltd, Edinburgh
Printed by Clays Ltd, St Ives plc

ACKNOWLEDGEMENTS

I'd like to thank: Saman, for the moment of fear; my parents, for double-checking facts and pointing out errors; my grandmother, Begum Jahanara Habibullah, whose memoirs were a wonderful source of information about courtly life; Marianna Karim, for helping with the historical details (the errors are all mine); Aamer Hussein, for correcting my Urdu, and other such helpful matters; the Haiders, for the lizard stories; Elizabeth Porto, for her insight; and Margaret Halton, for making this into a better book.

For Victoria Hobbs and Alexandra Pringle

THE HOUSE OF DARD-E-DIL

(showing those characters who appear in this story)

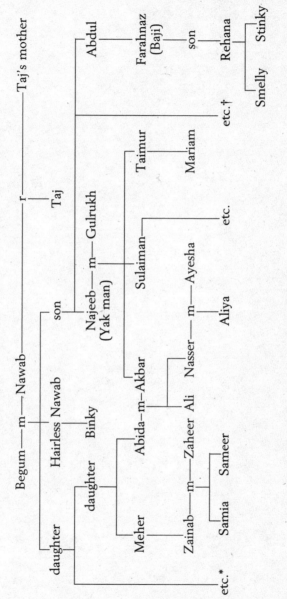

*Great-Aunt One-Liner, Booby, Usman related to Aliya through this line

†Starched Aunts, Mousy Cousin, Bachelor Uncle related to Aliya through this line

All right, don't scoff, mock or disbelieve: we live in mortal fear of not-quite-twins.

Of course, reduce all stories to their basic elements and you'll see all families are possessed of prejudice – that alternative name for 'fear'. The only thing that makes us stand apart is our particular choice of . . . I want to say 'bugaboo'. I often want to say 'bugaboo'. It's a word that demands to be said out loud, particularly among bilingual Pakistanis who recognize its resemblance to 'baghal boo' or 'armpit odour', but its meaning 'object of baseless terror' makes it misleading in this conversation. Nothing baseless in our terror; we have five hundred years of empirical evidence on which to base our fear of not-quite-twins. Ours has always been a scientific family, that way. So I suppose we are unusual. Because, though we are like all families in the almost religious fervour of our prejudices, all the other families we know can point to nothing but stereotype, ignorance and jealousy of their own privilege as a basis for those prejudices and, I'll admit, our contrasting historicity has always made us feel superior.

One of my earliest memories is of Dadi cackling when

she heard the news of Hussain Asif's marriage to Natasha Shah. 'Shia Muhajir marries Sunni Sindhi! How will the bigots react? Disown your own kind, or accept the enemy! Ming-ling! Ring-a-ling!' Of course, no multi-culti appreciation of marrying across both sect and ethnicity lay at the root of my grandmother's words. She merely wanted all other family biases confounded and challenged so that she could hold up her head and say, 'We of the royal family of Dard-e-Dil have always held true to our family fears.' No marriages, conversions or redistributions of wealth can change that. Not-quite-twins are not-quite-twins; no way around that. Oh, they may escape undetected for a time, but ultimately they are incapable of disguise, incapable of escaping the category into which they are born, incapable of causing our family anything but pain. I know. I've read the histories.

Confused? Would you rather I changed the topic to yak milk production?

Chapter One

Yak's milk is green. But, of course, I never got round to telling my fellow passengers that choice tidbit. It takes more than a Nepalese ox to distract attention away from my family. And the occupant of the aisle seat across from me was so grateful for my high-volume chatter – which replaced the usual boredom and non-recycled air of the transatlantic economy-class cabin with murder, war, jealousy, and rapidly reversing fortune – that he pulled my luggage off the conveyor belt at Heathrow while I was still stuck in the immigration line, waiting for a turbaned Sikh who dropped his aitches to finish scrutinizing my Pakistani passport.

'Here,' aisle seat said in an American accent, when I finally zigzagged my way to the conveyor belt through luggage trolleys, unknown languages and a hysterical Nordic man who had just been informed that his baggage had been mysteriously rerouted to Nicaragua. 'I figured this was yours. Any others?'

I wanted to say, Where are you from? You look Pakistani now that you've removed your baseball cap, though on the plane I assumed you were a tanned, possibly multi-racial,

American. But instead I shook my head, no, and hoisted my grey suitcase with its Gemini zodiac sticker on to a trolley. Aisle seat said I should go ahead, he was still waiting for his second suitcase, no point in me hanging around. He was just being polite, of course – that much was obvious by the pauses between words and the way his eyes darted around the terminal building to register his distaste for the surroundings – but at that moment I really didn't have the energy that the laws of reciprocal courtesy required so I just nodded and thanked him. We hugged goodbye (his initiative, but I saw no reason to resist) and when I turned to go he said, 'Hey, Aliya. How much of it is true?'

I smiled. 'A good storyteller never tells.'

I walked a few steps away and then turned back. My body had just begun to register the feel of his arms around me. What would my grandmother say if she knew I'd been hugging strange men in airports? He was facing away from me, staring at the leather flaps at the end of the conveyor belt through which the luggage emerged, so I could continue to look at him and regret that I'd spent so much time on the plane chattering to anyone who cared to listen (two girls had even sat cross-legged in the aisle, listening to my stories until the flight attendant shooed them away and then hung around herself, a pot of coffee cooling in her hand). If I'd been a little less intent on entertaining everyone maybe I would have leant over the aisle and talked, actually talked, to him. He knew all my family stories – all, except the most important one – and I didn't even know his name. I moved towards him, then felt absurd and walked away.

I stepped out into London. Filled my lungs with the 6 a.m. air of summer and slowly, in the lingering manner in which you might peel off a bandage in order to prolong the joy of seeing skin where last there was exposed flesh, I exhaled all residues of aeroplanes and airports from my system. I could have spread my arms wide and spun in tiptoed circles with the joy of terra firma and familiar breezes, but it seemed more expedient to flag down the nearest taxi instead.

'Where are you coming from?' the cabbie asked, after we had been driving in silence long enough for me to adjust the 'cultural expectations' knob in my brain from 'America: chatty' to 'England: not'.

'America,' I replied.

'But you're not American,' he said, in a tone which seemed to imply that I might not be aware of this fact.

'No, I'm Pakistani.'

'Ball tamperers,' he muttered. Even if he was merely talking about the not-so-long-ago cricket controversy between our two countries, that wasn't polite. I responded with silence. Not the kind of silence with which my cousin, Mariam, filled her days, but rather the silence of my grandmother, which was meant to inform those who received it of the lowliness of their stature. Dadi always accompanied those silences with an upward tilt of her head, as though she were posing for the head of a coin. Strange how, in remove, single gestures can be all that remain to us of people who once inhabited the daily tos-and-fros of our lives. In Massachusetts it was the memory of that tilted head which kept me from writing to Dadi. I suppose the tilt encapsulated for me the way Dadi behaved about Mariam Apa.

The cabbie pulled up to my St. John's Wood destination – after what seemed an unnecessary detour via Lord's – and

I tipped him a more than generous amount. (That was another Dadi trick for making the lowly feel lower, but it didn't seem to produce the desired effect.) I waited for him to drive away before sitting down on my suitcase in the tiny parking lot of Palmer House. Halfway to home, and not just geographically. There, two floors up, the red brick with its starburst of cracks, where the tenant of Flat 121 had slammed down a hammer and yelled at my cousins and me, 'If you don't stop that singing it'll be your heads next.' And there, behind the fence, the garbage bin in which I had hidden amongst green cans during a game of hide-and-seek, where curiosity taught me the taste of beer and my father, on finding me, taught me the meaning of 'backwash', embellishing details sufficiently to engender in me an unshakable paranoia regarding shared drinks. Oh, and up, between the white lace curtains of Flat 77, my cousin Samia staring down at me.

'What are you up to, Ailment?' she shouted. 'Have you gone mental?'

'No, just sentimental,' I said, and rolled my suitcase to the front door.

Upstairs, Samia flung her arms around me and pulled me into the flat. 'Look at you, you America-return! Graduated and all! Can't believe it's been five years since.' She held me at arm's length and scrutinized me. For a moment I felt as though I were a child again and she was the oh-so-cool elder cousin whose opinion mattered so much to me that I would go out of my way to annoy her just so that she wouldn't detect my devotion. 'You're looking so . . . I mean, *so*! Swear to God. When your mother told me you had cut your hair, I wasn't sure your face could bear the attention, but it can. It really can.'

'Thanks, and you look quite ugly,' I said, irritated at myself for feeling so grateful for that non-compliment. I glanced around at the new decor with its Bukhara rug and paisleyed floor-cushions and Mughal miniatures. Samia, it appeared, had become one of those *desis* who drink Pepsi in Pakistan and *lassi* in London.

'You lie so well, everyone will know we're related,' Samia said, handing me a mug of tea. She didn't add, No one would know it by looking at us, though that was true enough. She had the angular features, prominent clavicle and straight black hair of Dadi and my father, a throwback to the Rajput princess who was so beautiful that one of my ancestors from the Dard-e-Dil royal family abducted her and dragged her to a battlefield, hoping that her face would seduce enemy soldiers into dropping their swords and rushing for paper to compose *ghazals* of devotion. The plan might have worked had it not been that the princess, outraged that common soldiers were to look upon her, slashed her face with her fingernails before the battle began. My ancestor was so overcome by her proud courage that he married her, and went on to win the battle anyway.

Somehow, that story seemed quite romantic when I was fifteen.

Needless to say, I do not look like the Rajput princess. Which doesn't bother me much, though I really would have liked a prominent clavicle. Family members use words like 'agreeable' and 'pleasant' regarding my features, and go on so much about the beauty mark (no one ever says 'mole') on my cheek that it's obvious that's my only redeeming feature. My 'bedroom eyes' also attract much comment, but let's be frank, they only make me look like Garfield.

I have the unfortunate habit of looking very focussed when I am in fact distracted; a tendency that is a great asset in most classrooms, but has often landed me in trouble elsewhere. I suppose while my mind wandered down ancestral paths my eyes must have been fixed on some aspect of the flat's new decor, because Samia said, 'Look, Aloo, I know this has always been your home away from, so it must be just a little bizarre to think I've taken it over, but really, truly, I'm only here doing research for a few months.'

'Oh, please, Samia, you're such a moron sometimes. It's family property.'

'Yes, but—'

'Please,' I said. 'Can we avoid the tangle of family rights and privileges for just a few more seconds?'

Samia grinned. 'Yes. Good. Top Ten remark. I was just leading up to telling you that you're stuck in the spare bedroom.'

'No hass. It's where I always sleep when I stay here with my parents.'

'Yes, but there are new tenants next door, and their bedroom shares a wall with yours. They're newly-weds. The walls might shake a little. Speaking of which . . .'

'Yes?'

Samia raised an eyebrow at me. 'I just thought I'd generously provide you with a lead-in to any goosy jossip in your life,' she said.

'I think you're confusing my life with yours.'

'No goose?'

'Well, maybe a gander or two. Nothing worth mentioning.' What a thing to say about all the boys at college I had liked enough to consider liking even more. They were all

8

brimming with rage against the world's injustices, those boys. All of them. So how could I tell them the story I would have to tell them if there was to be anything approaching intimacy between us? I learnt many things at college, but the only art I perfected was the art of stepping away with a shrug.

'Hunh.' Samia fiddled with the heart-shaped pendant around her neck, but I wasn't about to sit through an exhaustive – or should I say, exhausting – account of her romantic entanglements, so I just sipped my tea and frowned at the calcium spot on my thumb nail.

'Oh, well. Good flight?'

I shrugged. 'I kept the galleries entertained with stories about the family.'

Samia rolled her tongue under her upper lip. With relatives, even those you haven't seen for many years, as I hadn't seen Samia since I was seventeen and she twenty-one, you can recognize what their expressions hide because someone you know well – in this case, my father – has exactly the same manner of concealment.

'No,' I said, skimming my palm on the underside of the mug before setting it down, and then wiping my palm vigorously on my jeans. 'Not that story. I take it you've heard some melodramatic family version of how I reacted to all that stuff four years ago.'

Samia tugged my earlobe. 'I wanted to come back home, you know. Mainly because of you. But between summer jobs and research and other stuff . . .'

'Like Jack, short for John.'

'Yeah, that loser.' We fell silent for a moment and then Samia said, 'Have you ever asked yourself why you don't tell that story?'

'*Uf tobah!* You're a historian not a psychologist, Samo.' I stood up and dragged my suitcase into the spare bedroom, pushing away my cousin's hand when she tried to help me. It was happening already. Five minutes with a relative and I was becoming a moody cow. Moo-dy cow. Well, that's all right. Still a shred of humour remaining.

'So, how long before you head off to the homeland?' Samia asked, following me into the bathroom.

'Tomorrow morning. You didn't read the e-mail I sent, did you?' I yanked my shirt over my head and tossed it at Samia.

'Not with any kind of obsessive attention to detail.'

I turned on the shower. The rest of Samia's reply was punctured by the needles of water that tattooed my body, so her words became indistinct and all that remained was the lilt and tempo of her voice, which could have been the lilt and tempo of any of my female relatives except one. I was not showering, I was carrying out a ritual, a ritual of arrival in London, and part of the ritual was to miss Mariam Apa, which I did, but the other part of the ritual was to imagine what she was doing, right now, and that I couldn't do. My imagination could accommodate aliens and miracles and the taste of certain men's sweat, but not that.

I turned off the shower and said, 'I don't tell that story, because it still doesn't have an ending.'

Chapter Two

'Is yaks' milk really green?' I asked Samia, settling down to my second mug of tea.

She shrugged and pulled my wet hair to check that it squeaked. 'That's really so not important.'

Which is the closest she's ever come to conceding ignorance. Fact is, I'm sure no one in the family knows any more than she or I do on the subject. But we all know that my great-grandfather's declaration, on 28 February 1920, that he had just heard yaks' milk was green and, therefore, he felt impelled to inform his cousin, the Nawab, he was giving up his courtier's life in order to become a scientist and study yak milk production, was what jolted my great-grandmother into premature labour.

Taj, the midwife, was summoned. A woman whose veins stood up a centimetre from the backs of her hands, Taj had delivered every member of my family born in Dard-e-Dil since 1872. By the time my great-grandfather was envisioning all the honours he would receive for investigating lactose colouration Taj was so shrunken and wrinkled that rumour had it she was regressing into babyhood and was only awaiting a suitable womb into which she could tunnel and complete the circle of her life.

When she entered my great-grandmother's bedroom, dressed as always in a *gharara* and looking like a deep-fried shrimp with wide, embroidered cotton trousers in place of a tail, all the hovering women, relatives and servants alike, scurried out. Only the Begum of Dard-e-Dil attempted to stay with her kinswoman and childhood friend through the birth, but Taj raised an eyebrow at her and, though the Begum may not have scurried, she did leave with a haste that was less than regal. It was all very well to have titles, and sufficient gold to cover all the streets and fields of Dard-e-Dil and still have enough to gild all the mango trees, but that didn't allow you to stand up to Taj, who had the family's umbilical cords. I kid you not. She never left a delivery room without one.

(Trace back the origins of the Urdu expression of disdain – 'Who do you think you are? Was your umbilical cord buried here?' – and you might just find it was first used to insult a member of the Dard-e-Dil family born between 1872 and 1920.)

Where, if at all, did Taj bury those Dard-e-Dil umbilical cords? No one knows. In 1890, immediately after my great-grandfather's cousin, the Nawab of Dard-e-Dil (Binky to his intimates), was born, his father, the hairless Nawab, told one of his courtiers to follow Taj when she left the palace and find out what she did with the umbilical cord. (The fear of not-quite-twins had been with the Dard-e-Dil family for over three and a half centuries at this point, and a miasma had arisen out of history to waft over any irregularity related to childbirth.) The courtier was discovered, two days later, in a neighbouring state, stealing pork from

12

the kitchen of the British Residency. He could offer no explanation for this act. After that, no one tried following Taj again. The hairless Nawab earned a reputation for his strong sense of justice by deciding that an umbilical cord, even a royal one, was not worth forfeiting a True Believer's place in heaven. It was pork, you understand, not theft, that marked the courtier for hell.

But I doubt any of this was on my great-grandmother's mind as she pushed and pushed and pushed and Taj held up first one and then another and then another baby boy, and said, 'Did you hear the midnight chimes?'

The quality of my great-grandmother's shrieks was different enough from her labour cries to bring the women of the family rushing back into the room. Taj handed the triplets to the Begum, who was the first through the door, and then disappeared out of the room, out of the palace, out of my family's life, three twined and bloodied umbilical cords in her hand.

So, three sons. One born just before midnight, on 28 February. One born just after midnight, on 29 February. One born at midnight, on the cusp of the leap year, his head emerging on 28 February, the rest of his body following the next day. My great-grandmother couldn't have been more successful in birthing not-quite-twins if she'd planned it. Though I don't suppose you can plan a thing like that. Of course, everyone still blamed Taj for the whole thing, quite overlooking her previous forty-eight years of midwifery, during which there were no not-quites and only three stillbirths.

'As a feminist I feel I should object to the Taj story.' I was lying flat on the floor so that Samia could pound airport tension out of my spine, my voice rising and falling with every thump. 'I mean look, it's got two of the archetypal female elements. The crone and the mother. The only thing it needs to fulfil all stereotypes is the virgin.'

'Well, don't look at me.' Samia practised dance steps along my back.

'I think you've just paralysed me.'

'Such gratitude!' Samia lay down and rested her head against my back. More than anything else, more than mangoes, *gol guppas*, *nihari* and *naans*, more than cricket mania, more than monsoon rains, more than crabbing beneath a star-clustered sky, what I missed about Karachi was the intimacy of bodies.

'Besides,' Samia said, 'aren't crones full of . . . What's that term? You know, like Ego in *Oh Hello*?'

'Iago in *Othello*. I hope you're just trying to be funny.' I traced the lozenge-shaped pattern on the rug with my forefinger and remembered playing a strange form of hopscotch in my grandmother's bedroom, along with Samia and her brother Sameer, with the geometrical designs on Dadi's carpet standing in as hopscotch squares.

'Motiveless malignancy, that's it. Can't get into Crone School without it. But Taj had a reason the size of Everest to hate the family.'

'If you're willing to consider the possibility that Iago is in love with Othello, then—'

'Oh, shut up. Who cares?' Samia rolled over, propped her head on her hand and looked at me. 'But listen, is it true that you once asked your Dadi if Taj's name appears on our family tree?'

'No.' Until Samia asked that question it hadn't really occurred to me that, yes, Taj was family too. God, it was even larger than I had thought, this pool of my relatives out

14

in the world, generations of people with Samia's hair, my father's eyes, Mariam Apa's smile, and if I saw one of those cousins on a street would I recognize something in them, would I say, We've never met but I know the jut of your clavicle, the curve of it. And what if, what if, in addition to the hair, the smile, the collarbone straining against the skin, what if there were also veins rising a centimetre above the backs of the hands?

'Really?' The disappointed voice of someone who's just had a family myth shattered. 'You never said anything like that at all?'

'Nuh-uh. Though there was that time I got frightened by a squirrel and Dadi just looked at me in such disgust and said something like, "And to think you are descended from the Nawab who killed a tiger with his bare hands." And I—'

'Did you just say, a squirrel?'

'It was a big squirrel. And I said to Dadi, "That paragon of bravery you just mentioned – isn't he the same guy who raped Taj's mother?"'

'No, wait!' Samia held up her hand for silence. 'Let me guess. She said, of course it wasn't rape. He was a Nawab.'

'Worse. She recited "Leda and the Swan".'

Samia fell forward, laughing. 'Abida Nani! Always full of surprises.'

If you're trying to understand how exactly Samia and I are related you might suppose from Samia's words that my Dadi is her Nani, which means my father and Samia's mother are siblings and, therefore, Samia and I are first cousins. It's never that simple. Dadi is my father's mother; she is not, however, Samia's mother's mother as Samia's use of the term 'Nani' implies, but rather Samia's mother's mother's sister, and so Samia and I are second cousins.

While I'm climbing up the family tree let me add that my grandparents, Dadi and Dada, or Abida and Akbar if you prefer the familiarity of first names, were also second cousins, and Dada was one of those three sons, the not-quite-twins, who brought such heartache to the family. But that comes later. Of course, it really came earlier.

'You can laugh,' I said, looking up at the painting of an emperor and his courtiers on a hunt, which has hung in the flat as long as I can remember. The emperor on a horse, surrounded by armed men on foot. What courtier would ever allow a ruler to get within wrestling distance of a tiger? 'But it really sums up Dadi's view of royalty. The Nawab as Zeus; I mean, consider the implications. She thinks he was a god. And he wasn't even a Nawab when he raped Taj's mother. He was still just heir apparent. Not that I'm saying the title or lack thereof makes the slightest difference.'

Samia stood up, pulled an anthology of poetry off the shelf, and thumbed through the pages. 'Suno,' she said. ' "How can those terrified vague fingers push/ The feathered glory from her loosening thighs?" Give your dadi a *qatra* more credit. The poem is about the seductiveness of power, right? Was it rape or seduction? The question is there. The fingers are terrified, the thighs loosen. Both things go on. We're too modern to appreciate the aura of kings-to-be. And of gods disguised as swans. And, hang on just a . . . Now that I think of it, in what rash of clairvoyance do we presume Taj's mother was unwilling?'

I turned away. 'Dadi doesn't understand complexity.'

'Your view of her has changed one hundred and twenty-three degrees since we last met.'

'Everything changed four years ago. Everything.'

Samia put her arms around me and pulled me close, my

16

head resting against her chest. 'Wasn't there something about Zeus's rape, seduction, *jo bhi*, of Leda that had something to do with twins?'

'You're right! Leda had sex with her husband, Tyndareus, on the same day that Zeus did what Zeus did. And nine months later Leda laid twin eggs. From one came Helen and Pollux, children of Zeus, and from the other came Castor and Clytemnestra, children of Tyndareus. Talk about not-quite-twins!'

'*Arré*, maybe we're descended from Leda.'

'It's mythology, cuz. And from a cultural tradition not our own.'

'Actually, Point A, ancient Greek texts were kept alive through Arab translations, which were translated from Arabic back into European languages when Europe was ready to stop being barbaric and have a cultured moment. My grandmother in her little house on the Mediterranean is very adamant about this matter. And, Point B, it doesn't sound a whole cartload more mythical than some of the stuff that's gone on in our clan. Speaking of which, did you hear about Sameer's lizard experience? In the loo. The bloody *chhipkali* practically attacked him. It was the same colour as the floor and it moved with speed.'

And then she was off, recounting a tale worthy of a place beside all the best lizard stories of our family. The one about Samia and Sameer's grandmother ripping off her sari at a state dinner because she thought she felt a lizard run down her spine; the one about Dadi's grandmother, who saw a lizard nestling between the pillows by her foot and reacted by leaping off her palanquin, thus showing her face to men who were neither eunuchs nor close relatives; and the one about the lizard, red and large-throated, which clambered on the grilles outside our cousin Usman's window, prompting screams that turned into full-blown hysteria seconds later when Usman's mother uttered the four most terrifying words imaginable: It's in the house.

At college I was famous for my storytelling abilities, but I never told anyone that my stories were mere repetition, my abilities those of a parrot. Oh, they are a talking people, my relatives, and I have breathed in that chatter, storing it in those parts of my lungs (the alveoli, the bronchi) whose names suggest a mystery beyond breath and blood. And yes, when the need arises I can exhale those words and perpetuate the myth that is nothing more than myth because it forgets Mariam Apa; the myth, that is, of my family's across-the-board, no-exceptions, one-hundred-percent-all-the-way garrulousness. But when I am my only audience, the wit and the one-liners, the retorts and the rebukes are just so much noise and I crave something silent as a wisp of smoke.

I can think of no one who knows me who would believe any of that. Maybe not even me. Maybe.

'But Aliya,' Samia said. 'A squirrel?'

Chapter Three

'So, please now, while I have your attention undivided and can threaten to withhold lunch until you answer, explain to me why, I mean why, are you planning to return to the Blighted Estates of America to get a Master's in Education?' Samia rolled up her sleeves as she spoke.

'What, are you planning to punch me?'

'No,' she said, taking my mug. 'I'm immersing dishes in soap suds. Come to the kitchen and answer my *savaal*.'

'Decisions,' I said, hoisting myself on to the kitchen counter. 'Where, what, why. Can't handle them. So I'm prolonging the indecision with higher education.'

Samia pulled on a pair of rubber gloves, which made me think irrationally that she really had grown up entirely. I wondered if the same could be said of me, even though I was quite liable to scald my hands while attempting to wash the dishes and I didn't care what the washing liquid did to my nail polish. Samia pointed a yellow finger at me. 'My quesh is, Education, colon, why?'

'Oh, the postcolonial why!' I shrugged. 'A friend of mine had application forms to various Schools of Ed.'

Samia threw a dish towel at me. 'What happened to studying history?'

'You're the historian in the family.'

'Aloo, when I was eighteen you knew as much about history as I did. And you were fourteen.' Samia could deliver the simplest comments in tones of high outrage.

'I knew more. But my first week at college I got a letter from Dadi.'

I would like to be proud of you again one day. But you can only make me proud if you first understand what pride means. Pride! In English it is a Deadly Sin. But in Urdu it is *Fakhr* and *Nazish* – both names that you can find more than once on our family tree. You must go back to those names, those people, in order to understand who I am and who you are. This is why it is good you are in America, where there are so many books. Study history, my darling Aliya, but not the history of the Mughals or the British in India, although our stories intersect theirs in so many ways. Study the Dard-e-Dil family. I know you don't trust the history that comes from my mouth, so go to that continent which denies its own history, and when you find yourself mocking its arrogance and lies, go to the libraries and search among the cobwebbed books for the story of your own past. And when you do that, and you see in print the old tales that thrilled you to sleep at night, I defy you to feel no stirrings of *Fakhr* and *Nazish*.

'Aliya? You got a letter saying what?'

'Saying she wanted me to study history. So I didn't.'

I opened the fridge and crouched down beside it. My cousin Samia had become a sandwich eater. Bread, mayonnaise, mustard, salami, sliced roast beef, lettuce, tomatoes, gherkins, tuna salad. Good God, how dreary.

Behind the loaf of bread was a sauce boat, not dissimilar in size and shape to Aladdin's lamp. I lifted it out of the fridge with both hands and held it to my face. Tamarind!

'What's in there?' Samia held out her hand for the sauce boat. 'Imli?'

'Friday nights.'

Fridays used to be Masood's day off. He'd cycle out at sunrise and be gone all day, leaving Ami, Aba, Mariam Apa and me to lay tables, wash dishes, heat up frozen food. More often than not, at lunchtime, Mariam Apa would end up eating last night's leftovers and Aba would drive me to the bazaar where we'd buy *aloo puri* with carrot pickles, and *halva* on the side to sweeten our mouths. Masood would return well after sunset, clothes wet, hair smelling of salt, sand glistening silver against his skin. He'd hold up two clenched fists like a boxer ready to jab, and when I tapped one he would twist his wrist, unfurl his fingers, and reveal a tamarind-based sweet wrapped in clear plastic. For a while, not so long ago, I had lost these memories of Masood; I'd like to say it was the better angels of my nature which restored the memories to me, but really it was embarrassment at the way my reaction towards him mirrored that of so many of my family members. Embarrassment, and also the visceral tug of food smells. When the taste of chillies sometimes brought tears to my eyes it was not because my palate was overwhelmed by the heat.

I held the sauce boat up to my nose again. Tamarind. It was only at college, when the racks of spices and international foods at Stop 'n' Shop forced me to confront the inadequacy of my culinary English, that I ran for my Urdu–English dictionary and discovered that *imli* was tamarind. It was several days later that I thought, Sounds a little like *Taimur Hind*.

Taimur Hind. To explain what that name means to me I must return to the triplets, those not-quite-twins. Their father, my great-grandfather, was so terrified to hear the circumstances of their births that he put yaks and their milk out of his mind and concentrated on averting disaster. He was well intentioned, of course, but in my family that's just a euphemism for stupid. He said, 'We'll call them Sulaiman, Taimur and Akbar.' He thought bearing the names of great kings would enable his sons to face up to any crisis, but he never paused to think what would have happened if their namesakes – Sulaiman the Magnificent, Akbar the Great, and Taimur, sometimes called Taimur Lang or Tamburlaine, but so unimpeded by his lameness that no one ever pictures him crippled – had been born brothers. Romulus and Remus, Aurangzeb and Dara Shikoh, Richard the Lionheart and King John would seem, by comparison, merely to bicker affectionately. (Though in the case of John and Richard it seems that their legendary disharmony may have been exaggerated by the Robin Hood tales, and incidentally I've never had much sympathy for the Crusaders.)

Of the triplets, Taimur was the one born on the cusp. His brothers adored him and were always arguing over which one of them shared the same birthday as Taimur. Are you born at the moment your head emerges into the light, as my grandfather, Akbar, claimed, or at the moment when every last inch of you is caressed by air, as Sulaiman insisted.

Taimur, when asked his date of birth, said, 'I was born between my brothers.' And when he grew older he added, 'There is nothing more arbitrary than the chime separating one day from the next.'

22

Things I know about Taimur: he was the most beautiful of the brothers, while Akbar was the most dashing and Sulaiman the most charming; when he was four he bit the nose off Dadi's stuffed reindeer and Dadi, in retaliation, bit his index finger; he was the sweetest timer of the cricket ball that you could hope to see, but at boarding school in England his run average remained lower than Akbar's because he so often forgot to ground his bat after completing a run; he loved the poems of Emily Dickinson; before he left for boarding school he had an English governess who called him Percy (Sulaiman was Alfred and Akbar was Gordie); he played the sitar; also, the harpsichord; it was he who persuaded his brothers to join him in leaping off a second-floor balcony in the Dard-e-Dil palace when home for the holidays at the age of sixteen, their broken legs and the intercession of the Nawab on their behalf finally convincing their father to allow them to finish their secondary education in Dard-e-Dil with their cousins, under the guidance of the private tutors at the palace; he despised politicians before it was fashionable to do so, but his most prized possession was a cane belonging to Liaquat, which he either stole or received as a gift from Liaquat after mock-pretending to steal it (the stories here vary, but I prefer the latter version); he could devour pounds of fried okra at a single sitting, though his appetite was otherwise unremarkable; in 1938, shortly before the brothers were due to leave for Oxford, he disappeared.

He disappeared and remained that way. For two weeks his family was made efficient by terror, until the arrival of an envelope with an indistinct postal stamp and Taimur's looping Ds made the postmaster spill his morning cup of tea and sent him pedalling frantically to my family's home.

Dadi was with her cousins, Akbar and Sulaiman, when the letter arrived and, though she swears she read it only once, she can still recite the letter from memory, her fingers tracing Ds in the air as she speaks:

My brothers, we were born the year after the Jalianwalla massacre. Think of this when you are strolling down paths in Oxford, studying how to be Englishmen and do well in the world. I lack your gift for erasing, nay! evading history. The writing of this letter is the last thing I do before entering into the employ of an English army officer, as a valet. I have accepted my historical role, and when you return from Oxford and take your positions in the ICS or in English-run companies the only real difference between us will be that I am required to wear a grander uniform. You will not hear from me again for I am repudiating English and, alas! those years of English schooling have robbed me of the ability to write Urdu. From the time of our births we have been curses waiting to happen, but now the suspense is over. This is our curse: Akbar, Sulaiman, we are kites that have had their strings snipped. We went to school in a place without sun, and believed this meant we had no need of our shadows. I am not an Englishman, nor are you. Nor can we ever be, regardless of our foxtrots, our straight bats, our Jolly Goods and I Says.

No more the Anglicized Percy, I.

I am now *Taimur Hind*.

Dadi always ends her recitations with a final flourish of D. And always, always she says, 'We thought it was a joke. How could it not be a joke? He wrote, Nay! He never said, Nay! except when he was mimicking our uncle, Ashraf.'

'What would you have done,' I once had the courage to ask Dadi, 'if you had been at an Englishman's house and saw a valet with your tooth mark on his index finger?'

If she had cried then, as I thought she was going to, our relationship might have survived what was yet to come. But, instead, she threw back her head and said, 'Family retainers were one thing, but what reason had I to look at other people's servants?'

Unconsciously I had dipped my fingers in the tamarind. 'You know the real reason they thought Taimur's letter was a joke?' I said to Samia, putting the sauce boat down. 'They couldn't believe that a Dard-e-Dil could possibly become a servant.'

Samia shook her head at me. 'Who says your version of events is less clouded than anyone else's? When I'm reading old historical accounts I like to find out as much as I can about each contributor.'

'Oh, no. You've become one of those deadly types like Sara Smith in my Intro Shakespeare class, who said it would be like, really, like, helpful, if we knew more about Shakespeare's relationship with his daughters, because then we'd, like, understand *King Lear*, like, better.'

'Shut up, shorty.'

'Take off those block-heels and try saying that.'

That kept her quiet for a few seconds. Then she said, 'They're here.'

'You do enigma so well.'

'Our Indian relatives. Some of them are here. I've accepted an invitation to their place for elevenses today. What do you say? Will you come?'

Chapter Four

I had met one of the Indian relatives, years before, in Karachi. On that day, I remember, I was wearing the T-shirt with a bullet hole in it. As far as I was concerned, the fact that I wasn't actually wearing the shirt at the time the bullet hole made its appearance had done nothing to detract from the glamour of the ravaged cloth. Our dhobi had been carting my family's freshly laundered clothes towards our house when someone shot at his donkey-cart. No one was ever able to determine whether the motives were sectarian (our dhobi was a Shi'a) or more literally asinine (the donkey was a champion racer whose three successive victories had reputedly angered a Mr Billo, who was missing a finger and was, therefore, dangerous). The donkey lost the tip of an ear, my shirt lost the embossed letter B and henceforth warned DON'T UG ME!, but the donkey only became more aerodynamic and I briefly acquired the nickname Ug, which I secretly loved.

Samia's brother, Sameer, once said, 'There is no digression, only added detail.'

So, as I was saying, I was seven or eight and a school friend was dropping me home from someone's birthday

26

party, except I was in no mood to go home so I directed her driver to Sameer and Samia's house instead.

No one saw me enter my cousins' drawing room, where a large crowd of my relatives was gathered around. All attention was focussed, instead, on a silver-haired woman in a sari who lit a cigarette and said, 'Cigarettes are to me what coffee spoons were to Prufrock.' I pictured this Prue Frock: a tall, thin redhead in a dress. I thought she must have been an Englishwoman from the Raj days of this stranger's youth, and I imagined her lifting the stem of a spoon to her mouth and exhaling silver smoke. I remember wanting to impress the stranger – except I didn't think of her as a stranger. There was something familiar . . . Is this memory or hindsight? But I did want to impress her, I know, so I fingered the bullet hole, hoping to draw her attention to it, to me. Instead, Sameer's mother – my aunt, Zainab – appeared in the doorway behind me and sent me home with her driver.

'One of Zaheer's relatives was over for tea,' Zainab Phupi explained to my mother later. 'And as luck would have it a whole *pultan* of my relatives landed up as well, so I was going crazy and one more child in the house to keep an eye on was not what I needed.'

To try and distract attention from my disgrace I asked my father, 'Who is Prue and what does she have to do with cigarettes and coffee spoons?'

He could offer no explanation, but the next day when he repeated this remark to Dadi I thought she was going to die. She put a hand over her heart and with the other hand caught me by the shoulder, her fingers digging into my flesh.

'Zaheer Phupa's relative,' I said, and repeated the silver-haired woman's remark. 'Dadi, what's wrong?'

27

Dadi pushed me aside and reached for the phone, her ring-laden fingers trembling as they dialed the six digits of her niece's number. 'Zainab, where is she?' Dadi demanded into the receiver. 'I know she's there. I'm coming over.'

I was close enough to the phone to hear Zainab Phupi say, 'She was only here for the day. She's on her way to England.'

Dadi's eyes closed and her head swayed from side to side. I don't remember any sound escaping her, but it must have because Zainab Phupi said, 'We were all so sure you didn't want to see her. You've always said—'

'Always! What do you know about always? We were girls together.' That word – 'girls'; she said it as a deposed monarch might say 'king'. 'More than thirty-five years I haven't seen her and you just assumed you understood my always. Blood is thicker than time, blood is thicker.' And she sat on the cold marble floor and wept.

It must be an instance of imagination plugging up a hole in my memory, but I could almost swear I remember Mariam Apa wrapping her arms around Dadi and rocking her into silence.

Samia nudged me and I raised my head away from its resting position against the smudged window of the Tube. 'Jet lag. Our stop already?'

The train was hurtling on, so Samia didn't even bother to answer. 'Racy *desi* viciously and vigorously checking you out. Sitting next to purple-haired woman.'

I casually flicked my hair aside, shifting the angle of my head as I did so. 'Where?' I said.

'He's on the move,' Samia whispered.

I looked up at the man walking towards me and felt a

terrible urge to stand up as well, meet him halfway between purple-haired woman and Samia and wrap my arms around him.

'Hi, Aliya,' he said, sitting down opposite me. 'Remember me?' He crossed one foot over his knee and rested his hand on his sneaker. His hand span extended comfortably from the toe of his shoe to his ankle bone.

'The aeroplane,' I said, as casually as possible. 'Aisle seat. And you handed me my suitcase.'

He extended his hand. 'Cal,' he said.

'You don't look like a Caleb,' Samia said, taking his hand before I could. 'I'm the older cousin.'

'Hi, the older cousin. Actually, I'm a Khaleel. But when you live in the Western world, and your last name is Butt and you're born in a town spelt A-T-H-O-L, pronounced "Athole", things are bad enough already. You don't want to add to the humiliation by admitting to a name that sounds to certain ears like you're expectorating. That "kh" you know.'

'Could be worse,' Samia grinned. 'You could be a Fakhr.'

'That's my older brother.'

'Liar,' I said.

He turned to look at me again. 'Maybe. But a good storyteller never tells.'

'All the way from Boston to London I could see your fingers tapping on your sneakers,' I said. 'That's some hand span.' On occasion, evil demons take hold of my voice box and force out remarks like that one. I reached across and held my hand against Khaleel's, palm to palm. His fingers bent forward at the topmost joint, pushing down against the tips of my nails, and his thumb rested lightly against the mole on my index finger. I thought of mosques and churches and prayer mats. Hands clasped together; one hand resting atop the other; fingers interlocked to mime a steeple. What sacred power is invested in hands?

This is not to say I was having pious thoughts.

I pulled my hand away.

'So it's safe to say your family didn't arrive in Amreeks via the *Mayflower*.' Samia has the Pakistani knack of finding out all she deems it necessary to know about someone's background within the first five minutes of conversation.

'PIA, actually. No, my parents are like Aliya. And like you, I guess. Karachiites. I've never been there, but there's a chance I might, really soon.'

'Are you related to Bunty and Yousuf Butt?' Samia's foot was pressing against mine as she spoke, signalling He's Gorgeous But Okay You Saw Him First.

'Bunty Butt! I don't think so. No bells ringing. But I wish I were. Aunty Bunty Butt.'

The train squealed to a stop at Green Park. 'Isn't this our stop?' I said.

Samia shook her head. 'So where'll you stay? If you come to Karoo?'

'With relatives. Place called Liaquatabad. What's that like?'

Samia jumped up, pulling me along with her. 'Aliya! It's our stop. Hold the doors please. Cal, nice meeting . . .' And we were out, watching the train pull away.

'I cannot believe you . . .' I closed my eyes and the world rocked around me.

'Sorry, Aloo. *Arré*, hold on.'

I pushed past Samia and ran, and kept on running until I was above ground, cars whizzing everywhere, and across the street the PIA office with a cardboard cut-out flight attendant smiling at me from the window. I was horribly jet-lagged, and as London jostled around me I thought, I want to be five again and willing to lie down in the middle of a busy London street to declare I'm tired; willing to weep that I want to go home to Mariam Apa; willing to talk to anyone who seems nice, regardless of where they come from and where their families live.

'Listen to me.' Samia put her arm around my neck in a gesture that was both affectionate and immobilizing. 'Have you ever, in all your days, in all your meanderings when Sameer first learnt to drive and you *chuker maroed* the city for the best bun kebabs, have you ever been to Liaquata-bad? If I asked you how to get there would you have the faintest?'

'Go away.'

'Not an option. Oh, *ehmuk*, he's an American. Green card and all that. If he really is planning a trip to Karachi his whole extended family is probably lining up its daughters as prospective brides.'

'Uff! The stereotypes . . .'

'What's stereotyped about thinking people want to get their children to safety? You know what most of Karachi calls our part of town? Disneyland.'

'Your point?'

'The poor live in Liaquatabad. The poor, the lower classes, the not-us. How else do you want me to put this? There's no one we know who would have exchanged Karachi phone numbers with him, Aloo. No one. And, do I have to say this, you especially . . .' She turned away in irritation, or perhaps it was frustration.

'Finish that sentence.'

'Try this sentence instead: after everything that happened four years ago no one, not even you, will ever trust any feelings you have for him. You can hit me, *Thaassh! Dhuzh! Dharam!* if it'll make you feel better.'

I might well have taken her up on that, had a man, stooped and rheumy-eyed, not twitched my sleeve and said, 'If I had amnesia and I saw you I'd pray you played a part in my life.'

'Perhaps you do,' I said. 'Perhaps I do.'

Tears came to his eyes. 'Our lives await memories. That's all.' He kissed my hand and walked away.

Samia knew well enough not to say anything. She started walking down the street, a few paces ahead of me, but aware enough of my footfall to look back when I stopped to scrape a bit of banana off the sole of my shoe. I refused to catch her eye. How could she just pull me off the train like that? How could she? Could she? Could she do such a thing if I were not willing? Could she have done it if in that split second between Khaleel saying 'Liaquatabad' and Samia's hand reaching out to grab mine I hadn't already thought of escaping? If I had amnesia, would I have stayed on that train? Imagine that. To be freed of remembered biases. To have nothing to consider but the moment itself; nothing but the moment and the touch of his fingers.

Our lives don't await memories, I decided; they are crippled by memories. Oh, I knew exactly which memories crippled me, crippled me into running away from him. (Mixing metaphors was the least of my problems.) But I've accepted what happened four years ago! I wanted to shout out. I've deconstructed it, analysed it, and I have refused to take on the attitude of my relatives with their centuries of

32

inbred snobbery. Why can't my heart be as evolved as my mind? Why did 'Liaquatabad' hit me so bruisingly in the solar plexus?

Perhaps there's no escape from wounding memories. Time was, I thought time was all it took to move on. But how could I be a part of my family and believe that? We are all the walking wounded. Take this relative we were about to meet: Baji. Fifty years on from Partition, and according to Samia she still couldn't talk about those who left for Pakistan without rancour. That whole generation of my relatives mystified me. How had they sustained, for so long, the bitterness brought on by the events of 1947? I could believe it of one person, or two, but good God! our family was huge and yet there was never any word of reconciliation across the borders of India and Pakistan. They grew up together: Dadi and Baji and the triplets and scores of other cousins. They were to each other what Samia and Sameer were to me, and I to them. They were to each other what Mariam Apa . . . Oh, Lord. How do you stop missing the people you loved before you could say 'love'? If I had the option of inheriting that ability, would I take it?

Change the subject, I told myself. Think of reasons to stop being angry at Samia.

'So, listen,' Samia said when I caught up with her minutes later, having finally convinced myself that exiting the Tube when we did was regrettable in the abstract but, practically speaking, had forestalled later embarrassment. 'Just don't say anything that could start a conversation about Partition. And do not even begin to start to think about somehow indirectly referring to your grandparents. She blames them more than anyone else for the split in the family. Your Dadi, especially; she's liable to start ranting at the mention of her name. I haven't dared to ask why.'

'You might want to tell me how exactly we're related to this Baji person.'

'Our grandmothers are her second cousins.'

'Well, bless my beehives. That's the least complicated explanation I've ever heard.'

'I haven't finished, of course. Your grandfather – Akbar—'

'I know who my grandfather was, thank you.'

'Shut up. And this isn't America, you need to look right, not left, to check for oncoming traffic. Akbar and Baji – her name is Farahnaz but everyone calls her Baji – were first cousins. Akbar's father—'

'The yak man.'

'Yes, the yak man had a half-brother named Abdul, and this is Abdul's daughter.'

'Anything else?'

'Her mother had tantalizing elbows.'

'Oh.'

The presence of 'people without family' on my family tree was always explained away in the following manner: she was walking this way, he was walking that way, she had tantalizing elbows, nine months later this one was born. I had heard a great deal about those women who had elbowed their way, so to speak, on to the family tree, but this would be my first time meeting the progeny of such a woman.

(By the way, Taj's mother did not have tantalizing elbows – perhaps that's why, unlike all those other women of low birth, she did not marry the father of her child and take her place in the zenana where the women schemed,

34

plotted, forged alliances, jostled for favour, laughed, be-friended each other, complained about men, teased the eunuchs, and conducted grand affairs with each other. This last detail was not part of the oral history of our family but Samia had once declared that it was absurd to assume otherwise and Dadi's response – disapproval but not denial – convinced Sameer and me that Samia must be on to something.)

Samia stopped outside a block of flats and pressed the buzzer to Flat 8. Before there was any response from the occupants of the flat, the doorman let us in and waved us towards the lift.

'This thing is as big as my dorm room,' I said, and stepped into the lift. It was only when I heard my own voice that I realized I was nervous. I lay down on the plush carpet and closed my eyes as the lift hummed its ascent.

'Up.'

The lift door opened and I took Samia's hand and levered myself off the ground. She brushed a few strands of dog hair off my shirt, straightened my collar, pinched colour into my cheeks and pushed my hair off my face. 'She should approve,' my cousin said and pushed open the unlocked door to Flat 8.

She didn't.

Chapter Five

'You!'

It wasn't a pronoun, it was an accusation. I blinked in the darkness of the hallway which opened out into a drawing room cluttered with furniture, pictures, books and no human being that I could see. 'You!' the voice said again, and now I saw the tiny woman on the sofa, surrounded by piles of fabric. Was it fabric or more tiny people? Samia manoeuvred her way gracefully through a maze of tables to bow down in an *aadab* before the woman and kiss her wrinkled cheek.

'Baji, don't do the imperious bit. You'll frighten her. Stinky! Smelly!'

A door opened and two children ran in, whisked away the piles of fabric, turned on the lights and disappeared back into the room from which they came. Even with the lights on I knocked my legs against two table corners before reaching a suitable *aadaab* position. Baji didn't respond to my *aadaab* with the traditional '*jeeti raho*' so I didn't kiss her. Whatever her feelings towards my grandparents there was no need for her to forego wishing me continued life. Manners above all. *Qaida*. *Saleeqa*. Hadn't anyone ever taught her that? It's those tantalizing elbow genes, I caught myself thinking, and refused to follow Samia's lead and sit down until I was expressly invited to do so.

'Be more considerate of your feet,' Baji said. Had I managed to sleep just a little on the flight from Boston I might have held out for something more gracious, but the situation being what it was I sank into an armchair.

'So,' Baji said. 'How is your dadi?'

I looked at Samia, who whisked a penknife out of Baji's reach. Very reassuring.

'Oh, Dadi,' I said, waving my hands vaguely. 'You know.'

'No, I don't. I haven't seen her since Partition.'

'Oh, that's right. Partition.' I wondered if ripping off my clothes and doing the bhangra would help steer this conversation towards less disastrous paths. 'Not a lot of interesting words that rhyme with Partition. I wanted to write a *ghazal*, in English, for a class. With Partition as the rhyme. Partition. Ma's mission. Pa's wishin'. Turns into a country and western song. Allowing for half-rhymes isn't too rewarding either. Partition. Fruition. Revision. Condition.'

'Division,' Baji said.

'Mauritian,' said Samia, and saved the day.

Baji leant back against the cushions and smiled at me, not altogether pleasantly. 'For Samia's sake, I won't say anything else on the subject. Except that if you ever write a poem about Partition, it must be a lament.'

'A *ghazal*,' I said, determined not to back down before her. 'It was to be a *ghazal*. And one of the reasons I love *ghazals* is that the mood can change entirely from one couplet to the next. Isn't that how it always is? One person's lament can be someone else's elegy.' Masood once told me that his grandmother walked over a hundred miles to reach Pakistan in August 1947, and when she arrived in her new homeland she fell to her knees and kissed the ground so repeatedly that the dust of Pakistan was permanently lodged in her throat and for the rest of her life she could not breathe deeply without coughing. When, years later, a doctor said he could cure her of the cough she threatened to break his legs. Who was Baji to imply that Masood's grandmother's story was not worth celebrating?

'My brother died in a communal riot just after Partition. Your grandparents, and all those other Dard-e-Dils who leapt on to the Pakistan bandwagon, had left by then, were in Karachi; so my brother died in their place.'

'In their place?'

'He died for what they believed in.'

She was making it up. I knew that with utter certainty. None of the Dard-e-Dils died in the Partition riots; they either left for Pakistan in first-class style, with armed convoys or in the safety of aeroplanes, or they stayed within the four walls of the palace in Muslim-majority Dard-e-Dil until the worst of the troubles died down.

'He was my half-brother,' Baji said, very softly. 'We had different fathers. I hardly ever spoke to him. He was not royal, you see. He was not too grand to be killed in something as common as a riot.'

Why weren't any of the windows open? I could barely breathe.

The doorbell rang and even Baji looked relieved by the interruption. Stinky (or was it Smelly) charged out of his room and into the drawing room, leapt over one table, rolled under another, somersaulted over a third, unlocked the front door and leapt, rolled, flipped back into his room before the bellringer had quite finished entering the flat.

'Rehana Apa!' Samia kissed the newcomer – a younger version of Baji, but with hair halfway down her back. Her elbows were quite ordinary.

'My granddaughter,' Baji said to me. And then to Rehana, 'This is Aliya.' Rehana Apa smiled at me, a lovely smile, and embraced me.

'These cousinly demonstrations can wait until later,' Baji said. 'Rehana, why don't you bring it out?'

It? I thought. Tea?

'Can I help?' I said.

'Not if the past is anything to go by,' was Baji's response.

Samia seemed as mystified by this as I was. We sat back in our chairs as Rehana Apa exited the room, and Samia started to talk to Baji about the difficulty of getting saris dry-cleaned in London. I tried to understand why I felt such hostility towards this woman whom I'd never before met. Because she hadn't greeted me with open arms? I was usually adept at receiving coldness with indifference. Why should she bother me so much, when I knew nothing about her except for that matter of the elbows (and it couldn't be that because I had no such animosity towards her granddaughter, who had provoked in me only feelings of warmth in the few seconds she'd been in the room)? So what else was there? She's liable to start ranting at the mere mention of my grandmother's name. Surely, surely, if anything, that should create a feeling of affinity between us. I'd done my fair share of ranting about Dadi in the last few years. Even as I thought that, I remembered Samia saying Baji blamed Dadi for the family split after Partition, and my face flushed with rage. How dare she? 'We were girls together,' Dadi had cried when she missed the chance to meet the mysterious Prufrock relative from India. She had cried. Slipped down on to the marble floor . . . My Dadi sat on that cold, hard floor and though I was only a child I knew the tears she was weeping were old, old tears.

I felt tears forming in my own eyes, so to distract myself I looked around at the framed photographs cluttering the walls and tables. A few of them were in colour, but by and large they were black and white and, here and there, sepia. Baji was still talking to Samia, but as my eyes wandered in her direction she extended a hand and pointed at a picture on the wall. I got up and walked over to it.

The setting was the grounds of the Dard-e-Dil palace. I recognized it instantly from the photographs and paintings that adorned the walls of Dadi's house in Karachi, recognized it well enough to know that to have snapped that particular vista the photographer must have been backed up against the marble statue of Nur-ul-Jahan, founder of the house of Dard-e-Dil. Behind the figures who posed in the foreground was the arched entryway to the verandah that led to the part of the palace where Dadi's immediate family lived. Her father, though related to the Nawab only through marriage, had the prized ability to make the Nawab laugh and, as such, was indispensable at court. Officially, he was a minister, but it seems to me he came closer to fulfilling the role of court jester. My other great-grandfather, the courtier-cum-yak-enthusiast, was somewhat more independent (or less favoured) and lived away from the palace. But not so very independent, or so very out of favour; if the photographer had angled his camera up, say, thirty degrees he would have captured that spot on the palace roof where you could stand and look through a gap in the trees to see the house where the yak-man and his wife raised the triplets, just outside the palace walls.

('House' is the word Dadi uses to describe the triplets' home, but within the boundary walls there were stables, a mosque, and fruit orchards, to name just a few accessories to the 'house'.)

All this I registered when I looked at the picture, but only to the extent that you might register the details of a frame when looking at the 'Mona Lisa'. My real interest was in the three boys and the girl who were the reason for the photograph. My first thought when I saw the brothers was how strange it was that I had never before seen a picture of all three of them together. Their arms around each other's shoulders, they stood so close they could have been Siamese triplets in *sherwanis*, their necks rising dark from the high white collars, their hair identically parted and slicked down. Abida – she was too young in the photograph for me to think of her as Dadi – stood in front of her three cousins, swaying back just enough to make it impossible to discern from the lens angle whether or not she was leaning against the middle brother's chest. But whose smile was that on Abida's face? Not Dadi's, certainly not. The peculiar expression, 'her face spilling over with laughter', made sense for the first time as I looked at that teenaged girl, her back arching towards the impossibly beautiful boy in the centre of the photograph.

'You see, I have a photograph of her, and of your grandfather, on my wall,' Baji said. 'Despite what I said earlier. Don't think my feelings are one-dimensional. Don't think you can dismiss me as an embittered old woman.'

'Baji,' Samia said. 'Please.'

'That's all I'm going to say about it. Now come and sit down, Aliya.' Baji waved me over to the floor cushion beside her. I hadn't seen Rehana re-enter the room, but

41

there she was, helping Samia pull a coffee table a little closer to Baji, a long roll of paper under her arm.

'I want to register my disapproval of this,' Rehana said.

'Yes, yes, you've done that. Now lay it out.'

'You know about Babuji, of course,' Baji said, motioning to Rehana to hand me a cup of tea from a trolley which had appeared without calling any attention to itself. I nodded my thanks to Rehana, and nodded a yes to Baji. Babuji was the keeper of the Dard-e-Dil family tree, as his father had been before him and his grandfather before that. It was said (which means none of my relatives in Pakistan wanted to admit to being the original teller of this tale because it implied contact with the Indian relatives) that Partition and the subsequent Age of Frequent Flyers had in no way impaired Babuji's family's meticulous record-keeping, and all Dard-e-Dil births and deaths made their way to the family tree, regardless of bristling borders.

'This is a copy – a pruned copy – of the family tree, as recorded by Babuji,' Rehana said, placing the paper on the table and unrolling it. This was a pruned copy? The coffee table must have been about four feet by four feet, and still the edges of the paper curled off three sides of the table and rolled down to the floor. There seemed to be some vastly elaborate colour scheme at work, involving purples, greens, yellows, reds, blues and a whole range of colours and shades besides. It seemed that those who were directly descended from the first Nawab via the patrilineal line had their name inked in purple, but what the other colours were supposed to signify I didn't know. They probably indicated how far you had strayed from being the offspring of a direct male descendant. Yes, true enough. My grandparents' generation was hanging over the edge of the table, but I could just make out Dadi's name in blue. Her mother was red, and you had to go back a generation further to locate Dadi's purple grandmother. How Dadi must hate that! But it must be some comfort that Akbar's bloodline allowed Dadi the privilege of purple children. Samia and my generation was hidden from view, but I didn't need to see our names to know Samia's direct line hadn't been purple since her great-great-grandmother. I was purple, but it appeared my children would be red unless I married a fellow purple. I wondered, If I were to marry a non-purple Dard-e-Dil, would my children still be red? Or was there a maroon or something for such cases? Why should it matter, either way?

'Are these what I think they are?' Samia pointed to a pair of black stars marking two names halfway down the tree. Now that she had pointed it out I could see pairs of starred names scattered across the paper, their familiarity rendering Samia's question rhetorical. The not-quite-twins. As a child, I had inked those names on to my skin after a hot bath, my pores thirsting for that spiral of legend wrapped around my limbs.

'This is the saddest of all the twin stories.' Rehana's thumbnail underlined the starred words 'Inamuddin' and 'Masooma'.

Baji sighed and laid a hand on my shoulder. 'What we are, we are.'

Baji was clearly like Dadi in one thing at least: she could state the obvious and make it sound like revelation.

'Although maybe I only think that because I'm an architect,' Rehana added.

Inamuddin and Masooma were twins born on either side of midnight, almost three hundred years before Akbar and his brothers performed that feat with an added twist. The twins' uncle, Nawab Hamiduzzaman, aware of the curse of not-quite-twins, ordered the royal physician to poison the babies and ascribe the deaths to natural causes. Someone should have told Hamiduzzaman the story of Oedipus. Or of Lady Macbeth, perhaps. Because after the deed was done, old Ham could not sleep. He could not sleep and he could not pray and he could not peel the taste of poison from his lips. Until at last a man with the dust of distance on his feet and the gleam of prophecy in his eyes won entry into the Nawab's presence and, bending closer than close, whispered a means to redemption. And it was this: raze to the ground the mausoleum you have just started building for the bones of your ancestors and your descendants and those who come in-between. Make that land a holy shrine for pilgrims from every everywhere.

You may wonder, Then what? And you may wonder, How did that lead to a fall in the family's fortune? I'll say this: Think of the Mughals. Think of an image that captures and preserves the glory of the Mughals, and if you have any sense of anything you'll say the Taj Mahal. Well, the fact is, Shah Jahan bought – in secret and in gold – the plans to that Dard-e-Dil mausoleum from the keeper of the Dard-e-Dil archives, and the only thing he changed when he had the plans copied for the benefit of the contractor was the name. But we know, though you'll laugh, that Taj Mahal is, was, should have been, Dil Mahal. Other not-quite-twins denied the family wealth, power, freedom, unity; Masooma and Inamuddin's curse was that they deprived us of posterity. And, oh God, we deserved it.

(When? you might demand. When did this happen? And now I'm forced to concede that it happened during the

44

glory days of the Mughals, when Dard-e-Dil was not a kingdom at all but merely part of the Mughal Empire and Nawab Hamiduzzaman was not a Nawab, not really, no; that title was only conferred upon him posthumously by the Nawabs that followed after Dard-e-Dil became independent of the Mughals. So really old Ham was merely a scion of a once important family which had the good sense to ingratiate itself with the Mughals early on and received, in return, the position of *subehdar* – chief administrator – of the province comprising those lands which earlier may have been, and later certainly became, the kingdom of Dard-e-Dil. The position was not hereditary and the Dard-e-Dils were sometimes sent to cool their heels in outposts of the Empire but somehow, in contravention of the standard Mughal policy of keeping administrators on the move, the Dard-e-Dils always returned to those lands. Because they were sycophants, competent as administrators, but otherwise so grovelling and seemingly ineffectual that the Mughals saw them as no real threat? Perhaps. But also perhaps because the Mughals trusted them, admired them, acknowledged them as cousins of the Timurid line, and felt that a few years away from Dard-e-Dil was all it took to remind those cousins that they were entirely dependent on the bounty of the Mughal for their own prestige and power. By and large the plan worked through the sixteenth and seventeenth centuries. By and large. But Hamiduzzaman was less than happy to play the role of needy relation. It was, I believe, the desperation to be ruler not vassal, coupled with an awareness of his own impotence against the Emperor, that made him so susceptible to an act as mad as infanticide. He saw that the reign of the Great Mughal, Akbar, was past and, sensing the faintly

45

glimmering possibility of breaking free from Mughal rule, he was willing to sacrifice anything that might stand in the way of an auspicious future for Dard-e-Dils, even if that thing was a pair of mewling babies.)

'Taj,' Baji said, interrupting my thoughts. I assumed she must have been thinking, like me, of Shah Jahan's architectural wonder. But no.

'Taj, the midwife,' she said, one manicured nail circling the name of the Nawab who killed a tiger with his bare hands. 'With her head full of family lore and no reason to love those oh-so-legitimate babies she brought into the world. How do we know she didn't invent, make up . . . Oh, let's say it straight. How do we know Akbar, Taimur and Sulaiman didn't enter the world on the same day, all just before or just after midnight?'

'Because their mother—'

'Samia, please. I've given birth in the days before these super painkillers and epidurexes – Rehana, you wouldn't laugh if you'd been through it yourself – and I would have believed anything, yes anything, anyone said to me afterwards about when the clock chimed and when it didn't.' She smiled, as though thinking of something that pleased her inordinately. 'Maybe Taj saw triplets and wondered if they qualified as not-quite-twins. And then maybe she saw the clock and thought, Why not. Let me make them believe it's so. Let this be my revenge for their treatment of my mother and me.'

I was thinking, believe me, of my earlier conversation with Samia about Taj. I was thinking that, and thinking also that of course I wasn't the first woman in the family to be bothered by Taj's role in our narrative. So I said, 'Well, I can understand why you feel a sense of affinity with Taj.'

Was it the air, the company, the tilt of my head? I don't know. I just know that as soon as the words were out something transformed them. At the periphery of my vision, Samia was shaking her head at me and Rehana had turned her face away, but Baji only laughed, throwing her head back and showing all her cavities. 'Oh, I see Abida in you. I see her so clearly. You with the untainted blood. Here . . .'

She swooped forward and picked the trailing end of the family tree off the floor, unrolling it on to my lap. 'Here's a pair of not-quites you don't know about.'

Beside Mariam Apa's name, a star.

A diagonal dotted line connected it to another starred name.

Mine.

Chapter Six

I'd had the opening line of Mariam's story ready for a long time: *In all the years my cousin, Mariam, lived with us she only spoke to order meals.* The next line varied, according to my mood. Usually it was: *Strictly speaking, she was more aunt than cousin, though I always called her Apa.* But when I was feeling more fanciful I sometimes replaced that with: *She taught me the textures of silence, the timbres of it, and sometimes even the taste.*

My first thought when Baji showed me those stars was, the opening line will have to change. The story must begin with the curse of not-quites.

I should have thought, How is this possible? Given chronology, given science, given my life. How? But Rehana Apa was up and moving towards me, distracting me with her purposefulness as she pulled me up and said, 'Baji, remember Hamlet? I'm taking Aliya out for something to eat. Samia, stay and look after my grandmother. She's about to go into regret.' She turned to me. 'Where to?'

I thought, Hamlet? I said, 'Any doughnut shop.'

'To Piccadilly Circus then,' Rehana Apa said. She allowed me silence as we walked. I suppose she thought I was thinking of that star beside my name. But actually I was thinking of America. My college days, so recently finished, were days of empty spaces in my head. Spaces without chatter, spaces without textured silences. I was so utterly foreign there, so disconnected from everything that went on that I could afford to be passionate about the tiniest injustice in the domestic news.

'I don't really want a doughnut,' I said. I put on my best academic voice. 'The word "doughnut" is a sign, the visual image of the doughnut is the signifier and a nostalgia for another life is the signified.' I gestured vaguely with my hand. 'Can we just go and sit under a tree instead?'

Rehana Apa said she knew a wonderful tree, and indeed she did. A shady beech in Green Park. Or perhaps it was an elm. Or an oak. I know nothing about trees, but I've read enough novels set in England to be pretty sure no other trees of importance exist there.

'What about Hamlet should Baji remember?' I sat down, unmindful of the damp.

Rehana Apa touched her palm to the tips of the grass, found the grass wet, dried her palm with a tissue and sat down anyway. 'When Polonius says he'll treat the players as they deserve, and Hamlet says, "Use them after your own honour and dignity; the less they deserve, the more merit in your bounty." '

'Such an aristo remark,' I said. 'Combat abuse with nobility; it'll make the other guy look so small.'

Rehana Apa shook her head at me. 'I love Hamlet in that moment. It makes me weep for everything he's forced to become.'

I leant against the tree trunk and tried not to stare at her. My cousin. She must have been a dozen or so years older than me, and suddenly that didn't seem very much. And here we were, talking about Hamlet. With everything else there was to talk about, we were talking about Hamlet.

'Those kids at Baji's. Are they yours?'

'Stinky and Smelly?' Rehana Apa laughed. 'Yes. When the older one was born Baji said he had eyes like the old Nawab, Binky. So I said to my newborn child, "Should we call you Binky?" and he put his hand to his nose and scrunched up his face. My husband said, "He's saying not Binky but Stinky." And it stuck as such names do. The second born didn't have a chance.'

'Their real names?'

'Omar and Aliya.'

'Really? Aliya?'

Rehana Apa nodded. 'Samia told me there's a Stinker in the Pakistani side of the family.'

'Yes. And his brother is Pongo. Weird, isn't it? How our names overlap despite, you know, the complete lack of communication between the two sides of the family. How did Samia get in touch with you?'

'We met at an art exhibition. Treasures of the Indian princes. We both kept circling back to a cabinet which displayed the sword our illustrious ancestor, Nur-ul-Jahan, used in the Battle of Surkh Khait. Once we started talking it took about seven seconds to work out the connection. Do you think your – our – relatives in Pakistan will criticize her for fraternizing with the enemy?'

'No. Well, maybe one or two will. But I suppose the overwhelming emotion will be curiosity about how you've all fared. And the Indian relatives?' It occurred to me suddenly that we didn't support the same cricket team, this cousin and I. We'd never share that joy or camaraderie

50

or heartrending despair that Samia, Sameer and I – and various other cousins – had so often experienced as we sat together in Sameer and Samia's TV room, digging our nails into each other with anticipation during the final overs of a one-day game.

'Probably react the same. Except, as you say, for one or two.' Rehana Apa pulled a twig out of my hair. 'Besides, almost everyone who stayed in Dard-e-Dil is now locked in some kind of property dispute with other relatives, so we're expending our quotas of familial animosity within the national borders. And, for the record, I think Pakistan was a huge mistake.'

'For the record, I don't see it that way. Glad we've got that part of the conversation over with.'

She laughed and slapped my hand lightly. For a while we were silent and I found myself thinking again of him. Khaleel. I tried to picture him in Liaquatabad, but I had no idea what Liaquatabad looked like, so I just imagined tiny storefronts and burst sewerage pipes and cramped flats with laundry hanging over the balconies, spattered with crow droppings. I didn't know if I was imagining a place I'd seen, or one I'd had nightmares about when I had night-mares about Mariam Apa. I looked at Rehana Apa's elbows and I knew I had lied to myself when I said that crippling memories were what made me recoil at the prospect of Liaquatabad. I was born into a world that recoiled at such prospects. If Rehana Apa were to tell me that she was in touch with Baji's mother's family, I'd be shocked. I'd wonder what she could possibly have to say to them, and how she could bear to be reminded that she was one of them just as much as she was one of the Dard-e-Dils. But for all I know, I reminded myself, they could have risen in the world in the last few generations. They could be as polished and urbane as Rehana and I. They could be as polished and urbane as Khaleel.

Rehana Apa must have seen my brows furrowing deeper and deeper because she put a hand on my arm and said, 'If I understand correctly, Mariam's older than you, older than me. What I mean is, you do realize that this twin stuff is absurd, don't you? Babuji won't say why he added it to the tree, but you know, just because we claim he's always right, it doesn't mean he is.'

So I told her the story of Mariam Apa's arrival, and of mine.

It started with a letter to my father; another one, like Taimur's, with an indistinguishable postmark. It was addressed to Sahibzada Nasser Ali Khan, and my mother was still new enough to our family to laugh at the pomp of that address. The letter (my mother still has it) said:

Huzoor! Aadaab!
    I hope you are well and I hope you hope the same of me. I am writing because there is a young lady, Mariam, who soon before was motherless but since last month is an orphan. Her father (late) was Sahibzada Taimur Ali Khan whose name you must know and maybe even his face if you have old pictures. But even if not his face is your father's face and so you will recognize her also because she has the familiarity. She is coming to look you up and I like her so much that I want to say take care of her because even though she may come back here if you don't and that will make me happy I do not want her to be sad and so please make her happy. And also this way I can dream but when she is here I can only wait for what is never!

52

In true Hollywood fashion the gate-bell rang as soon as my parents finished reading out the letter and, in a further cinematic twist, my mother was so surprised by the sound she spilt her tea over the paper and it washed away the signature, which my parents had read when reading the letter, but could not afterwards remember because the letter's sentence structure convinced them that the writer was no one they knew.

So the bell rang and my father, certain that the laws of Hollywood had no part in his life, frowned at the spilt tea and told my mother it was probably just the night-watch-man come to collect his monthly gratuity (which was and still is a tiny amount, but how much can you pay a man for riding through the neighbourhood on a bicycle while blowing a high-pitched whistle which sounds as if it's the shriek of something supernatural).

At this point in my tale, Rehana Apa stopped me to enquire what I thought of Pakistani movies. I had to concede I'd never seen one of Lollywood's productions, though Samia's brother, Sameer, once went to see a local flick with his driver and cook and came home howling with laughter. 'So the hero's at this party, looking suave in his safari suit, and a waitress – not a waiter, a waitress! I ask you, From where? – asks him what he'll have to drink. And I'm thinking, Is he going to do a shocker and ask for alcohol? But no, he asks for Coke with ice. Except he says it in English in some pseudo-smooth accent, so how it really comes out is "Cock on rock." '

Rehana Apa laughed. 'You must tell Baji that. She'll look offended, but she'll love it. But now get back to the story. You said the bell rang.'

Yes, the bell rang. A few seconds later the ayah, recently

hired in preparation for my arrival into the world, knocked on my parents' door and told them that a begum had arrived and was seated in the drawing room. She hadn't said anything but she'd brought two suitcases.

'Well,' Ami said. 'Well. It must be her.'

'What do we do?' Aba held the letter up to the light as if looking for a secret message written in lemon juice. 'I mean, what kind of a person do we think she is?'

Ami laughed. 'If the servants in all their snobbery think she deserves to be seated in the drawing room, she obviously isn't a valet's granddaughter. Most of your relatives only make it to the TV room, and they all think they're princes and princesses.' My mother can be dismissive of lineage in such a manner because, although she never mentions it, everyone knows she can trace her family tree back even further than the Dard-e-Dils. She's from a family of Syeds, yes, descended from the Prophet Mohammed, and there were at least four great poets in her family – one of whom was exiled from Dard-e-Dil by one of the Nawabs who fancied himself a poet. My mother's ancestor read the Nawab's poetry and said, 'This poem proves Allah's justice. How can religion reconcile the privileges you were born into with the hardship I have had to face from birth? This is how: you have power and emeralds; I have talent. And history has shown that fine couplets live longer than fine banquets. God is great.' My father's family claims that the Nawab showed his greatness by banishing, rather than executing, the offending poet. But they never say so within my mother's earshot.

'You're diffusing the suspense,' Rehana Apa said.

Mariam Apa was never about suspense.

She stood up as my parents entered the drawing room,

quite assured. 'Made us feel as though we were the needy relatives, not her,' my mother recalls. 'Though once we'd taken a look at her we couldn't really think of her as needy.' She was dressed in a blue chiffon sari, three gold bracelets adorned her left arm, and a gold chain with a diamond-studded pendant in the shape of an Arabic Allah hung around her neck. My mother looked at her cheekbones, her clavicle, her straight black hair, and knew she was a Dard-e-Dil.

'Hello,' Aba said. 'You're not . . . Mariam?'

She just smiled that smile of hers which once made a rose burst into bloom, and Ami reached out to hug her. It is always possible to measure my mother's reaction to a person by multiplying the time, in seconds, that she speaks without pause by the number of words she utters in that time. The greater the result, the greater her affinity for the person. When she met Mariam Apa she went into seven digits. So my father says, and he's always been good at calculations. At any rate, the warmth of my mother's reaction to Mariam Apa's smile was so overwhelming that whole minutes went by before my father realized that Mariam Apa hadn't said a word.

Rehana Apa pulled a pen out of her handbag and started writing numbers on a leaf. 'Seven digits?' she said. 'Really truly?'

'Now who's diffusing the suspense?'

Aba stopped Ami's monologue with a tap on her shoulder and said, 'We just received this letter –' he waved in the direction of the room where the letter lay – 'and were very sorry to hear about your father. What happened?'

Mariam Apa looked heavenward and raised her hands and shoulders in a gesture of resignation to a higher will.

'Well, yes, of course there's that,' Aba said. 'But can you be more specific?'

Mariam Apa tapped her heart.

Ami reached over, grabbed Mariam Apa's hand. 'Can you speak?'

Mariam Apa nodded.

'Oh,' said Ami. 'Well . . . well . . . oh. I suppose I should show you your room. Of course you're staying; the issue doesn't arise of not. We only found out so the bed hasn't been made up but it's a lovely room, my favourite in the house actually. I prefer it to our room but Nasser doesn't like it because of some reason he's never seen fit to share with me. But I know you will . . .'

That's when Masood walked in. He had come to work for my parents a few months earlier, and had been hailed by all who had sampled his cooking as 'a cook to be hired but never fired'.

'Begum Sahib,' he addressed Ami in Urdu. 'What should I make for dinner tonight?'

Before Ami could answer, Mariam Apa said, '*Aloo ka bhurta, achaar gosht, pulao, masoor ki daal, kachoomar.*'

And my mother was so stunned that Mariam Apa had ordered her favourite meal that she went into labour.

Mariam Apa held her hand throughout the birth, while Aba sat in the waiting room practising the self-hypnosis exercises the gynaecologist had taught Ami to help ease the rigours of childbirth. Between contractions Ami revealed that she and Aba had been planning to name their child Mariam, if she was a girl, but there couldn't be two Mariams in the house. Fortunately they had (given the Dard-e-Dil history) considered the possibility of twins, so there was a second name: Aliya.

'Don't tell me that for this reason you think you qualify. As not-quite-twins,' Rehana Apa snorted.

Mariam and Aliya were supposed to be twins. And Mariam Apa and I entered a world, not *the* world I'll admit, but a world – one inhabited by my parents and Dadi and Masood and Samia and Sameer and all the rest of them – on the same day. But that's not all. Everyone I know grew more garrulous than normal around Mariam Apa, except for me. I've heard that twins communicate in the womb before tongue and throat and larynx form, so they know how to speak to each other without speech.

Am I saying Mariam Apa was in Ami's womb with me? Not quite.

Chapter Seven

I fell asleep under the tree and woke up in the spare room of the Palmer House flat, with memories of a dream which involved Rehana Apa pulling out a mobile phone from her bag, Dadi asking me about the quality of Baji's teaset, me lifting myself off the ground and stumbling into a cab with the help of Samia, and Ami saying, 'But of course you're twins; did I forget to tell you?'

The scent of Samia's perfume and a set of door keys were gone when the eddying noises in my stomach finally convinced me to get out of bed, but in their place was a still-hot *haandi* of chicken *karhai* on the stove and a note instructing me to 'add whole green chillis and *pudina* – or is it *dhaniya*? That green thing, you know what I mean – and cook on medium heat for two minutes'. A spoon covered in spices and the juice of cooked chicken lay next to the *haandi*, but I ignored it and reached for a clean spoon to stir in the chillis and coriander. Masood always used to say that two hands on one spoon spoilt the flavour of a dish. I watched the clock for the two minutes to be up. ('How much time?' I heard Masood's voice, incredulous. 'How can I tell you how much time it'll take? When the spices and the meat dissolve the boundaries between them and flavours seep, one into the other, then it is time.' The day he said that I added new words to his English vocabulary so that he could laugh at, 'For the true chef, thyme is only a herb.' English is the language of advancement in Karachi, and I taught Masood as much as was necessary to enable him to laugh at my jokes.)

The chicken was good, but it wasn't spiritual.

Someone was calling my name. I looked out of the window into the parking lot, and it was him. Khaleel. Cal Butt from Athol, Mass. My knees buckled absurdly, and I pretended to be leaning into the sink to cover that moment of unsophistication. Although how sophisticated can you look while leaning over a pile of dirty dishes? I pulled a teacup out of the sink and waved it at him. Thumb hooked into the pocket of his jeans, sneakers replaced by brown leather boots, fingers twirling a pair of shades, he looked like an American cliché. I said to myself, 'I'd like to be clichéd by him.'

'Hey!' he called out. 'These are for you.' He held up a bunch of flower stems.

'Am I being stalked?'

He laughed. 'I promised myself if you didn't get it, I'd leave.' His expression changed to embarrassment. 'I can still leave. I don't mean it's my decision to make.'

'Hang on.' I grabbed the spare keys and ran down the stairs until I came to the final bend leading to the lobby with its glass doors, and then I ambled. 'How?' I said, when I was through the doors.

'Your luggage tag. From the airport. I remembered the address on it because I have a friend who used to live in that building.' He pointed across the street. Adam's arm reaching towards God. When I first stood in the Sistine Chapel I wondered if Michelangelo was aware of his blasphemy. Who even noticed God when naked Adam lolled so sensually?

Khaleel dropped his arm. 'Look, I'm sorry. This is stupid. It's just that I was thinking of you and then you were there.'

'And then I wasn't.'

'Just after I mentioned where my family lives.'

'What? No, no. Samia just realized it was our stop, that's all. She's a little scatty sometimes.' If I had said a UFO had landed behind the Ritz and its occupants had activated Samia's homing beacon, I might have pulled it off. I can tell stories, but I can't lie particularly well. Samia, scatty!

'Did you say "catty"?' He grinned and leant back against a car, with arms folded. The I'm-cool-enough-to-handle-anything pose. 'So what's so terrible about Liaquatabad that you had to run away at the first mention?'

'Karachi's huge. Really. What was sea and swamp and wasteland not so long ago is now tarmac and concrete and, well, another kind of wasteland.'

'Tell me about April's cruelty,' he said. 'Or answer my question.'

It didn't surprise me that he knew his Eliot. On the plane he'd had a copy of John Ashbery's *Selected Poems*. 'I've never been to Liaquatabad. But it's on that side of Karachi.'

'Which side?'

'That.'

'Are you planning to elaborate?'

'I'm feeling minimalist.' He raised his eyebrows at me, and I thought he was going to walk off. So I said, 'Don't tell me you don't know about the great class divide of Pakistan.'

'Oh. It's like that, is it?' He scuffed the toe of one shoe

against the heel of the other. 'So I'm the boy from the wrong side of the tracks.' Before I could quite decide how to respond to that he said, 'I had a hard enough time growing up in the States knowing the other kids were laughing behind my back at my parents' accents, their clothes, their whole foreign baggage. The way I dealt with that was by telling those kids to either lay off or stop pretending they were my friends. Most chose the first option. But what I'm saying is, I decided pretty early on that I'd rather risk unpopularity at school than feel embarrassed at home. So don't expect me to start getting defensive about my family now just because . . .' He put his hand to his scalp. 'Aaah, hell. Can we go somewhere? And talk?'

Of course we could. But not upstairs; he didn't even suggest that, but followed me around the corner towards a café. When we came to a crossing his hand lightly touched my elbow, convincing me not to make a dash for it between one speeding bus and the next. At the café we sat down at an outdoor table. I ordered coffee; he asked for tea.

'Tell me about Karachi.'

I dipped a lump of sugar into my coffee and watched it change colour. He hadn't said, 'What's Karachi like?' as so many people did, as though they thought I could answer that question with a single, simple analogy. My stock answer was, 'Like a chicken.'

But to Khaleel I talked of June, July and August, the three months that were all I had known of Karachi during my college years. The spring semester always ended by the middle of May, but I'd spend a month or so with college friends, or cousins in New York, having instructed my travel agent to book my flight home for 16 June or as soon thereafter as possible, by which point Dadi was sure to have departed for Paris, where she spent three months every year with her younger son, Ali, always making a point of being there for his birthday on 16 June.

'But summer in Paris is horrible,' Khaleel said. 'Hot, and still. All the Parisians leave for the countryside.'

'Dadi hates the monsoons. If they come early, she leaves early.'

'Why?'

'I've never asked.' I had my suspicions though. In avoiding the monsoons Dadi was avoiding memories of her youth in Dard-e-Dil. Dadi's sister, Meher, had once told me that Dadi's favourite festival of the year when they were children was the festival that marked the first of the rains. In the Dard-e-Dil palace grounds lengths of silken cord were looped around the boughs of trees and held coloured planks of wood a few feet off the ground. The young girls of the family would rush out, bangles clinking together, and would sing the monsoon songs as they swung higher and higher in the air. Beneath numerous tents great feasts were laid out, with special emphasis placed on mangoes. At the height of the mood of dizziness and gaiety the Nawab would produce a rain-shaped diamond from his pocket and bestow it on the girl who swung the highest without faltering in her singing. Dadi left Karachi before the monsoons so that she wouldn't remember all those girls she sang with and all the lustre of her early life.

'But I thought the monsoons were unpredictable,' Khaleel said. 'Don't they sometimes start early, sometimes start not at all?'

'Aren't you the expert on global weather conditions? Karachi monsoons, French summers . . .'

'I'm French.'

'Shut up.'

'No, really. My parents are professors. Physics. Both of them. And bitten by the travel bug. So they get teaching jobs all over the place. And when we were in France I got citizenship. They didn't want me to be a US citizen because it was the seventies, Vietnam and all that, and they had visions of me growing up and being drafted to fight in some war they considered morally repugnant. Which pretty much covers all wars.'

'But the French require you to do military service.'

'Well, maybe I'm lying. Maybe I'm not French. Or maybe I have done military service.'

'What's your point?'

'Don't pigeon-hole me, or my family, in Liaquatabad.'

I looked down into my coffee. 'I try very hard not to pigeon-hole Liaquatabad.'

'So what's the problem? Why didn't you jump back on the Tube before the doors closed?'

'It was my stop.'

Khaleel poured his tea into a saucer, blew on it and tipped it into his mouth. My eyes swivelled round to check that no one I knew was watching. I knew right then everything my family would need to know about Khaleel's parents. They were hardworking, decent people. Not professors, though. Somehow they'd made it to America, land of opportunity, with barely more than the clothes on their backs, and worked absurd hours for even more absurd wages, swearing all the while that for their son it would be different. And it was. He was smart enough and lucky enough for scholarships, and he'd assimilated; maybe he'd even been offered (and accepted) the chance to live as an

63

exchange student in England or France while still in school. At college, perhaps he'd studied abroad for a year, and now he was thinking of going back, back to Karachi, to show his parents' families that yes, the Butts had succeeded in the US, and you wouldn't even know how humble his parents' origins were, except in moments when he revealed little habits he'd picked up at home, like slurping tea out of a saucer.

'If I tell you I just drank in that manner to see your reaction you'll never know if it's true, or if I'm saying it precisely because I did see your reaction.' He wiped his mouth with a napkin. 'So for that reason, and also because I did see your reaction, let's shake hands and say goodbye.'

'No.' It was time to unlearn the art of shrugging. But, even as I thought that, I knew that this time the option to step away didn't exist. Run away, yes; but for reasons so complicated I couldn't cope with thinking about them, and also for reasons as obvious as his smile, there could be no pretence that I was capable of ambling away with only the barest backward glance.

'If I come to Karachi, will you visit me in Liaquatabad?'

Moments when the whole world holds its breath. 'There was a boy I knew at college. No one important. But the last time we attempted to have a conversation he said, "The insurmountable problem is that when you think of me there's logic to your thoughts."'

'So what are you thinking now?'

'Every night, Mariam Apa – Did I mention her on the plane? My father's cousin? – she used to stand in our dining room just after we'd finished dinner, while Masood was clearing away the plates. She'd look out of the glass doors that led into the garden, straight at a hibiscus bush with one branch that curved out from the rest of the plant. With her index finger she'd trace in the air the length, the curve of that branch. And she never let the mali go near the hibiscus. Tended it herself. Cut, watered and manured it. And traced it every night. I don't understand that. I would really like to understand that.'

'Who's Masood.'

'Our cook. He's the only person I've ever known her to speak to.'

'All right. Time out.' He waved his napkin in the air. 'That's it. There's no way you're not making this up.'

'And the only food she ever ate was the food he cooked. You still want to shake hands and walk away?'

'What is this? Are you doing some Sheherazade thing on me?'

'No. I can't live in anticipation for one thousand and one nights.'

'What exactly are you anticipating?'

He could be swallowed up by the earth right now and I would never forget the touch of his finger against my elbow. Absurd, absurd thought. Memory does not preserve. How horrifying that morning when you wake up and your first thought is not of the person who has left. That's when you know, I will never die of a broken heart.

I moved my elbow. Closer. 'What now, Khaleel? What do we do now?'

'Why can't we roll with it; see where time and tide take us?'

'Because Liaquatabad.' I couldn't believe I'd said it out loud. But instead of looking offended he smiled at me, as though grateful for the truth.

He paid the bill, and we started walking. 'A history lesson,' he said. 'After the Mutiny of 1857—'

'Revolt.'

'Sorry?'

'Not a mutiny. A revolt. Mutiny implies it was confined to a section of the armed forces, and though it's true that it started with the Bengal Sepoys—'

'Whatever. The point is, after it was crushed the Mughal Emperor was stripped of all his rights, his privileges. He died poor; his children lived poorer. They were born princes; they died beggars on the streets of Delhi.' He stopped at a grocer's to buy a bag of apples. Took one out and started munching it.

There was a photograph in an old history book of mine, showing the last Mughal Emperor, Bahadur Shah Zafar, after the Revolt. He lay on a charpoy in a dusty courtyard, no robes of state, no jewels, not even an attendant. His head was turned in the direction of the camera, but that seemed merely accidental. I have never seen anything as pathetic as those eyes. I wanted to look at that picture and say that even in these conditions he looked like a king. But he didn't. He looked bewildered, and so sad.

'So there could be descendants of those princes living in Liaquatabad. Have you thought of that? Maybe I'm one of them. Would it make you happier if I told you I was a Mughal prince?'

I shook my head. 'You don't understand. You think this is some simple complication of me believing that lineage is all. On the plane, when I talked about the not-quite-twins, I didn't mention the first pair. You want to hear about them?'

'I want to hear. Anything. Just keep talking.'

I had heard their story for the first time at Baji's flat that morning, between the time Samia first pointed out the stars on the family tree and Rehana Apa mentioned the not-quites who cost us the Taj Mahal. So perhaps I should have mentioned it earlier, but I think you'll agree it fits in better here.

Cast your mind back to Baji's crowded flat and the unrolling of the family tree.

'Hang on just a little tiny minute,' Samia said. 'Who're these two miscreants?' Right at the top of the page beside the name Nur-ul-Jahan, the founder of Dard-e-Dil, victor of the Battle of Surkh Khait, were the names of his two wives, Kulsoom and Shahrukh. Their names were starred.

Kulsoom I knew. Her father, Qadiruddin Shah, fought alongside Nur-ul-Jahan during the Battle of Surkh Khait in 1423. There is nothing original in Qadiruddin's story. Scion of an old royal line from Persia, Qadiruddin dreamt of restoring his family to its former debauchery, but lacked the means and the ability to do so. In the Central Asian marauder, Nur-ul-Jahan, Qadiruddin saw, as his memoirs report, 'a man so high in ambition that he would tear out his own liver and eat it to secure advancement'. Which means, I suppose, that Nur-ul-Jahan had ability, while Qadiruddin had only the knack of recognizing ability in others. Determined to tie his fortunes to those of Nur-ul-Jahan, Qadiruddin presented himself to Nur in the cere-monial garb of the kings of Persia and, by his own account, so impressed the hardened military man with his manner and deportment that, within minutes of their introduction, Nur-ul-Jahan offered Qadiruddin the position of advisor. (Many of my relatives find this account somewhat suspect, since Nur-ul-Jahan was from the royal and cultured Timurid line and was hardly likely to be taken in by some old Persian robes. It is true, however, that his grandmother,

67

Tamburlaine's daughter, was married off to a man known more for his warmongering than for his finesse, and it was in this man's tribe that Nur-ul-Jahan grew up. It is also true that Nur-ul-Jahan had many many advisors.)

After the Battle of Surkh Khait and the little skirmishes that followed, a marriage was arranged between Qadiruddin's daughter, Kulsoom, and the new ruler, Nur-ul-Jahan of Dard-e-Dil (no one knows why he chose that name for his realm). Shortly after providing the new royal family with an impeccable Persian lineage to add to their somewhat diffused Timurid blood, Qadiruddin was poisoned.

I had heard enough stories of Nur-ul-Jahan to know the name of his wife, so when Samia pointed out the starred names on the family tree I recognized immediately the name of Qadiruddin's daughter, Kulsoom. But her not-quite-twin, this Shahrukh character, I had never heard of.

Baji laughed at Samia's and my confusion. 'Poor Shahrukh! Exiled to the fringes of history.' She leant back in her chair and smiled, and I knew from her expression (such a familiar expression! I'd seen it often enough on Dadi's face) that she was about to tell a wonderful story. 'Qadiruddin's wife had died in childbirth and the baby, Kulsoom, was suckled by a wet-nurse. This wet-nurse had a daughter, Shahrukh, born the same day as Kulsoom. They say Shahrukh's father was Qadiruddin's brother, but this may just be a rumour born of the fact that Kulsoom and Shahrukh were twinned in appearance, voice and mannerism. Qadiruddin himself could not tell them apart. Now, after the marriage of Nur-ul-Jahan and Kulsoom, Qadiruddin's enemies told Nur that Qadiruddin had sworn he would never

68

taint his own bloodline with that of a barbaric marauder, and so he had given Shahrukh – illegitimate daughter of a wet-nurse – to Nur in marriage.'

'That's why Nur poisoned Qadiruddin.'

'Exactly, Aliya Begum. But he still needed Qadiruddin's lineage to bolster his own claim to power, so he married his wife's foster sister.'

'Shahrukh!' I said.

'Kulsoom!' Samia said.

Baji laughed again. 'Well, no one knows. Qadiruddin's enemies might have been lying, or they might not. The foster sisters never revealed which was which, and with the wet-nurse dead no one else could tell them apart. All their lives they each answered to both "Kulsoom" and "Shahrukh"; each claimed to belong to the royal family of Persia, each referred to that wet-nurse as her mother.'

'So they were the first not-quite-twins?' I ran my fingers over their names. When Baji nodded, I said, 'But then the myth is untrue. The first not-quite-twins didn't bring ruin to the family. Okay, so they didn't do Qadiruddin any good, but as far as the Dard-e-Dil family goes, they were . . . that is, Kulsoom was, I mean . . . Oh my God.'

Baji clapped her hands and sat back, watching Samia and me gape at each other. 'We're all descended from the illegitimate child of a wet nurse,' Baji giggled. 'As likely as not.'

'So you see,' I told Khaleel, 'the Liaquatabad problem isn't about lineage as such. If it were, if that was the issue I was having to struggle with, I wouldn't just be reprehensible, I'd be stupid. Right?'

'Er . . . well. Hey, is that your cousin?'

In a newsagent's doorway stood a woman I'd never seen

before, with dark hair and beautiful eyes. 'We all look alike to you, don't we? You Americans!'

He checked to make sure I was teasing, and then laughed. 'Don't tell me you don't see the resemblance. But no, I guess it's pretty obvious that woman is not related to you.'

'Why's that?' By now we'd walked past her, and I looked back once more because really, she did look a little like Samia.

'Didn't you see her hands? She's clearly not from a privileged background.'

'What, you read her palm as we walked past?'

'No. But she's grown up having to do some kind of manual labour. Didn't you see the veins bulging out from the back of her hands?'

There was a bench nearby, so I sat down. I looked back at the woman with beautiful eyes whose collarbone was hidden entirely beneath her high-necked shirt. Khaleel said my name, twice, and when I didn't answer he put his hand to my forehead, his wrist just inches from my lips. His other hand rested on my knee and when I looked down I saw him holding the half-eaten apple, his teeth marks embedded in its flesh. I looked up at him and smiled. 'As I was saying, it's not about lineage or, to give it its more modern term, family background. It's not that simple.'

The woman with beautiful eyes walked by, talking to a man. I heard him say, 'How's the new sculpture coming along?'

'A sculptor. Hence the hands.' I stood up. 'I was just about to go up to her and say . . . I don't know . . . Show me your clavicle, or something equally suave.'

'So what is it about if not lineage?'

'Do you know what I found out today? That I'm fated to bring ruin to my family. Me and Mariam.' I said it, and then I stopped to think about it for the first time. Oh, I told the stories often enough. The curse of the not-quite-twins. The inevitability of destruction trailing in their wake. But if you'd asked me whether I believed, truly believed, the stories, I'd have laughed. But seeing that star against my name, seeing that other star against Mariam's name and thinking of what she'd done and how my family had reacted, something more primeval than logic or cynicism or nineties cool had made me feel – still made me feel – so sick, so trapped.

'Cal,' I said, taking the apple core from his hands and dropping it in a garbage can. 'In another life, maybe even in another year, we'd meet each other's friends, we'd watch movies together, we'd talk on the telephone about nothing, and I'd order such meals for you in restaurants! But, instead, I'm going to get on a plane tomorrow and go home. And it's still May. This time I booked my ticket back for May. And look, Khaleel, we've reached my flat, and I can see Samia through the window, so even if it had occurred to me to invite you up, now I won't. So you're right. Let's shake hands and say goodbye.'

'Aliya, I'm not going to shake your hand. No way. No civilized goodbyes, or sorry-our-timing-was-bad speeches, okay?'

'What then, Khaleel?'

Samia was watching television when I walked into the flat, minutes later, but she turned it off when she saw me. 'Where have you . . . What's wrong? You look mighty odd.' She walked closer to me. 'Are you drunk?' She leant in, smelt my breath. 'Is that cider?'

Chapter Eight

That I hadn't told him what time I'd be leaving in the morning did not prevent me from looking for him as I exited Palmer House and moved towards the waiting cab. Samia, her tongue thick with sleep, told me not to be a fool, and no, I didn't have a few more minutes before I had to leave and, please, did I really expect her to believe I wanted those extra minutes because I hated saying goodbye to her.

'Well, I do,' I said.

'Are you getting misty-eyed?' She blinked and stared at me. 'You are! My God, Aliya, I haven't made you cry since that time you had mumps and I told you the only cure was surrounding yourself with dirty undergarments. What did I say MUMPS stood for? Malodorous Underwear Might Provide Succour.'

It's a family tradition. When you leave, you leave laughing.

But airports and aeroplanes kill all laughter. Things I find funny anywhere else seem like signs of the coming Apocalypse in an airport. This time was no different. While I was still queuing up to get my boarding pass an airline official walked past, checking that everyone had passports and tickets ready, and told me my suitcase was 'not appro-priately proportioned'. Was it too large? Too wide? Too high? He sniffed and conceded, no. And walked on. At the ticket counter I was told that the computer 'doesn't seem to want to recognize you'. 'Well, force it,' I said. The man behind me whispered, 'Farah' and started humming the *Charlie's Angels* theme. It's what every airport experience needs: a touch of seventies magic. But at least the airline person took me seriously and thumped on the computer until it yielded up my name. In return for this affront, the computer gave me a seat in the smoking section.

Aboard the flight, I waited patiently for take-off and the subsequent extinguishing of the no-smoking sign, at which point a small group of men – blatantly ignoring the earlier breathy instructions of the flight attendant – got up from their seats in the no-smoking section and walked back to light up, scant feet from my face.

'Excuse me,' I said. 'Would someone mind swapping seats with me? I don't want to be in the smoking section.'

'Who does?' said a man with beautifully manicured hands, puffing away at his Marlboro.

But by now I had spotted my targets. There were three Pakistanis grouped together, labourers by the look of it, and for their benefit I repeated the question in Urdu.

'Give the lady your seat,' one said, gesturing at a wiry, bearded man.

'Yes. Do you want her to travel in discomfort all the way to Karachi?' another said. 'Didn't anyone ever teach you any manners?'

The wiry man turned to me. 'Our seats are 8D, E and F. Go and sit in any one. We'll decide who should stay here.'

I took the aisle seat. Sat down and closed my eyes,

pretending to be asleep by the time two of them came back, having left the wiry man amidst the swirl of smoke.

The man in the seat next to me said to his companion, 'Why is it that the desire for a cigarette is even stronger on a flight during take-off than it is just before Iftari, even when Ramzan falls in summer and you're without a smoke for over fourteen hours?'

There are only two things I can do to while away time on a plane: talk, or remember.

I remembered Ramzan.

Officially the month of fasting, Ramzan has always seemed to me synonymous with feasting. Through the first eighteen years of my life, abstaining from food and drink from sunrise to sunset had less to do with religious devotion than it did with culinary devotion. For in order to truly appreciate the Iftari meal that Mariam Apa ordered – yes, since her arrival she had been the one responsible for ordering meals and everyone swears that, though Masood had been a fine cook to begin with, he only became a magician when she started telling him what to cook. (I might be inclined to view this comment with suspicion if it wasn't for the fact that I've seen people attempting to replicate Masood's recipes in their kitchens, even going to the extent of borrowing his pots and pans and chopping board and knife, but never, not once, has anyone succeeded in producing a meal that could be mistaken as Masoodian. '*Haath mein maza hai*,' Dadi always said – the delight is in his hand – but perhaps the delight was really in Mariam's voice.) Regardless of cause and effect, what I was saying was that to appreciate the Mariam–Masood Iftaris we had to build ourselves up to a pitch of hunger that enabled us to sit and eat and eat for an hour and a half without pause.

In drawing rooms across the country frazzled Begums complained that all this fasting, combined with the heat, made their cooks so horribly bad-tempered. Of course, one felt guilty asking them to stand over a stove and cook under these circumstances. Masood, however, loved it. He liked nothing so much as to shoo us out of the kitchen with the warning, 'If you smell my food you will be so overcome with temptation that you'll break your fast on the spot. Leave, leave, before you make me into an instrument of Shaitan and I send you to hell.' The only person he allowed in was Mariam Apa, who would chop and stir and watch, as she never did during any other time of the year.

And oh! the meals that resulted. We started with the requisite date, of course, to symbolize fidelity to the first Muslims in the deserts of Arabia, but then . . . on to gluttony! Curly shaped *jalaibees*, hot and gooey, that trickled thick sweet syrup down your chin when you bit into them; diced potatoes drowned in yogurt, sprinkled in spices; triangles of fried *samosas*, the smaller ones filled with mince-meat, the larger ones filled with potatoes and green chillies; *shami* kebabs with sweet-sour *imli* sauce; spinach leaves fried in chick-pea batter; *nihari* with large gobs of marrow floating in the thick gravy, and meat so tender it dissolved instantly in your mouth; *lassi* that quenched a day-long thirst as nothing else did and left us wondering why we ever drank Coke when a combination of milk, yogurt and sugar could be this satisfying; an assortment of sweetmeats – *gulab jamoons*, *ladoos*, *burfi*.

There were always at least ten people gathered at our house by sunset for Iftari and, at some point, someone would look up from his or her third helping and say, 'Mariam, have you finished eating? That's an insult to the food. It's divine!' And Mariam Apa, who always ate just enough to show she appreciated the food, would make a gesture as though plucking the words from the air and swallowing them, to indicate, 'I am eating your praise.' Then she would look across at Masood, who had walked in with hot *naans* to go with the *nihari*, and smile her smile of congratulations. Masood would incline his head in a gesture that was not so much a salaam of deference as an acceptance of well-deserved praise.

(When I start to talk about Masood's cooking to people who've never tasted it, I'm often greeted with looks of scepticism. All I'll say is this: the Dard-e-Dil relatives of Dadi's generation swear the finest meals they've eaten have all come from Masood's kitchen. Such a compliment is not to be slighted when it comes from people who've eaten food from the fabled kitchens of the Dard-e-Dil palace where legions of cooks plied their trade, each one specializing in a different kind of food. So, for instance, there was one cook for the rice dishes and one for the *parathas*, one for the sweetmeats and one for the kebabs.)

In our house, the only meal that ever surpassed those Ramzan meals was the one Masood and Mariam Apa conjured up for me the day I was accepted at a college in America. Halfway through the meal I burst into tears to say, 'But who will cook for me when I'm there?'

Masood almost touched my shoulder, said, 'Don't worry, Aliya Bibi.' It was the first time he'd ever called me '*Bibi*' and the deference it implied made me feel even more miserable. 'When you come home for the holidays I'll feed you so much they'll have to roll you back on to the plane.'

'Promise?' I said.

'Promise.' He smiled back.

Two weeks later he was gone.

I pulled the airline blanket over my face and tried to regulate my breathing, which had become ragged just thinking about Masood's departure and what followed.

When I told Samia that I never told Mariam Apa's story, I wasn't entirely honest. Admittedly, I'd never said it aloud in one go, but in dribs and drabs I'd hinted at, implied and blurted out every fragment of it at college to my room-mate, Celeste. Brilliant, artistic, revolutionary, multi-multi-ethnic and entirely unpindownable Celeste, who moved into our room at the start of freshman year while I was still in transit and decided to make me feel at home in Massachusetts by customizing her reproduction of Che Guevara. Imagine me, walking into the airy, brightly co-loured dorm-room and seeing a six-foot-by-three-foot paint-ing of a long-haired man with beautiful eyes, a mango in one hand and a cricket bat in the other, his teeth red with blood.

Betel-nut juice, Celeste explained weeks later, when I felt I could query her artistic judgement.

The first thing Celeste asked me when I'd unpacked was, 'Who is she?' She was Mariam Apa, captured in black and white, framed and displayed on my desk. I evaded answer-ing in any detail until the end of that semester, when Celeste announced, 'I'm going to make a painting of your cousin, Mariam. You got any input on that?'

'Yes. Can you paint her older? So I'll have some way of knowing how age might change her face.'

Celeste turned her attention away from the picture of Mariam Apa and towards me. 'It's more common for people to want a painting to remove a few years from the sitter.'

I laughed. 'The thought of Mariam Apa older . . . older

and happy. Can you, who never knew her, imagine that? I so wish that I could.'

'So she died?' Celeste was never one for cloaking brutality in euphemism.

'My grandmother would doubtless say it would be better if she had.'

'Okay, spill.'

How Celeste made sense of the garble that followed, I'll never know. But I'm clearer now. So, deep breath, forget about Massachusetts, forget about the flight, and let me take you to the day of Masood's disappearance, two weeks after he called me Bibi.

I knew something was wrong the moment I returned from school and the only smell to assail my nostrils as I walked up the driveway was that of the manure recently delivered to my neighbour's garden. Ami was standing in the kitchen as I ran in, staring in mystification at Masood's rack of spices.

'What's happened? Where is he? Is he ill?'

'No, no, he's not ill. He had to leave. His father has died. Masood's the head of the family now. So he's gone.'

'For how long?' I didn't stop for a moment to think about Masood's loss; I just wondered how long I'd have to do without his cooking.

'*Jaan*, he's gone. They need him there. It's feudal land, you know. It seems his father was the cook at the home of the *zamindar*, and Masood will be taking over that position. He said to tell you he's sorry he didn't have time to say goodbye, but he had to catch the morning train.'

'But how will we . . .' I looked around the kitchen, cavernous and strange. 'What about Mariam Apa?'

Ami shook her head. 'I don't know. We've already found

a new cook – the one who worked for your dadi when Mohommed was on leave – and he's starting tomorrow, but I don't know if Mariam . . . I don't know what. I don't know.'

All I was thinking was, I'll never hear her voice again. But when I saw the flutter of Ami's hands across the spice jars and her refusal to meet my eye, I thought, Oh dear God.

It's not just that she only spoke to speak to him of food; she also only ate when it was his food she was eating. When Masood had taken his father on haj, two years earlier, he'd frozen a week's supply of food for Mariam Apa so that she wouldn't starve.

'Where is she?' I said.

'In her room. When Masood was leaving he told her to keep eating, otherwise she'll fall ill and cause him much pain. And she smiled and . . . hugged him. Briefly. She hugged him goodbye.'

I stared. A hug – across class and gender. And he wasn't even much older than her. Before this had their fingers even touched as they passed a tomato from one to the other? I doubted it. A hug! I wouldn't have, and Masood had carried me piggy-back style when I was a child.

But when I entered Mariam Apa's room she was reclining in bed, reading the afternoon papers, as though it were just another day. I stood in the doorway, watching for the throbbing vein in her neck, for the inward curl of her fingers, for the awkwardly angled shoulders or the tooth biting down on her lip. But all I got, instead, was the tiniest alteration in the curve of her mouth to tell me she knew she was being watched.

'Will you eat?' I burst out, and flung myself across the bed. Without looking at me she shook her head. I touched her wrist and, still not turning her eyes towards me, she reached out and pushed my hair off my face with fingers so stiff I jerked my head back in fright. Rigor mortis, is what I absurdly thought when I should have been thinking of how hard she was trying not to tremble. But right then I could only see the hollows of her form. Hollow between clavicle and neck, hollow of cupped palm which held itself just short of supplication, hollow of her mouth.

I backed away and stood up. 'You can't do this to me.'

Her eyes closed and opened. And closed again.

Three days later she still hadn't touched a morsel of food, and Aba was raging through the house, railing against the stubbornness of women. He was looking for a fight, of course, but Ami and I were too despondent to rise to the challenge.

In the silence that followed a protracted outburst we heard the door swing open. Auntie Tano, an old family friend, walked in.

'Guess who I met?' she said, after proffering her cheek all around to be kissed.

'Why don't you just tell us,' Aba said.

'Pinkie!'

'I thought she was in London.'

'No, no. The other Pinkie. Rash's wife.'

Ami attempted interest. 'Oh, really? How is she?'

'Why do we care?' Aba asked.

'You care, my dear man, because she has just spent a week on the family lands with her brother, Jahangir.'

'Jahangir! How is he?'

'Really, why do we care?'

Ami slapped Aba lightly on the wrist. 'Of course we care. Haven't seen him in what? Three years? Ever since his wife

80

died. He just stopped coming to the city. I don't know why. You'd think he would get so lonely on the lands.'

'Such a tragedy,' Auntie Tano murmured, pressing the back of her hand against her forehead. 'So young. I have a picture of them at our New Year's party. They look so happy.'

'Yes, well, it was a masquerade party,' Aba observed.

'Honestly. What a thing to say. Ayesha, look at what your husband is saying. They were quite happy together.'

'Happy? Oh please. It was common knowledge he was having it off with any number of women.' Aba picked up a newspaper and opened it with the air of one who has nothing further to learn from the conversation proceeding around him.

'Ye-es. But that was his habit, you know.'

Aba lowered the newspaper. 'What?'

'Yes, yes. He acquired the habit before he got married. You can't expect a man to change his habits just because he gets married.'

A long pause followed this remark. Finally Aba said, 'Why are we having this conversation?'

'Well, this is what I've been trying to tell you. Masood is Jahangir's cook!'

Next door, in Mariam Apa's room, the bed creaked.

'Of course,' Ami said. 'How stupid of me. That's why the name of Masood's village sounded so familiar.'

'Don't you see?' Auntie Tano said. 'Don't you see how you can solve Mariam's problem? Jahangir, widower. Masood, his cook. Mariam, single and starving to death.'

I try to remember how I reacted to that. I can't.

'Are you mad?' Aba said, regarding Auntie Tano as though she needed spraying with pesticide. 'Do you think

I would send my cousin off to be married to a man she barely knows, in some remote village? And not just any man, but a man of those . . . habits. Just so that she can dine well? Over my dead body.'

'No,' Ami whispered. 'Her dead body.'

I remember my reaction to that. I thought, How scripted. How absurd. I wanted to say, Auntie Tano, you've done your bit; you've told us where he is. Thank you, thank you. I've never said that more sincerely. But now you can go. I'm taking over.

'So she can live there or something,' I said. 'Buy a house in the area.'

'Alone?' Auntie Tano raised her eyebrows.

Aba tossed the paper aside and waved his finger in the air to indicate a Thought. 'No, of course not that. But maybe now that we know where Masood is perhaps . . . Yes. Why didn't we consider this before? We can pay him to send a supply of food over every week. Send it by train. Or by plane even, if such things as airports exist in that god-forsaken rural farmland. We could arrange that.'

Mariam Apa glided into the room, a newspaper in her hand. She lifted Ami's hand, pointed to her wedding ring, then pointed to her own unadorned finger, and nodded.

'No,' I said. 'You can't.'

For the first time ever she ignored me. She held the newspaper out to Aba, pointing to something on the page.

'What's this? Train schedules? Mariam, you can't be serious.'

But she was. I knew it immediately by the sudden burning at the back of my eyes. I could not stay then. Could not stay for Auntie Tano's confusion about how to react now that one of her ridiculous schemes was being taken seriously; could not stay for Aba's baffled rage; could not stay for Ami's pleas to wait a while, don't be hasty, even if you decide to marry, not him, and if him, not now, wait, weddings have to be planned, this is not the way things are done. I could not.

I ran to my room, locked the door, and wept, though I didn't quite know why, my fists banging against the wall. And when half an hour went by and Mariam Apa did not knock on the door, I wept some more. But when I heard Aba dragging suitcases down from the store-room shelves, I pushed myself off the bed, out of the room, into her room where she was waiting for me, arms open just wide enough to fit me in. Something of the sickness inside me dissipated then, for though I knew she would leave, I also knew he – Jahangir – would not be able to help but love her.

'There was a boy in my class called Jahangir,' I gulped between sobs. 'We used to call him *Jangia* – Underpants.' And then we both laughed, our heads thrown back, our shoulders shaking, our arms still around each other.

She and Aba left the next day. She had packed all her favourite clothes and books, much to the consternation of Ami, who kept saying, 'But you're only going to meet him now. That's all. The wedding, if there is a wedding, won't be for a while yet.'

But she knew Mariam Apa well enough to know there would be no planning and preparation and attention to custom and drawing up guest lists that would include everyone whose shadow had ever crossed paths with Mariam Apa and her closest relatives.

There was a strange silence in the house when they left. Ami and I retired to separate rooms to try to imagine what would await Mariam Apa at the end of that train journey.

But I could not imagine the Underpants Man as anything other than a caricature, and found myself wondering over and over how she would greet Masood, and would she hug him again? And why, why, I wondered, I finally wondered, why was it that when we tried to think of ways to save Mariam Apa there was one we never mentioned?

Several times that day I paused to think of living in a house without Mariam Apa around, but I never allowed myself to linger over that thought, telling myself instead that soon I'd be gone as well, and perhaps by the time I came back for the holidays Mariam Apa would have found a way to convince Underpants to move back to Karachi and build a house in the empty plot next door to ours, with an extra-large kitchen for Masood.

Aba returned the next day, alone.

'Well?' Ami and I greeted him at the door.

'Well, she's married.'

I looked at Ami, and she looked at me, and I knew she was thinking what I was thinking, only she was thinking it with greater horror, and we both wondered, How? How can we say it? So we just said it the simplest way we knew: 'To whom?'

I had lived all my life in that house but, I swear, I asked the question because I did not know the answer.

Chapter Nine

To set foot once more on the soil of one's homeland. Modern airports deny us this symbolic gesture. No soil, not even tarmac. Instead we step into an elevated corridor which carries us through to passport control, luggage claim and customs clearance. Denied my Richard II moments ('so weeping-smiling greet I thee, my earth') I've learnt to crane forward, or sideways, towards a window, to await the dip of the plane's wing, the descent from the clouds and – almost there now – the giant expanse of Karachi glittering under the darkened sky. I've always loved the brashness of that city, the resolve that turns on lights, night after night, not really in the hope of outstarring the sky, but just for the sake of contesting. Skyscrapered skylines, for all their self-vaunting, seem far less ambitious by comparison; the buildings shouting out, 'I'm taller, I'm more brightly lit, hey look at me!' vie merely with each other for attention.

As I watched the land below, an area of lights winked once, twice, and disappeared. A sigh, half exasperated, half amused, went round the cabin. '*Bijli* failure,' someone behind me said needlessly, and we all waited to see how many lights would flicker on, signifying back-up generator power. Only a handful did, and the voice behind me said in Urdu, 'Well, looks like it isn't Clifton or Defence.' The passengers around me started laughing at this mention of the élite neighbourhoods, except for the woman across the aisle from me who caught my eye and gave me a rueful smile. We both recognized the other as someone who did, or easily could, live in the most upmarket parts of town.

At passport control the same woman and I regarded the long line ahead of us, consisting almost entirely of men, and simultaneously set up a cry of, 'Ladies!' The cry was picked up by the men in line, 'Ladies! Ladies please!' and a path opened up, despite a few grudging noises, to the front of the line.

The airport official looked at my passport picture, which had been taken the year before on what was, by the look of it, the most glamorous day of my life. The official sniffed, squinted at me, and said the photograph was of my older sister. He turned the picture towards me to make his point, but the men standing near me waved off his suspicions. 'Oh, you know the studio photographers; when they're developing the picture they do a little artistry of their own,' one man said. Another interjected, 'Touch up. Touch-up job.' And a third sealed the argument. 'These are women's matters.' The official grunted, 'Sometimes I think we place too much importance on women's matters.' But he let me through.

The wait for the luggage was mercifully short. As a porter wheeled my suitcase out of the terminal I heard a voice announce over a loudspeaker, 'No cigarette smoking or *paan* chewing in the terminal.' The end of the remark reminded me of Che's reddened teeth and I realized I was glad Celeste hadn't been able to afford to take me up on my offer to spend part of her summer in Karachi.

My cousin Sameer was waiting for me when I exited the terminal, and he hugged me with an exuberance that prompted a cat-call from some unknown person.

'Good God, girl!' Sameer grinned. 'You're a sore for sight eyes.'

'You're a bit of a sore yourself,' I laughed. 'But, oh God, Sammy, the heat!'

'The problem's the humidity.' He gestured in the direction of his car. 'Your parents were planning to come and pick you up but I had to drop a business associate at the airport in any case, so I said I'd just hang around and wait for you.'

'Business associate.' I raised my eyebrows at him. 'And how's the corporate world treating you?'

He made a face. 'It would help if this country had an economy to speak of. My advice is, keep studying as long as possible.' He put an arm around my shoulder. 'But, honestly, other than my overwhelming desire to greet my favourite cousin, I'm here because the BS called. Beloved Sister. She told me what happened and that maybe you're a little shaken up. So I'm here with my shoulder.'

I shrugged. 'He bought me a cup of coffee. Not much more to it.'

'He who?'

'He who? Well, what did Samia say?'

'Baji. The family tree. What the stars say about you and Mariam.'

'Oh. That.'

'That.' He didn't say anything else as we got into his olive-green Civic (brand new – obviously the economy wasn't treating him too shabbily), paid the porter (ignoring his plea for US dollars) and drove away from the

87

comparative order of the airport into the crush of brightly coloured buses and honking horns and zigzagging scooters. Open-backed trucks carrying huge, mushroom-shaped bales of hay lumbered past, and Sameer veered off to the far lane and slowed down until they passed. A man rolled down the tinted windows of his car and raised an eyebrow seductively at me from behind eighties-style dark glasses. My view of him was cut off by a van that zipped past, letters of the alphabet stuck on its back window, spelling out I AM TOM SAWYER.

I laughed so hard at that I almost wept. 'The absurdities Karachi proffers up to keep our sense of humour intact.'

'Of course it's not as absurd as believing old family myths.'

'Sam Mere!' I boxed his shoulder. 'If it were one set of twins, or two, it could be coincidence. But so many, over the years, and each time . . .' We overtook Tom Sawyer and I saw he was a woman. 'Of course I know it should be absurd. And you have to really stretch definitions to believe that Mariam and I . . . but still. Something feels unresolved.'

He was gracious enough not to laugh at my expectation of resolution. 'Is that why you're finally here before the middle of June?'

'Has she said anything about that?'

'Your dadi? Not exactly. But she called me a couple of hours ago and gave me a lecture on driving carefully and not exceeding the speed limits.'

'There are speed limits?'

'In the abstract. Are you nervous about seeing her again?'

Nervous? That wasn't inaccurate, but the word seemed wrong somehow. Who was it who first decided that something as complicated as an emotion could be summed up in a word with consonants neatly spaced between vowels? Of course, there had been a time with Dadi when my feelings were as uncomplicated as a monosyllable, vowels politely alternating with consonants. A monosyllable such as 'love'. And then, after that, there had been a time when I tried to convince myself that my feelings for Dadi were as uncomplicated as that other monosyllable, love's opposite. But I could never quite bring myself to believe that.

'She's not at my house, is she?' I asked Sameer.

'What, now? No. Don't suppose so. Think she's had her share of family-related tensions for the day.'

'Why? What happened?'

'Mummy just broke the news to her. My grandmother's coming to town.'

'Meher Dadi? God help us all.'

Don't misunderstand that remark. Dadi's sister, Meher, is the grandmother I'd always wanted. Born two years after Dadi, she early on perfected the role of rebellious younger sister. At thirteen she announced that one day she would elope, and five years later she did just that. Mind you, the man she eloped with was from a very good family and, on his own merit, was a particular favourite of my great-grandfather's, so both families were delighted with the match. (Once, watching a stage production of *The Tempest*, Dadi laughed at Prospero's plans to unite Ferdinand and Miranda and said, 'My father was Prospero to Meher's Miranda.') Meher's husband died long before she was ready to settle into respectable widowhood, so she took to spending her evenings playing bridge with my father and his friends and demanding to know when one of them was going to marry her daughter. One of them finally did – my father's old friend, Zaheer. Immediately after the wedding Meher sold her house and declared she was going to Greece, and maybe she would take flying lessons while she was there. She said to her daughter, Zainab, 'Zaheer's rich, and I don't foresee divorce for the two of you, so you won't mind if I squander all my money, will you?' Then she took off in the direction of the Mediterranean and proceeded to multiply her wealth with a few wise investments in the European stock markets. Every so often she'd return to Karachi for a visit and – this is why I said, God help us – she and Dadi would get into the most bitter rows about the most trivial things. I was almost fifteen before I realized that 'Apollo', who missed her while she was away, and because of whom she couldn't stay in Karachi long, was not a dog. And yes, she had learnt to fly. She had the aviator goggles to prove it.

In London, Samia had said that once you scratched the surface those two sisters, Meher and Abida, were really quite similar. I pointed out that Meher might scratch the surface, but Abida would consider it a most common activity.

'So what did you think of Baji?' Sameer waved away the young boy who had darted into the middle of the road to wipe the Civic's windscreen at the red light. The boy ignored Sameer and wiped vigorously with a dirty cloth, leaving streaks of grease on the windscreen. Sameer rolled down his window and yelled at the boy, who darted around to my side and wiped with more vigour. I picked up the two-rupee note lying, half torn, by my foot and handed it to him just as the lights changed.

'I was too terrified to think. But Rehana Apa's lovely.' Something that should have occurred to me long ago finally did. 'Sameer, how many of the Indian relatives do you know?'

Sameer shook his head and turned on his wiper spray. 'Me personally? None. Samia and Rehana Apa found each other in London a couple of weeks after my last visit there, so I haven't met her or Baji or Stinko and Skunky, or whatever the kids' names are. And you remember that old Indian relative you saw at our house when we were kids? The one you thought was talking about someone called Prue Frock? Well, she wrote my grandmother a letter of condolence when my grandfather died, which Mummy answered, along with some polite if-you're-ever-in-Karachi kind of note. No one really expected Prue Frock to take the offer up, and there was – I can't believe we haven't talked about this before – there was a huge *tamasha* when she wrote back weeks later to say she'd be in Karachi for a few hours. A major deal was made of keeping the whole thing secret from your dadi. But we haven't heard from her since then. I think she might have died.' His hands left the steering wheel in a gesture of incomprehension. 'Our more distant cousins – you know, the Starched Aunts and that whole side – probably keep up some of their old ties. I think some of them may have done some border hopping from time to time. And now that everyone's moving around so much . . . You know little Usman's got a conditional offer for Oxford? Akbar and Sulaiman's old college, no less. So yes, I suppose there are increasing opportunities for meeting on neutral soil. But I think, the more closely one's connected to your dadi, the less likely one is to hear about all the family reunions going on. I love her, you know, but she's always been a little nutty about the Indian relatives.'

'Can you imagine doing that? Cutting off all contact with me? Or Samia?'

Sameer's hand touched one ear and then the other. 'God spare us all from such horrors.' He said it with a fervour I didn't expect, and for a moment I thought he was mocking me.

'There's a strong chance the bank's going to post me to Hong Kong. It's an attractive proposition and God knows there are days I just want to get away from the inefficiency, the violence, the corruption . . . Fact is, if it happens I'd be stupid to turn it down. Professional suicide. But no place will ever be home like this. And no company is as comforting as the company of family. That's what I learnt at college.'

I turned off the air conditioner, and rolled down the window. We were much closer to the sea now and, coupled with the speed at which Sameer was driving, it made for a pleasant breeze. I inhaled the musky scent of *motia* that wafted over boundary walls, and turned up the volume of the stereo. Dire Straits with my perennial favourite, the *Brothers In Arms* album. This could be any day, any year, in the last decade. Sameer driving, me controlling the music and the ventilation, conversation drifting between what we would do in the future and what we didn't know about the past, and Sameer as inclined as ever to treat a red traffic-light as a suggestion rather than a command.

Karachi boys have a distinctive one-handed way of driving, though I hadn't realized that until I went to America. They push their seats further back than is necessary, keep one hand on their left thigh, ready to shift over to the gearbox, extend the other arm forward, absolutely straight, and grip the top of the steering wheel. When the time comes to turn, they unfist their right hand, hold the open palm against the wheel, and make the turn, the circular motion of their hand suggesting that they're miming the actions of a window-cleaner with a wash cloth. It's only silly when it isn't sexy.

'So, go on. Spill the beans,' Sameer said.

'About what?'

'Who is the "he" you mysteriously alluded to at the airport? The one who bought you coffee?'

'I was just wondering how he drives. You'd like him. Have you ever been to Liaquatabad?'

'I hope you've just changed the subject.'

'Why? Dammit, Sameer, why?'

'Because petrol prices have shot up. Name?'

'Khaleel. New topic.'

'Khaleel? So he's a *desi*.'

'New topic, Sameer.'

'And he lives in Liaquatabad? Aliya, seriously?'

'New topic. Please. Sammy, please.'

'Okay. But we're going to have to talk about this later. Hey, did you hear about Godziloo? The lizard in my bathroom?'

I closed my eyes and leant back. 'Yes. It was the same colour as the floor and it moved with speed. But go on, tell.'

When I opened my eyes again, the front door of my house was on the other side of the windscreen and my father was leaning in through the window, pulling my nose. 'Oh, Zsa Zsa GaSnore. Madam Snooze Jahan.'

My mother clipped Sameer's ear. 'Sammy, you so-ter-rific soporific.'

Home.

93

Chapter Ten

When I finally awoke the next morning, my first thought was that I would see Dadi today. So I skipped over the first thought.

Wasim was in the kitchen, squatting on the floor and kneading flour for *chappatis* when I pushed through the swing door minutes later. He smiled when he saw me. 'Who is this guest in the house? The mali was going to water the plants outside your window earlier this morning –' he gestured as though holding a hose, and produced the sound of spurting water – 'but I told him not to because it might wake you up. Guests receive every courtesy around here.'

'I have every expectation that I'll receive nothing less from you,' is what I wanted to reply. But my Urdu, never up to par, swapped *umeed* with *amrood* and I ended up saying , 'I have guava that I'll receive nothing less from you.'

Wasim laughed and put the kettle on to boil. 'Always thinking of food.'

In Masood's kitchen, how could it be otherwise? I sat on the counter, with my feet resting on the stool beneath. In the early mornings between waking up and leaving for school I'd sit just so and watch Masood prepare lunch. He was always up by sunrise, preparing the miracles Mariam Apa had asked for the night before. 'The sun can climb or it can burn,' he said, more than once. 'The first stages of the sun's ascent are the more sheer and slippery. It's like climbing K2. So Aftab Sahib climbs the sky and does nothing but climb. By the time he is near the top it's as easy as climbing a hill, so his attention can wander and then he starts seeking out kitchens and angles his rays through the windows.'

My only moment of glory in an Urdu class was when I put up my hand and said, yes, I knew a word for sun other than *sooraj*. It was *aftab*. I almost flubbed the moment by appending a Sahib, but decided, instead, that I could be on a first-name basis with someone who Masood referred to with formality.

Wasim asked, 'Have you started cooking there?'

'There' was America. I shook my head. I'd watched Masood cook, seen shape and colour transformed into texture, witnessed odour becoming aroma, observed vegetables that grew away from each other in the garden wrapping around each other and rolling through spices in his frying pan. Cook? I may be proud but I know my limitations.

Wasim handed me a cup of tea and I left the kitchen. When Wasim first came to cook for us, four years ago, I was sure he wouldn't last. How could anyone attempt to replace Masood? One cook had already tried, but he was gone, passed on to a newly-wed relative just days after Mariam Apa eloped with Masood. But Wasim was different; he recognized, early on, that everyone in our house had some hesitancy about ordering meals and, without question or comment, he took over the kitchen entirely, serving up meals which, by any standards other than Masood's, were very good indeed. I suppose he must have known about

Masood and Mariam. After all, Auntie Tano, the greatest purveyor of gossip in Karachi, reputedly got most of her salacious tidbits from her children's ayah. Aba, commenting on this, said that if you put together the servant's information network with that of Dadi's bridge-playing crowd you'd eliminate the need for Intelligence Services in Pakistan.

I sipped my tea and approached Mariam Apa's door. Time for the ritual that in the last four years had become an integral part of my first morning home. But there was a Post-it Note stuck on the door, its bright yellow cheeriness disrupting my attempt to evoke a meaningful atmosphere. 'Child!' said the note, in my mother's hand. 'You've just come home after nine months away and we (your parents) aren't there to feed you buttered toast and rumbletumble eggs when you wake up. Hai hai! Crisis at work. Hotshot politico has decided he wants a longer driveway for more dramatic red-carpet entrances when he's entertaining VIPS and VVIPS, not to mention VVVIPS. And construction has already started on the house! Real *musibat*. But we'll be back for lunch unless death threats happen. You might even still be asleep then, in which case we'll tear up this note and pretend we were never away. Lots of love, Ami.' All this on one Post-it Note. She used both sides, but still.

I put it out of my mind, closed my eyes, opened the door, and walked in. Memory conjured up a picture of Mariam Apa's room as it used to be. On the walls, Sadequain's pictorial rendition of one of Ghalib's verses. The illustration showed a paper, half filled with Urdu words. In the foreground, a pair of hands with bloodied fingertips. One hand held a red-tipped quill, poised to scratch a finger which dripped blood. The accompanying couplet was one I could recite at the age of three:

درِ دل اے لاہور کتب خانہ جاوید اُن کو دکھلاؤں
اُنگلیاں فگار اپنی، خامہ خونچکاں اپنا

Conventional translations would render it something like this: 'How long shall I write of my aching heart? Come! I will show my Beloved/ My wounded fingers, my pen dripping blood.' But my family always treats the 'dard-e-dil' near the beginning of the couplet as an invocation of our name, rather than allowing it to represent its literal meaning of 'aching heart'. And so we read the line as: 'How long shall I write of the Dard-e-Dils?' And that undefined pronoun generally assumed to refer to the Beloved? We insist the pronoun stands for all of us who ever were and ever will be. No wonder we have such a skewed sense of things. By the age of three I imagined Ghalib – Ghalib! – showing me his blood-stained hands, implicitly beseeching me to allow him to stop.

There was more Ghalib to be found in the bookshelves that ran along the length of a wall. And not just Ghalib, but also Woolf, Faiz, Faulkner, Rumi, Hikmet, and a whole shelf devoted to Agatha Christie. Some thought it strange, but to me it made sense that such a worldless woman should surround herself with books. Celeste had once asked me, 'Could she . . . did she write? To communicate with you?' No, she did not. But, of course, she could have had she chosen to. The bedside-table drawer was filled with an eclectic mix of music, each tape labelled in her sloping hand. A portable stereo took up the lower ledge of the table.

Why was the stereo portable?

I opened my eyes. Mariam Apa's room was no more. I stood in a drawing room, with plump divans ready to form

97

a makeshift bed in the event of houseguests. Even the curtains had been replaced since my last trip home, the lemon-yellow of Mariam's choice ripped down to make way for a geometric pattern of blue and white. Now, more than ever, only my ritual of memory preserved Mariam Apa's room, awaited her return.

I walked across the marble floor, lay down on the divan, and looked out of the French doors leading to a terrace and to a garden beyond. Mariam and I shared this terrace, our adjacent rooms both leading out on to it. I sipped my tea and looked at my saucer. Cal's hair was short at the back and the space between his hairline and his collar was the width of a hand. When we said goodbye I slid my hand around to the back of his neck, my fingers straying down to his spine.

Why was the stereo portable?

Four years ago Sameer had said, 'Do you think they . . . you know? In your parents' house?'

'Don't be a moron,' I replied. 'Of course not. Of course not.'

It's true, my parents and I were light sleepers and, as the number of burglaries increased among people we knew, we'd become increasingly vigilant for late-night noises. So we'd have heard a squeak of door, a rustle of cloth, a tip of toe. But it's also true that four years ago desire was an abstraction for me.

I rested my hand on the wall behind the divan. This used to be the wall behind Mariam Apa's bed. It was also – though I hadn't realized it until last year – a wall partially shared by Masood's quarters. I knocked on the wall, put my ear against it. Solid. When my parents designed this house, almost fifteen years ago, they envisaged this as my room and, thinking ahead to my teenage years and the inevitable blare of music that would accompany them, they made certain the walls were soundproof. How I ended up in the room next door no one remembers.

I stepped out on to the terrace. Not long ago I'd woken up in the middle of the night at college, imagining Mariam Apa easing open the French doors, walking out into the garden in her nightdress, and turning the corner to Masood's quarters. But there was a wall at that end of the garden, separating the grass from the concrete paving outside the kitchen and the servants' quarters, and a large, spreading *falsa* tree grew in front of the wall. With such relief I had curled around my pillow, remembering that wall and remembering, in particular, the outdoor lizards – *girgits* – that skittered along the *falsa* tree, keeping away everyone in my family. I told Celeste about the dream, and when she said, 'Oh, come on. A celibate love affair for possibly eighteen years?' I stubbornly replied, 'Pakistan isn't as obvious as America. Our love stories are all about pining and separation and tiny gestures assuming grand significance.' But Celeste rolled her eyes. 'Hormones are hormones,' she said.

Khaleel. Khaleel. Khaleel.

I traced his name on my wrist, in Urdu. Wrote the letters separately خ ل ی ل and thought, Too curvy, then put them together خلیل and traced the word over and over. In the earliest days of Islam the drawing of portraits was forbidden. I'd always heard that ban was meant to discourage the semi-idolatry that might arise if people made pictoral depictions of Allah, or of the Prophet. But was it possible that the ban also recognized that words have a power that remains untapped? When artists turned from portraiture to

calligraphy the dazzle of their art restored to words the
power to make our eyes burn with tears and longing.

خليل خليل خليل

The ringing phone startled me out of my reverie.

'Awake?' Aba said, when I finally found the phone,
hidden behind a pile of books, and answered it. 'A miracle!'

'How's the driveway?'

'With my usual brilliance I've convinced the illustrious
minister that the driveway should stay as is.'

'How did you achieve that?'

'Well, I told him that instead of doubling the length of
the driveway he should double the intensity of the redness
of the carpet.'

'And this was seen as an acceptable solution?'

'Why not? There's no originality in a long driveway. But
to have the reddest carpet in the country, that's something.
Only problem is, now your mother and I have to find the
carpet.'

'I sometimes forget how amusing you are.'

'You sometimes forget a lot. Your dadi's on her way to
see you.'

'Now?'

'Now. I told her your mother and I were at home. I lied.'

'Why?'

'I love you. 'Bye.'

I stood with the receiver beeping in my hand. Impossible
now to skip over, avoid, forget, the first thought of the
morning.

Dadi.

Chapter Eleven

She'd always been strange about Mariam Apa.

At the time of my birth and Mariam's arrival Dadi had been staying with my uncle in Paris. She had started that holiday tradition the summer after my grandfather, Akbar, had died much too young. His hair had begun to silver and his eyes no longer had their hawk-like vision, but Dadi's sister, Meher, doesn't mention that when she recounts her last glimpse of him, the evening before his stroke. Just arrived in Karachi from Greece, she had driven over to my grandparents' house and pulled into their driveway in the failing light. Among a group of cricketers in the garden she saw a man silhouetted against the sun, bat in hand. The delivery was short of a length. The batsman danced out of his crease, went down on one knee, and swept the ball to the boundary with the grace of . . . 'With the grace of the triplets in their youth,' Meher Dadi said, the first time she mentioned it to me. 'Taimur, Akbar, Sulaiman. He could have been any one of them, young and gorgeous with the world at his . . . at their feet. It was the first time in a long while that I'd thought of what he'd had to learn to live without. Aliya, I backed out and drove away. I didn't want to wait for the light to change, didn't want him to step forward and become the gruff man I'd known for so long that I'd forgotten that other Akbar.' She closed her eyes and I knew she was imagining that other Akbar, and in her imaginings he stood with his brothers.

Dadi was inconsolable after his death, though it always seemed to me that whenever any of my older relatives mentioned this fact it was with an element of surprise. So when my uncle, Ali, suggested she come to visit him in Paris the whole family agreed she needed a break. Before the summer was over, Ali Chacha and his wife had convinced her that the trip should become an annual ritual. The only time she even considered changing her mind about that was when Ami was pregnant. Dadi offered to stay, but Ami told her, 'No. Just come back sooner rather than later.' She did, and on her return Aba greeted her at our front door with, 'Guess what, Mama! I've kept a secret from you. There isn't just one new addition to our family, there are two.'

'Twins?' Dadi gasped.

'No, no,' Aba said. 'Taimur's daughter, Mariam, has come to stay.'

Ami was standing behind Dadi, arms braced, and caught her as she swooned. 'Honestly, Nasser,' Ami said.

I'm on my father's side. Dadi's reaction seems a bit extreme. But I suppose, even given how long it had been since she'd seen him, it wasn't extreme that she cried and cried when Aba told her Taimur was dead. She wanted to know how and when and where had he been and what had he been doing, but when Mariam Apa walked into the room with me in her arms, and Dadi asked all these questions, Mariam just offered me to Dadi to hold. Dadi kept repeating the questions, ignoring me entirely, so Ami took me from Mariam Apa, who still did not answer or even attempt to. Dadi said, 'Who was your mother?' Then Mariam Apa's expression changed to something like pity. She put her hand on Dadi's arm. Dadi shrugged her off. 'Some upstart, no doubt, who raised her daughter without manners.'

I'll admit that, when I was old enough to understand the story, it annoyed me that Dadi was too concerned about Taimur, whom she hadn't seen in decades, to coo and fuss over her first grandchild. But, looking around the room that used to belong to Mariam, I tried to imagine decades passing by with no sign of Mariam Apa, until one day a young girl purporting to be her daughter appeared. And if this girl refused to tell me anything of Mariam's life? I'd shake that girl, yell at her, curse and cajole. No baby would detract me from my purpose.

'So that's why,' I said out loud. That's why Dadi was always so cold towards Mariam.

Cold didn't entirely cover it, of course. That's what made me even angrier at Dadi than I might have been had their relationship consisted of nothing but animosity. But there was more to it than that. I know. I was there when they laughed together at the sight of me parading around in Dadi's old wigs; I was there when Dadi described to Mariam Apa meals at the Dard-e-Dil palace; I was there when Mariam Apa told Masood to make the lightest soup in the world for Dadi when she was too sick to keep anything down, and I was there when Mariam Apa fed Dadi that soup herself.

But none of this seemed to matter when Dadi learnt that Mariam had run away with Masood. Just seconds after Aba had told us what had transpired on the farm, while I was still too stunned to feel anything, Dadi walked into the house. Aba told her, simply, in one sentence, 'Mariam has eloped with Masood.' Despite my shock I remembered the story of Dadi's reaction to Mariam's arrival, and I moved to catch her if she should fall. She did not fall. She stood up straight and said with icy regality, 'That whore!'

Then she staggered and almost fell.

Because I slapped her.

She left early for Paris that year. Packed her bags and was gone within forty-eight hours of that echoing slap which I can still hear, along with my words: 'I hate you. I hate this whole bloody clan.' I would not apologize, would not say goodbye, though everyone in the family – even Sameer – said I must. I had not seen her since.

Oh, they had tried, of course; everyone in the family, I mean. Letters, phone calls, lectures, I got them all from three generations of relatives in the year just after the slap. Sameer and I'd had our only serious fight, ever, over the matter of my refusal to apologize.

'What's the point of an apology if there's no forgiveness?' I said to him, the first time he called me at college to say Dadi had just got back from Paris, and it really would be a good idea for me to call her.

'I think she will forgive, Aliya.'

'Who's talking about her?'

That's when he called me obstinate, stubborn, and even stupid. He'd called me these things before, and I'd returned the compliments, so I wasn't too ruffled by any of it. And then he said, 'Look at it from her point of view.'

'Sameer,' I said. 'Even you?'

Within minutes we were yelling. I was the first to slam

down the phone, and then he called back so that he could do the same. If it hadn't been for Samia making a three-way call and telling us both off so thoroughly that we had no recourse but to band together and gang up against her, who knows how long our stand-off would have continued.

Sameer never mentioned the matter to me again, except through oblique hints which I ignored, and after my first summer home no one else brought the matter up either. I think my parents must have told everyone that Dadi and I would just have to work it out on our own. They only said that, of course, because they'd spent that whole summer doing everything they could to make me pick up the phone and call her but I'd been intractable. It was the worst summer of my life; worse even than the summer before, when we were all in too much pain about Mariam Apa's departure to talk about it, or about my fight with Dadi, in anything except quick exchanges which rapidly became silence.

But now, unmistakably, those were Dadi's footsteps progressing down the hall. I could drum out the beat of those steps, with their pauses in between one footfall and the next, which had always suggested to me that someone had told her, when she was just past crawling, never to drag her feet while walking. She lifted each foot up, entirely off the ground, and then placed it down, firmly, without any slipping or sliding. I caught myself praying that she hadn't aged.

Wasim opened the door. 'Bari Begum Sahib,' he announced, and fled.

I stayed seated on the divan and stared down at her feet and the hem of her sari. I wanted to fall to my knees and wrap my arms around her calves as I had done more than

105

once in my childhood when she was leaving for the airport. If we'd been in any other room in the house, I probably would have. But instead I waited for her move and, after a long pause, her move was laughter.

'And you're still so young,' she said.

I flushed and looked up. She wasn't more wrinkled or stooped or sagging, and I could have kicked myself for having come back now, before June, because I was afraid she would die and I'd be left with nothing but guilt and anger to remember her by. To hell with guilt.

'Better young than old,' I said.

'Oh, Aliya.' She sat down and shook her head at me. 'I wasn't insulting you.'

'No?'

'No. The last time we saw each other –' her hand went to her cheek in a gesture that was supposed to look unconscious – 'just after that, when I was on the plane to Paris, I realized how young eighteen is. So young. How can you hold people responsible for things they did at eighteen? How can you go on clinging to something from that stage in your life?'

'You want me to forget Mariam Apa existed?'

'Aliya, I'm not talking about you. Now stand up and greet me properly.'

I stood up, performed an *aadaab* and bent lower to kiss her cheek. Her arms wrapped around me for a moment, then disengaged before I could respond.

'Aba and Ami aren't home yet.'

'Yes, I know. Your father isn't always clever.' She reached into her handbag and pulled out a mobile phone. 'He said he was calling from the house, but the display showed his office number.'

106

'You have a mobile phone?'

'I'm an uppie. A yuppie no longer young. Sameer suggested prefixing "geriatric" but I will not be a guppie.'

I wouldn't allow myself to laugh, so instead I said archly, 'Nothing less than smoked salmon for Dadi.'

'I was thinking along the lines of a swordfish.'

Had she always possessed this virtue of self-parody? Yes. That's partly why I'd loved her so much. Why had all those relatives wasted so much time in *talking* about rapprochement? If they'd only thought, instead, of a way of bringing us together, physically together, so that I could see her ear lobes. Yes, I said ear lobes. As a child I was always fascinated by their softness; I would grip a lobe between thumb and finger and fall asleep, and nothing on earth would persuade Dadi to move while I still had her in my grip. When I'd wake up and say, 'Dadi, you could have pushed me away,' she'd reply, 'My darling, one day you'll push yourself away. I'm making the most of this while I can.' I swore that would never happen.

I looked at her ears and felt an overwhelming anger towards myself. 'I shouldn't have slapped you.'

'No shit, Sherlock, as your Americans would say.'

'Dadi!'

She leant back and looked at me, amused. 'English is capable of such vulgarity. But sometimes that's good. When you live in euphemism you can't speak to people who are accustomed to direct speech.'

'Is this a euphemistic jab at me? What haven't I understood?'

'Love, Aliya. You never understood love.'

What I had never understood, I now saw quite clearly, was her. I had left at an age when understanding had only

107

just become possible, and I'd spent the intervening years reducing her to a tilted head and a cheek that provoked slapping. How had I let myself do that? How could one remark undo eighteen years of love? Because hating Dadi was easier than facing the truth. I thought that, but then I didn't know what it meant. What truth?

'Sameer says you met Baji?'

I hadn't been at all sure how to bring this up. But she seemed only curious; perhaps even relieved. 'Yes.'

'What did you talk about?'

'The first not-quites. Kulsoom and Shahrukh. A story I'd never heard before.'

'If you'd been around at all over the last few years I'm sure I would have told it to you by now.' Her tone was entirely matter of fact. My anger caught me off guard. This time the anger was all outward. I really did hate her for the pretence that nothing had ever been wrong; the pretence that my absence meant nothing more than a few missed opportunities to tell family stories. I had felt, just seconds earlier, the urge to cry for having stayed away from her for so long, and she couldn't even bring herself to acknowledge that there were moments when she had missed me.

'Touché,' I said, matching her tone of indifference. 'I don't believe you, but touché.'

Dadi raised her eyebrow just enough to let me know that I had come perilously close to accusing her of lying. 'Did Baji mention me?' And now I saw that she was, unmistakably, hungry for news of her family. My God, I thought, it's only pride that's kept her from writing a letter, making a phone call, doing something, anything, to get in touch with the family on 'the other side'. Pride, and the fear of being rebuffed. Were those absurd reasons partly to blame for *my* decision not to call Dadi or write her a letter these past years? What else? What were my other reasons?

'She asked how you were,' I said. 'Then she said she saw you in me.'

'What did you do to deserve that?' Dadi smiled sadly, and I thought back to that laughing girl framed in Baji's apartment. No trace remained. 'I always liked her, though I don't think she knew that. I told you that once. Remember?'

I couldn't say I did. Dadi persisted, 'When you were studying twentieth-century thought at school. Condensed in one chapter of seven pages. The green history book. Remember?'

Yes, I remembered. Remembered that I had fallen asleep with the history book on my lap, and when I awoke Dadi was sitting beside me. She started talking about a cousin of hers whose mother had tantalizing elbows. She asked me two questions: 'How does royalty treat a washerwoman? How does a daughter treat a mother?' Before I could answer Dadi said, 'What do you do when the two questions are really just one question?' That was Baji's story – convinced her father's relatives considered her their inferior; equally convinced that her mother's relatives should treat her as their superior. Dadi pointed at the bearded man on the open page of my text book. 'Although she couldn't demonstrate any sympathy for the lower classes herself, it was Baji who made a Marxist of me.'

A decade later, recalling that remark, I found it even more absurd than I had at the age of twelve. 'Baji made a Marxist of you?' I said to Dadi.

'You're thinking, If she's a Marxist, I'm an eland,' Dadi said. 'But I was. So was Taimur. We were both so young.'

Elands. Yaks. We couldn't be common and deal in dogs

and goats. 'And Akbar?' I asked. 'Did the two of you fall in love over shared political views?'

'Akbar? He said the difference between a royal who inherits power and a plebian who achieves it –' she used the word 'plebian' without a grain of self-consciousness – 'is that the royal is tutored in the arts, in social graces, in subtlety. So his misuse of privilege is blanketed in *ghazals* and *aadabs*. The plebian, unused to power, hungry for it, desperate to grab it while it lasts, does not bother with niceties. And niceties, Akbar said, cannot be undervalued.'

'You disagreed with this?'

Dadi shrugged. 'Yes, but politely.'

'With subtlety and art.'

'Precisely.'

I didn't know what to do with the silence that followed, so I picked up the morning newspaper and looked at the front page. 'Who's flaying who?' Dadi asked.

There is no institution in the world which uses the word 'flay' as wantonly as the Karachi morning papers. *Government flays opposition. Opposition flays PM. Politician flays bureaucracy. Journalists flay censorship. Batsmen flay bowlers. Hygienist flays fleas. Foreign Minister flays Foreign Hand.* The other wantonly used word is 'miscreant'. Whenever anything untoward happens – be it the spread of vulgar graffiti or the detonation of a bomb – miscreants are blamed. No one seems to realize that the seriousness of the crime is undermined by the use of the word 'miscreant', which conjures up an image of little gnomes scampering around with flaming torches in their hands. When the papers are feeling particularly reckless they'll print a headline which announces that someone has flayed a miscreant.

'I'll say this for Akbar Dada's theory.' I tossed the paper

aside. 'If a politician flayed someone in verse, he'd get my vote.'

'My darling, relative to the times, you're a bigger snob than I was at your age.'

'It's intellectual snobbery.'

Dadi laughed. 'Around here who but the privileged have the luxury to commit poems to memory?'

'Your butcher, for one.' Dadi's butcher had his shop miles away from where she lived, but she wouldn't hear of patronizing anyone else in the meat trade, because no other butcher could quote poetry so beautifully while slicing through hunks of flesh. 'I wouldn't vote for your butcher if he took to politics. I can't dissociate him from the image of a cleaver.'

'Advancement without bloodshed.' Dadi polished her solitaire ring with the *puloo* of her sari. 'Unheard of at one time.'

'Well, yes.' I sat up. 'At some point, when whatshis-name, the founder of Dard-e-Dil, swept down into India with his forces . . . Dadi, we were the nouveau riche.'

'The word then was "marauders". Actually, whatshis-name was a Timurid from Samarkand, so you're wrong about him.' Her tone suggested reproach, but this time I didn't mind. She was reproaching me for having forgotten, if only for a minute, the stories of our family that she had so often told me, and in that reproach was an acknowledgement of all the hours we'd spent together. Dadi held her ring up to the sunlight and checked for smudges, then slipped it back on and tried to smooth out the wrinkles on her fingers. She grimaced, then smiled in resignation. 'But go back far enough and, of course, we were all swinging from trees.'

'So, we've had our turn. Power, wealth, the whole

tamasha. Too bad we were born during the downward swing.'

'That is our chief blessing. Now we can fade with dignity.'

'A moment ago we were monkeys. Now we're cloth. *Milao*-ing your metaphors, Dods.'

It was the old nickname that did it. She put her hand on mine, and absently scratched away the curve of nail polish that my swab with the polish-remover had missed. 'Akbar knew my Marxist ideals – unformed and uninformed as they were – were based on a world that did not exist. In this world, the one we must live in, Baji will never fully belong to either side of her family. And if Mariam has a daughter, as beautiful and intelligent as Baji was when I knew her, you'll never be able to forget that her father was a servant.'

I'd been wondering how I'd feel when she first mentioned Mariam Apa's name. Sorrow, and an overwhelming physical exhaustion. And somewhere deep down, somewhere horrible, the nausea of knowing I agreed with her. It came to me then – that truth about why I'd tried so hard to hate her: when I told the story of Mariam's departure . . . No, when I told *my* story of Mariam's departure, I could allow myself to figure as the heroine. Here was the story as I'd told it to myself over and over and over: Mariam eloped with Masood and I was shocked to hear about it, but then Dadi walked in and called her a whore so I slapped Dadi because whoever Mariam might have married she was still Mariam and I would defend her against all those who couldn't see beyond their own class prejudices.

Bravo, Aliya.

But I *had* felt something other than shock. When Aba told me she'd eloped I felt humiliation. Also, anger. Worse,

I felt disgust. *She's having sex with a servant*. Those words exactly flashed through my mind. Not Masood; just, a servant. How could I possibly have acknowledged that reaction as my own? So much easier to remember, instead, that I championed Mariam, seconds later. So much easier to say that in slapping Dadi I proved I did not think like her.

I felt a terrible emotion, too complicated for a mono-syllable, well up inside me. I cried out, 'But Dadi, at the end of the day can't we at least hope to be better than ourselves!'

'What we are, we are.'

Chapter Twelve

I had planned to tell Dadi and my parents about Baji's copy of the family tree over lunch, but just as we sat down at the table Sameer sauntered in.

'*Aadaab*. Hello. Hi,' he said, pushing me over so that he could sit on the edge of my chair. He raised an eyebrow, silently enquiring about my meeting with Dadi, and I rolled my eyes slightly and smiled. He seemed to understand what I was trying to say. I hadn't forgiven and forgotten what she'd said four years ago; but I had remembered why, prior to her terrible words about Mariam Apa, I had adored her so completely. Of course, I now adored myself a lot less completely than I had a few hours earlier . . . but no, that wasn't quite true either. At least now I could put my finger on why it was I had so often felt the urge to smash my fist through my reflection in the mirror in the weeks after Mariam left. But how much had I changed in the last four years? That really was the question. I had learnt to reclaim my old affection for Masood, and it had been a long time since I felt anger at Mariam Apa. But there was still that matter of Liaquatabad.

Sameer touched my ankle with his foot, to let me know

how glad he was that things were approaching normality between me and Dadi, and he and my parents exchanged looks of relief. He raised my glass as in a toast, then thought better of it and turned to Dadi. 'Abida Nani, Mummy was about to call but I volunteered to deliver the news, person-to-person. Some relative just had an ultrasound.'

'Mini,' said Dadi. 'Booby's daughter. Everything's okay, I hope.'

Sameer spooned *haleem* on to my plate and sprinkled green chillis and ginger over it. 'Twenty fingers and twenty toes.'

Aba rolled his eyes. 'More twins.'

There had been much holding of breath a couple of summers ago when some random cousin whose existence I was only dimly aware of had an ultrasound which detected twins. I was back at college by the time the twins were born and Aba left a two-word message on my answering machine to announce the event: 'They're quite.'

Sameer tore a *naan* in two, and gave me one half. 'The Starched Aunts are clearly thrilled because it gives them something to speculate about. Particularly since the father's name is Farid. Short for Fariduddin, which is supposedly significant.'

Dadi jangled the little bell which was always placed within her reach when she ate with us. When Wasim appeared she said, 'Quickly give my driver something to eat. Tell him we have to go to Booby Sahib's house as soon as I've finished lunch. And didn't you see Sameer Mian walk in? Set a place for him straightaway.' Before he was out of earshot she said, still in Urdu, 'I remember the days when servants were fired if their hands shook while they were serving food.'

Marx would have liked that. I decided to relay the thought to her telepathically and it must have worked because she paid me no attention.

'There was a famous Fariduddin in your family, wasn't there?' Ami said. 'Wasn't he the twitchy one?'

'No, the twitchy one was the necrophiliac,' Sameer said.

Aba clicked his tongue. 'The stammerer was the necrophiliac, and for the record he wasn't a necrophiliac as such – he just had some difficulty accepting his wife's death.'

'I thought the stammerer and the twitchy one were the same person,' said Ami.

'I didn't know there was a stammerer.'

'Sameer, everyone knows there was a stammerer.'

'Are the stammerer and the stutterer the same person?'

Dadi jingled the bell so softly I wouldn't have heard it if I hadn't seen it. When I was very young she had taken me to a *kathak* performance. It was my first experience of classical dance and I was transfixed by the sound of the ankle bells – the *ghungroo* – which accompanied the tabla and sitar as the dancer whirled and glided across the stage. Dadi, however, declared the performance amateur. A real *kathak* dancer, she said, such as the ones she remembered at the Dard-e-Dil court, did not rely on a 'crowd-pleasing chhing-chhing' of hundreds of bells. A real *kathak* dancer demonstrated mastery by isolating one bell from all those hundreds, through sheer muscle control, and ringing it with the clarity and purity that was lost in multitude. It was that way with family histories, too, she said. One could not simply say that our family was involved in battles and treaties, patronized poetry and dance, was sometimes generous and sometimes cruel. To say someone committed patricide and someone infanticide, that heads were severed and hearts broken, that there was great glory and also falls from grace, with no symmetry to the reversals unless chance has its own peculiar symmetry, to say all this is not enough. You have to isolate each life, have to say that here lies the first discordant note and look how it is echoed in this life and see the discordance transformed into a necessary part of the whole as it, through contrast, heightens the harmony of this chord.

'Fariduddin was the ugly Nawab,' I said, and everyone aahed.

So ugly that all the paintings of him show a tall, strikingly handsome man with lashes so long and luxurious you ache to run your fingers through them. Of course, the painters were all his subjects, so what do you expect? (Besides, one of the Starched Aunts noted, none of the paintings show the back of his head, and that omission must mean something.) Regardless of details, the bottom line is he was ugly, and he knew it. He knew also that his wife's brother, Askari, was not ugly and he knew his wife knew it, too. But he didn't realize the extent to which she knew it until she gave birth to twins. One, the spitting image of Fariduddin. One, the spitting image of Askari.

Perhaps Fariduddin had read too many Greek myths and too few biology texts. It was the middle of the eighteenth century – literature was more important than science in the education of a prince. Yes, yes, I'm referring to Leda and her twin eggs again. One egg encased the mortal children of her husband, Tyndareus; the other egg incubated the immortal children of Zeus. No one tells us what Tyndareus thought when he saw his children hatch and saw, also, that other egg from which the children of Zeus – Helen and Pollux – emerged. Let's face it, Tyndareus could do nothing about the fact that his children, Clytemnestra and Castor, were twinned with twins who were no relation to Tyndareus. There is nothing to do against a god but rage, and quietly. But Fariduddin, having read his mythology, saw his wife's children and knew that those twins were not-quite-twins in the way that Castor and Pollux were not-quite-twins. Except, it was no god who held Fariduddin's wife in his beak and his wings. It was Askari who thought he could take that which was most forbidden to him and escape without detection. But Askari's beauty – his eyes, his smile, his rose-shaped mouth – was his doom. Fariduddin saw his wife's children, saw one who was ugly and would never be anything else, and saw another who was beautiful in the way that only one other man in the kingdom was.

Fariduddin said to his wife, 'I will kill Askari first. Then his son. Then you.' You'd do well to suspect the veracity of this part of the story. We've watched enough movies, all of us, to know that when you say a thing like that all three of your intended victims will survive, and you'll be the one with the bullet through your heart. You see, I'm not even pretending there's suspense attached to this bit. Did I mention that by now the Dard-e-Dils were well and truly independent of the Mughals and had their first real chance of becoming great princes, free from all overlords, enlightened rulers of a stable kingdom? Did I mention that the year was 1773? Guess which trading company in India was dealing in more than spices by now.

Yes, when Askari heard Fariduddin's cry of rage he galloped away to a neighbouring state, where the East India Company had something between a toe- and a foot-hold. What exactly Askari said to the Englishman, Fraser, I don't know, but he might as well have held out a silver platter with the soil of Dard-e-Dil sprinkled on it, and a gout of blood added for good measure. The rest is painfully predictable. The troops loyal to Askari, with the aid of the English, overran Dard-e-Dil. Fariduddin was killed. Askari became regent to the infant Nawab (the ugly one, who grew up to be beautiful despite all predictions). Did Askari think the English would tip their hats, collect their gold, and go? Did he think? Clearly not, because in addition to the fifty lakh rupees he paid out, he also made a treaty of mutual assistance with the English.

Were they involved, the Empire builders, in stirring up trouble for Askari? Every time the state lurched towards peace another nobleman would carve out an alliance to unseat Askari, and every time that happened Askari turned to Fraser and his men. By the time the Nawab attained his majority and Askari died in a drunken brawl at the banquet to celebrate the Nawab's birthday, Dard-e-Dil was just another de facto vassal, and Fraser, that man of common birth, was a lord. The rest of the story? This is how the history books sum it up: 'Near the turn of the century the state's fiscal debt to the English was so vast the Company annexed half the lands of Dard-e-Dil in commutation of arrears.' Half the lands. Those three syllables cannot begin to convey the orchards and rivers and mosques and temples and shrines and people, yes, there must have been people on those lands, too. I only just thought of that.

(Has anyone asked what became of Fariduddin's wife? Fariduddin killed her. Though some say Askari killed her when she shielded her husband from Askari's drawn sword. This, at least, is incontrovertible: she died. So much for movie rules.)

I looked up from my *haleem*. Touched my foot to

119

Sameer's for support. 'Don't worry about Mini Apa's twins.' Sameer, now with his own place setting, moved his chair a little closer to mine. 'There's never been more than one pair of not-quites co-existing at one time. And if that pattern holds, her twins will be fine. After all, I'm still alive and, though god help us we have no way of being sure of this, so is Mariam Apa.'

Ami tapped my cheek with a piece of *naan*. 'Aliya, I love you truly-truly, so don't take this badly, but I have no idea what you just said and why and don't dip your sleeve in the *haleem*.'

'It's my sleeve,' was all I could say.

'No, Aliya, it's mine. But it looks a lot better on you so you can have it.'

'Just the sleeve,' Aba said. 'The rest of the *kameez* goes back to your mother's cupboard. What's the matter, little bug?'

So, finally, I told them about the family tree.

Aba snorted.

Ami rolled her eyes.

Dadi looked at me. And nodded. And sighed.

Aba turned to his mother. 'Mama, don't you dare,' he said.

Dadi stood up in her most regal way. 'The one thing left to us was the ability to hold our heads up high. She took even that from us. The curse has already come to pass.' She looked at me. 'You had no part in it. The histories teach us that the twins aren't always directly responsible for what happens. Sometimes they are victims of others. Sometimes only one twin is responsible. Sameer, escort me to my car.'

Sameer glanced at me, and I loved him for that moment of treason. I nodded, inclined my head towards Dadi.

120

Should I be angry with her for saying Mariam had brought a curse upon us; or should I be grateful for her declaration that I had no part in the curse? Just before she turned to walk out with Sameer, Dadi bent down and kissed the top of my head.

Aba watched her go, his expression bordering on petulance. 'She gets worse with age.' He threw a stick of ginger at me, his expression of paternal command restored. 'Ignore what she said. The twin thing hits a raw nerve in her.' He pointed at Ami. 'Your mother didn't want her filling your head with all of that from such an early age, but I said they're good stories. Nothing more.'

'Are you saying you don't believe any of it, Aba?'

'I don't believe it,' Ami said. 'He wants not to. But he was raised on the stories, too.'

'You and Mariam aren't twins. Not in any sense of the word. What she did, she did. She would have done it even if you'd been born a day later.' Aba folded and unfolded his napkin repeatedly. 'I should have fired Masood when—'

'Nasser!' Ami said. 'Be quiet.'

Sameer came back in and sat down. 'Clones,' he said, picking up the stick of ginger that had bounced off my shoulder, and pointing it at me. 'Human cloning. Theoretically, it's possible.'

'Point?' I said.

'If someone . . . say, Ghair Insaan, is cloned, then he and his clone are . . . what?'

'Used to settle the nature versus nurture debate?'

'Wrong. They are twins. More than twins. So they're not-quite-twins. Yes?'

'Point?'

'Theoretically, in the next generation or two of Dard-e-

121

Dils there could be dozens of sets of clones. Imagine every baby cloned in all the extended family. If that were to happen it would be impossible for every set of not-quites to bring downfall upon us because, after all, there's only so much downfall that can happen in one generation, and only so many people who can be responsible for it.'

Aba nodded. 'Point.'

I shook my head. 'Rubbish.'

Sameer threw the ginger at me. I ate it before it could be used as a missile again. 'Theoretically, it's possible. Theoretically, a mass cloning across the family would prove that the theory of not-quite-twins fated to bring about disaster is rubbish.'

Ami stood up. 'This whole family is mad, *bhai*, cent percent banana bread. I'm going to lie down with cucumbers over my eyes.'

'There's something you should know, little bug,' Aba said. 'Your Dadi didn't believe the legend of not-quites when she was young. It's just that with Partition, the horror of what went on then, and the whole Akbar and Sulaiman thing, believing the legend was the easiest way of making sense of things. Even your mother admits it was strange how everything unfolded – the break-up of the family and my father and uncle's roles in it. It makes it hard to dismiss family lore.' He walked out of the room, turning in the doorway to glance briefly at me.

He still couldn't dismiss family lore entirely.

Chapter Thirteen

A couple of days later, at Dadi's house, the Starched Aunts entered the room and I said, 'At last! The tarts are here.'

I was referring to the lemon tarts which Dadi's bearer wheeled in on the tea-trolley, just after the aunts entered, but it was an inauspicious start to the evening, nonetheless. The two aunts did their round of the room, kissing their aunts and uncles and cousins and nephews and nieces, and when it was my turn they both pinched my cheeks and said to each other, 'She still gets excited about pastries. Like a baby! Sho shweet.'

They pulled their signature crisp, starched kurtas taut as they sat down, so that the material wouldn't crease, and the older sister spread her hands as though to ward off any accusations. 'So sorry to arrive in this *haalat* –' she pointed at the incongruous running shoes on her feet – 'but we've both been for a walk and came straight over from the park. *Bhai*, I said maybe we should skip the walk today, but you know, have to look good for Kishoo's wedding next week. We saw Kishoo's mother yesterday and *tobah!* She's put on so much weight and was wearing a sari on top of that and I swear a tidal wave of fat came lurching towards us when she walked into the room. And Kishoo's in-laws-to-be are so stylish. I mean if I looked like that at my daughter's wedding I'd do her a favour and stay away altogether.'

'Or claim overflowing of religion and cover yourself in a *burkha*,' said Younger Starch.

The sisters beamed and looked around. 'So good to be with family. Why don't we do this more often?'

Any of the twenty or so relatives in the room who might have been asking the same question minutes earlier were not doing so any more.

'Kishoo? You mean Kishwar? Lily's daughter? *Hanh*, I heard she was getting married. Who to?' While Dadi was asking the questions she was also using hand gestures to direct two of my young cousins to hand around plates and tea things and find out how much sugar everyone took in his or her tea. Sameer and I watched this with great satisfaction; not too long ago we were the two considered both old enough and young enough to have this chore placed on us.

'Quite a catch!' Younger Starch said. 'The oldest son of the Ali Shahs. He has the family seat in the National Assembly.'

'Really?' Great-Aunt One-Liner sniffed. 'Lily's daughter is marrying a Sindhi?' Great-Aunt One-Liner generally made only one comment in an evening. She usually waited until late to make it; just when she realized everyone was about to leave and she hadn't said anything memorable to leave her stamp on the occasion she'd speak, and then everyone would feel that the evening had truly come to an end. The only exceptions to her policy of delayed vocalization occurred, as now, when someone gave her an opportunity to reveal her disdain for anyone not from Dard-e-Dil or the states around it.

124

I glanced over at Sameer's father, whose mother was Sindhi. He winked at me.

'They're very important people, the Ali Shahs,' Older Starch said. 'Kishoo's parents are thrilled with the match. After all, why should the Ali Shahs have settled for a girl who isn't from a political family? They won't get any mileage from the match. And yet, they're conscious of lineage, they understand these things matter, so they're welcoming her with open arms.'

'In fact –' and here both the sisters looked at me – 'the Ali Shahs have a younger son. Unmarried. Very intelligent, very ambitious. They say he won't remain in the shadows long. In fact, some say, if democracy survives, future prime minister. And he's looking for a girl from a good family. He'll be in Karachi for the wedding. Aliya, you should come with us to all the functions. We've been invited to everything – even the really small *dholkis*.'

I opened my mouth and Sameer shoved a sandwich in it. Cheese and tomato. Too much butter.

Great-Aunt One-Liner leant forward and, shockingly, spoke again. 'Have they expressed an interest? In Aliya.'

'My granddaughter is not a confectionery item,' Dadi said. 'And in any case, she's got two years of university ahead of her.' I felt the urge to stand up and cheer.

A bachelor uncle shook his head. 'She'll be twenty-four then. Her "best before" date will nearly have passed.'

Aba turned to him. 'I have a stone aimed at your glass house. Should I throw it?'

'The lemon tarts are really wonderful,' Ami said. 'For years they were too sweet, but this is how I remember them from my childhood.' She put a hand on Sameer's mother's wrist. 'Zainab, remember how your mother

125

always used to have two lemon tarts waiting for us, by the side of the pool, when we finished our fifty laps at the Club? When is your mother arriving?'

'Don't have the exact date yet. You know what she's like. Loves the element of surprise. For all we know she could be in the air right now, halfway between Greece and here.'

The bachelor uncle returned the conversation to its earlier topic. 'Aren't the Ali Shahs related to that Jahangir? The one whose lands Mariam was on when she . . . What's the preferred family euphemism? . . . Disappeared.'

I had the desperate urge to yank off his toupee.

'Oh, everyone is related to everyone,' my mother laughed. 'And you have ketchup on your silk shirt. I think it'll stain.'

'Well, I think this is as good a time as any to say it,' Older Starch said. 'My children, as you all know, have both, Allah *ka shukar*, been admitted to Karachi Grammar School and Maliha will be joining the Senior School. You know what kids are like at that age. Anything to tease about they'll tease about. So I've said it plain to them, if anyone mentions Mariam they're to say she is no relation to them. She was an imposter. And I'm not just saying this for my children's sake, because of course you have to teach them to speak the truth. I truly believe it and why no one else has thought of it already I don't know.'

I had been about to pick up the lemon tart on my plate, but drew my hand back when I heard the word 'imposter'. Anything I ate now would taste like ashes.

'Thought of what?' Ami said, and now she wasn't even pretending to keep her voice cordial.

'Ayeshoo, this is no reflection on you, sweetie.' If there's one thing my mother dislikes more than being called 'sweetie' it's being called 'Ayeshoo'. 'We were all taken in by her, and no one has anything but praise for the hospitality you showed her, but what proof did we ever have that she was one of the Dard-e-Dils?'

'She looked just like her father,' Great-Aunt One-Liner said. She was having a wild, wild day. 'Didn't she, Abida?'

'Just like him,' Dadi said. 'Right down to her smile.'

What a smile it was. I had taken with me to college the one picture in the world which captured it and Celeste, remarking on it, said, 'Looks like she's seeing angels beckon in the camera lens.'

'Well, Booby looks like Orson Welles,' Bachelor Uncle said, pointing at his stocky cousin. 'That doesn't mean he should be getting percentages from video rentals of *Citizen Kane*.'

Older Starch leapt upon that with alacrity. 'Exactly! I'm not saying she wasn't clever, probably looked around to find a family she could fit into and, let's face it, we're prominent. Pictures in the papers all the time. Social pages. Business pages. Art pages. Front pages. My theory is this . . .' She leant forward, and I tried to determine the trajectory of my lemon tart if I were to get so engrossed in her theory that my hand pressed down with all its weight on the edge of my plate. I shifted the plate slightly. But I couldn't help listening. 'I'm not saying Mariam was some *dehati* who'd never seen a big city before. Clearly she had learnt social graces somewhere. But we've all heard the stories of girls from good families who go bad and are disowned. Usually because of some man. So what if Mariam was disowned. Because of some man. Probably lower class. And then he didn't want her because it was only her money he was after. And maybe somehow she'd heard the story of our family. It's no secret. And she saw pictures and saw her features repeated in those pictures. So she wrote a letter, sent it to Nasser and Ayesha. The address is in the phone book, always has been. Then she arrived. But she couldn't speak because speaking would mean answering questions which would mean revealing the truth. So she remained quiet. Except about food because she knew if she developed one eccentric trait it would shield her. Then if she ever did something odd, something out of keeping with the way our family behaves, we would just say, "Oh, that's just Mariam. She lives by her own rules." And we did. We said it often.'

You bitch, I thought. You absolute stupid bitch.

'And what about Masood?' Bachelor Uncle asked.

Younger Starch raised a hand for attention. 'That letter which announced she was arriving, we've all read it, we all agree it's strange. Clearly not written by someone like us. So what if this man – the one who waltzed her up the garden path – what if she made believe, to herself, that he was the one writing the letter. To make herself feel better about him not wanting her. She imagined she was the one choosing to leave and he was the one writing the letter. So she wrote it the way she imagined he would write it. That tells us what kind of man he was. Lower class. Definitely. So from him to Masood was no big leap. For some reason she's just attracted to that type.'

'She had no birth certificate, it's true,' Bachelor Uncle said. 'Remember all those strings I pulled to have a passport and ID card made for her? Broke the law, but anything for family, I said. But there's no way of knowing if that's what she really was.'

Around the room I saw people nodding their heads,

murmuring to each other. Great-Aunt One-Liner seemed to be crying; Aba had gone red; Ami had gone white; Sameer's mother was trying to restrain her husband from attacking the Starched Aunts, though it might have been the other way round.

The oldest of the relatives, a woman who had doted on Mariam Apa said, 'Perhaps it is best to say just that. For the sake of our grandchildren and great-grandchildren. Family reputation is the most precious jewel in a young bride's *jahez*.' She sighed. 'There was a time we were so close to the heavens no stigma could reach us. But what we were we no longer are.'

I could almost hear the scissors snipping away the strings which bound Mariam Apa to our lives. Here, now, the story was shaping; the one that would be repeated, passed down, seducing us all with its symmetry. In parentheses the story-tellers would add, 'There are still those who say she really was a Dard-e-Dil, but a new identity was fabricated for her by those who felt she blemished the family name.' Would she hear the story one day, wherever she was, whatever she was doing? Was her life so separate now from ours that even the wind carrying our lies would never play with her hair, swirl it away from her ears and make all hearing possible?

Or did she know us better than we knew ourselves?

Who starred her name and mine on the family tree?

If Mariam Apa were ever to send me a message it would be wordless. A strain of music pushing open my window and creeping through; a fistful of saffron sprinkling over my eyelids while I slept; a shell yielding to my cochlea the whisper of waves allied to the sound of footsteps running away from the rushing tide. These were the signs I waited for. But how could I forget the stars?

Mariam Apa used to point out constellations to me; she'd show me the clusters of light as a lesson, not in astronomy but in our lives. No star, except the brightest, has meaning on its own. During nights at the beach she'd sweep her arm in the direction of the sky, showing me this star and that and the other one there, and we could not discern the difference between them. But when we saw the middle of Orion's belt or the handle of the Big Dipper, then the stars ceased to be interchangeable, one no different to the other. Mariam would point out a star and make a shadow picture of a bear against the wall of the beach hut. Her hand would reach out as though to extinguish that star and as she did so the shadow picture would disappear. Without that star, there's no Ursa Minor. Without Ursa Minor the sky is less than it can be. Somehow Ursa Minor became our favourite and we'd talk (so to speak) of buying a boat and sailing for ever within sight of that constellation as the seasons shifted and the bear moved away from us.

She had starred the family tree. She wanted me to know we were bound together, she and I and all of us. I had to buy that boat. I had to find out where she had gone. Maybe the only way of doing so was to find out where she had come from.

'It could be true,' I heard. It was a mousy cousin speaking. 'It could be true that she's not a relative. But if I ever see her again I'll put my arms around her and I'll hold her so close. And there's no one else in this room about whom I can say the same.'

Dadi rang the bell to have the tea things cleared away. 'She is Taimur's daughter. If she wasn't, don't you think I would know?'

Chapter Fourteen

The next morning, reclining on the sofa in Mariam Apa's old room, I thought that the only thing shocking about the Starched Aunts' version of Mariam's life was that it took them four years to come up with it. Still, after four years you'd expect them to do better than the psychobabble of 'she imagined she was the one choosing to leave and he was the one writing the letter'. Not to mention 'she knew if she developed one eccentric trait it would shield her'. Honestly. That made about as much sense as the theory my cousin, Usman, had propounded when he was little more than a toddler: 'Maybe she doesn't know any words that aren't about food.'

It wasn't just toddlers, of course. Virtually everyone in the family had a favourite theory about Mariam's silence, long before she became our official black sheep. My father's theory was among the most succinct. 'She's taking the notion of a woman's traditional role a little too literally,' he had said after one of his attempts to get her to talk about her early life. Mariam Apa had smiled and walked towards the kitchen, from where I heard '*biryani*' just before the door swung closed.

But my mother had laughed at my father's explanation, and reminded me of Mariam Apa's encounter with Dr Tahir.

I was very young when that happened. It was winter, and Karachi's social elite were feverishly getting married and throwing parties before the hot weather and riots and curfew returned and impeded social activity. (Mariam Apa was, incidentally, extremely popular in the social milieu, praised for being discreet, a good listener and never interrupting anyone's flow of loquaciousness.)

My parents and Mariam Apa were at a party, the last of their social stops for the evening. Mariam Apa was draped in a sari that was covered in intricate sequinned designs. As she and my mother wandered to the buffet table, a liveried bearer tripped on the uneven ground and sent a dozen glasses of pomegranate juice crashing to the floor, splattering Mariam Apa's sari with red blots.

'Oh, too bad,' a male voice exclaimed, and she turned to see Dr Tahir – the man infamous for diagnosing mosquito bites as measles bumps – standing behind her. 'Well, you'll never wear that again,' he said cheerfully. 'That's the problem with these fancy sequinned clothes. Can't wash them. I always say that if you want proof that men are more practical than women you should go compare their clothes.'

Mariam Apa did not sleep that night. She sat in the TV room and unstitched every single sequin in the area around the stained section of the sari. When I woke up to get ready for school she was in the bathroom handwashing the sari. And when I returned home that afternoon she had just finished stitching back every sequin in its original place. That night she did the unthinkable and rewore the sari to a dinner where she knew she would see Dr Tahir.

'So you see,' my mother told me, 'she has this, I don't know, determination, stubbornness, whatever, that allows her to do things that most people wouldn't. For all we know she's like this because she lost a bet long ago, and someone said she would never be able to stick to the winner's terms.'

I never found out which of my parents was right, or if they were both as far from the truth as Usman. To be quite honest, I didn't really care.

It was enough for me to sleep curled beside her in the afternoons, our heads sharing the same pillow; enough to watch her fingers rise, curl, tap, fall as she listened to Beethoven played or Ghalib sung; enough to know she was watching me as I did my homework, watching me for the simple reason that I was not invisible in her world. And enough to eat the meals she ordered.

My enjoyment of summer holidays abroad, in London or Paris, was always tempered by two factors: the absence of Mariam Apa and the absence of Masood's food. We always tried to persuade Mariam to come with us but a simple lift of the eyebrow was all it took for her to remind us that she wouldn't be able to eat anything. One summer, when he was feeling particularly flush, Aba offered to buy a plane ticket for Masood. It was the only time I saw Masood exhibit anything approaching anger. He stood up straight and said that, of course, he was just a servant, he would cook in whichever kitchen we wanted him to cook in, even if it was in a country where he knew no one and couldn't speak the language. Aba never broached the issue again.

Well, of course I've wondered what went on in those weeks when Masood and Mariam were alone in the house.

I always used to imagine that they used that time to cook

together. Maybe they did. Early in the morning, before friends and relatives dropped in. I can see them both in the early morning light as they slide the skins off scalded tomatoes, unzip the casing of pea-pods, pour golden oil into a sizzling pan.

I should have invited Khaleel up for dinner.

Just seconds after that thought entered my head, Wasim brought a pile of letters into the room along with my morning tea. There was a letter for me. Mailed in London. My heart thudded so violently against my ribs it must have ricocheted back into my spine.

The letter was from Rehana Apa.

Dear Aliya,

My cousin for whom my degree of affection must prove that blood and water rule. I've been thinking a great deal of our conversation in the park, and have extracted from Baji the confession that she didn't really believe that you would take the myth of not-quites seriously. It's important you know this so that you know she wanted only to surprise you with the family tree, not to set you wondering how you, and Mariam, will bring down the family. She was stunned when I said I, too, believe there is something to the old legend. She's quite sure, you see, that the story of not-quites is a self-fulfilling prophecy, or a tool used to others' ends. Like Taj, the midwife, whose quest for revenge may have led her to say the brothers were not-quites when really they were plain and simple triplets. I do believe the not-quites are special. But does that mean (putting aside the question of whether you and Mariam are qualified to enter their ranks) they always trail destruction? Remember Zain and Ibrahim?

But here my eyes scanned ahead and caught the word on the next line which emptied my mind of everything that had gone before.

Remember that photograph of Bahadur Shah which you mentioned to Khaleel (Samia and I ran into him when we were having tea together at a café round the corner from your flat. Samia introduced us and then had to take off, so Khaleel and I had a very pleasant time talking about how we both know you so little and yet think of you so much and also think so much of you. He's really quite delicious. I've invited him over to meet Baji. Samia will be there, too – I'm sure she'll report all).

Write to me.

Love,

Rehana Apa.

P.S. The photograph is from Baji. As a token of apology, though she won't admit that.

I looked at the postmark on the letter. Only four days ago. Why didn't she say if Khaleel was planning to come to Karachi? The café round the corner. That had to be the one we'd been to together. Surely it wasn't just coincidence that had brought him there again. Liaquatabad had to be a lie. He'd said it just to test me. He'd talk to Baji and Samia for just a few minutes before they'd ferret out names of his relatives who were known to our family, either pre- or post-Partition. Maybe it would turn out he was somehow distantly related to us.

Damn.

I looked at the letter again, the flat of my hand hovering

135

slightly above the paper to block out that part which referred to him without running the risk of smudging his name.

'Remember Zain and Ibrahim,' Rehana Apa had written. Zain and Ibrahim? Dadi had a cousin called Zain, but as far as I could remember the only thing noteworthy about him was the absence of his left eyebrow. And who was Ibrahim? I picked up the phone and dialled Dadi's number. I had never got out of the practice of dialling Dadi's number. In the past, whenever I was home for the summer, I would dial that familiar configuration of digits, just to allow myself to believe that she would answer the phone and everything would be as it used to be.

This time, for the first time in four years, she did answer. 'I had a feeling it was you,' she said. 'Are you calling about Usman's piece?'

I picked up the newspaper, which was lying unread beside me. My cousin, Usman, was interning at the newspaper office, and every day the whole family would scan the papers for his name and call each other up to discuss his journalistic strengths and weaknesses. 'No, which page?'

'Two,' Dadi said. 'So why are you calling?'

I turned to page two. OFFICIAL FLAYS FLIGHT FAILURE, ran the headline. The story below read:

Saboteurs are responsible for sabotaging the runway controls which caused chaos at Karachi airport yesterday, says an airline official. Further details will be unveiled when an enquiry has uncovered further details. Other sources say shady people were seen lurking near the control tower. When questioned by airport police they claimed they were not lurking but loitering. When this reporter asked the airline official if miscreants were involved, the official responded, 'We have not yet looked into the creant factor.'

'Little Usman!' I said. 'Never realized he had the Dard-e-Dil humour gene.' Dadi's earlier remark struck me for the first time. 'Did you say, "So why are you calling?" Can't I call you on a whim?'

'Well, we haven't really clarified that, have we? Or should I say, you haven't decided whether we're friends again yet.'

'I love you Dods.' I'd been wanting to say that ever since I heard her footsteps in the hall, the morning after I had returned home.

'That's not quite the same thing.'

'We're friends, so long as we don't talk about Mariam Apa.'

'A strange kind of friendship.'

'We're a strange kind of family.'

She laughed. 'All right. For the moment, all right. So you're really just calling on a whim?'

'Well, no.' I felt light-headed with relief that we'd got that conversation so painlessly out of the way. 'Who are Zain and Ibrahim?'

She made a noise of exasperation. 'Have you forgotten everything? Ibrahim and Zain . . .'

'Oh, Ibrahim and Zain! Now I remember. Thanks Dadi. I have to go. There's a letter I'm trying to understand. I'll come over this evening, is that okay?'

'Yes, fine. There are still lemon tarts left over. I'll see you at five.'

Ibrahim and Zain. Of course I remembered them. They

137

were one of the not-quite pairs. Their father, Nawab Assadullah, had two wives. One was high-born; the other was the Nawab's favourite. But he couldn't have been entirely discriminatory in his treatment of his wives because they were both found to be pregnant within days of each other. For months the court was gripped by rumour and speculation, and a lot of heavy gambling. Which of the wives would bear a son? If both, which would bear a son first?

Cliques formed around each wife, praying, fasting, bringing unguents and holy water from distant lands (those were less prejudiced times – distant lands were trusted). Midwives were consulted. What was the earliest a child could be induced without greatly reducing chances of survival?

Sometime around the seventh month of the pregnancies, the high-born wife's father, cousin and Vizir to Assadullah, could take the anxiety no longer. He swallowed a diamond and waited for the sharp edges to lacerate his insides and catapult him into the embrace of an afterlife without intrigue. It didn't work. After a few minutes of lying in bed feeling mildly uncomfortable, the Vizir got up, drank a glass of water, and realized that his father – a man who lost all sense of judgement at the mere sight of a pack of cards – had gambled away the family jewels, cunningly replacing them with fakes so as to avoid detection by his wife. With his fortunes lost and the future holding a fifty percent possibility of bleakness for his family, there remained only one course of action for the Vizir.

That afternoon, a midwife, her pockets heavy with diamonds and pearls, entered into the presence of the high-born wife. Within minutes the word went round the palace: she was in labour.

Another midwife was summoned to a different part of the palace, and for the rest of the night the courtiers couldn't move anywhere without tripping over someone prostrate on a prayer mat. At dawn, at opposite ends of the palace, two umbilical cords were snipped; two premature sons were born. One must have been born first, if only by seconds, but no one was ever to know which. Two sons. Brothers. Princes. Twins? Well, no. But sort of.

Nawab Assadullah declared that Zain, the son of the favourite, was his heir, and Ibrahim, the other son, was not. But he showered the Vizir with money and jewels all the same, and when the old man tried diamond suicide again he died smiling.

So where's the calamity?

Assadullah died in 1525. Zain ascended the throne. The next year was 1526. The year of the Battle of Paniput and the beginning of Mughal rule in India. Zain, sent his envoys to Babur, founder of the Mughal Empire, shortly after the battle. The envoys found a man who spoke not of wars or empires, but of melons. Read Babur's memoirs if you want confirmation. To him, India was an 'unpleasant and un-harmonious' place, a second-best territory he'd settled for when it seemed clear he would never again rule over his ancestral home and one-time kingdom, Samarkand. He was, in modern parlance, homesick. This homesickness manifested itself primarily in his yearning for the honey-sweet melons of Central Asia. (A great deal of attention is paid to fruit in the *Baburnama* and, by and large, India failed to impress Babur in that all-important regard. While he appreciated the mango he thought it unworthy to be considered, among all fruit, second only to the melon. Still, at least the mango fared better than the jackfruit – which, he wrote, 'Looks exactly like sheep intestines turned inside out' – and the fruit of the clustered fig – 'an oddly insipid fruit'.)

Zain had heard of Babur's homesickness and so he sent his envoys with this message: 'I, too, am from the Timurid family, and there are many still in Samarkand and Bukhara who tremble in awe at the name of my ancestor, Nur-ul-Jahan, founder of Dard-e-Dil, a prince of Transoxania by birth. We are brothers, you and I, and brothers must help brothers. My armies are at your disposal to recapture Samarkand, land of fabled beauty and honey-sweet melons, where the power of the Uzbek is weaker than it outwardly seems. In return, I ask only that I may administer your lands in Hindustan, and rely upon you to help me defeat the infidel forces of Rana Sanga.' (I blush, of course, to know my ancestor used the religion card to claim an alliance.)

The throne of Samarkand in return for his portion of India? Babur did not hesitate to say, 'Let us meet, my brother, to talk of this.' Zain's envoys galloped home to find Zain assassinated, and Ibrahim on the throne. By the time Ibrahim had consolidated his position and cooled his rage towards his brother sufficiently to realize what a brilliant offer Zain had made the Mughal, Babur had decided that a mango in the hand was worth two melons in his dreams. I did not intend for that to sound vulgar.

Dard-e-Dil was absorbed into Mughal territory soon after, with little fuss or fanfare, and spent most of the next two centuries reduced to an administrative unit of the Mughal empire.

'Those Johnny-come-latelies,' my relatives are wont to say when the Mughals are mentioned. 'You know, their empire could have been ours. Those not-quites!'

(And here, again, we must pause to account for the history books which show that the Mughals were certainly not willing to allow powerful rulers to remain powerful once the Mughal Empire was established. And Dard-e-Dil was a northern state, not one of the Deccan kingdoms out of Mughal reach. So why don't we hear of any marriage alliances – except fairly minor ones – between the Mughals and the Dard-e-Dils? Why don't we hear of Mughal plans to cut the Dard-e-Dils down to size? Before answering those questions, consider this one: Why don't we see the kingdom of Dard-e-Dil on maps of pre-Mughal India? The truth, according to the history books, is this: the founder of Dard-e-Dil, Nur-ul-Jahan, was indeed from the royal Timurid line, but after his victory in the Battle of Surkh Khait he failed to consolidate his power, and the Dard-e-Dils remained minor figures in the power game, so minor you wonder if Babur could have taken Zain's proposal seriously, so minor it's no surprise the Mughals allowed the Dard-e-Dils (on an on-again, off-again basis) to administer the land which Nur-ul-Jahan and his descendants sometimes held and sometimes didn't in the years between Surkh Khait and Paniput. The sad truth is that Nur-ul-Jahan's so-called kingdom was little more than a patch of land and it was only after the fall of the Mughals that his descendants gained control of enough of the surrounding areas to claim real power (and to confer upon their ancestors the posthumous title of 'Sultan' which those early Dard-e-Dils never really held in their lifetimes – and later, when the British invented the term 'Nawab', the Dard-e-Dils decided they preferred that title, and airily replaced 'Sultan'). That's what the history books say, but they also acknowledge that the Dard-e-Dils were among the first northern kingdoms to throw off Mughal rule, soon after the eighteenth century had dawned and Aurangzeb, the last Great Mughal, had died, which is not explicable if they really were as insignificant as the historians make them out to be. Who says it's true just because it's in print?)

Still, given our family's belief that it was the not-quites alone who prevented us from replacing the Mughals, Rehana Apa was kind to point out the obvious: those sad, sad eyes of an emperor deposed could have been Dard-e-Dil eyes. So perhaps, in the case of Ibrahim and Zain, the not-quites indirectly brought about a blessing. That's what Rehana Apa was trying to say; but, of course, taking the throne of the Mughals would not have meant replicating the actions – and the downfall – of the Mughals. I know what prevented us from being deposed, and worse, after the débâcle of 1857. It was not the fact that we didn't sit on the throne of Delhi. It was all down to Taj's mother. Yes, the woman whom Dadi had compared to Leda.

All right, let me clarify. Skipping ahead over three hundred years from the days of Babur, let's consider what happened to the Dard-e-Dils during the Revolt or Mutiny or War of Independence, or whatever your preferred name for the events of 1857. Near the start of the fighting, when Bahadur Shah Zafar, last Emperor of the Mughals, found himself whisked away from his poetry and music to become the figurehead around which the Rebels banded, the then Nawab of Dard-e-Dil sent his heir apparent to meet the Emperor's representatives and assure them of Dard-e-Dil support. The heir apparent dawdled. Not because he thought joining the Revolt was a bad idea, but because he was lazy, dedicated to pleasure, and saw no reason to be galloping around the country like an ordinary messenger.

142

He feared if he proved too efficient his father would make a habit of sending him off on such expeditions. He couldn't dawdle around the palace, of course, because his father's spies were everywhere. So he rode into the fields around Dard-e-Dil instead, where he saw Taj's mother who looked him in the eye.

Why do we know this and nothing else, except what we can naturally assume given Taj's birth, nine months later? *Her elbows were not tantalizing, but she looked him in the eye.* That's the one line the family devotes to Taj's mother, the woman without name. Did she look him in the eye to let him know she thought him worth looking at? Or to show she was no bowing and scraping royalist? Or to clarify that he was not worth a bow or a scrape? Did he find her gaze attractive? Offensive? Diverting?

She died in childbirth, so even her daughter could do nothing more than speculate. But the Dard-e-Dils don't speculate, because motives and emotions aren't pertinent. What is pertinent is that Taj's mother delayed the prince, giving the Nawab's chief messenger those few extra seconds needed to intercept him just before he extended a hand of support to the Revolt. The Nawab had dithered after his son rode away. Unable to decide whether to back Bahadur Shah or the British, he told his messenger, 'Leave now. If you reach my son before he delivers a promise of assistance, then tell him to return at once. If he has made the promise, tell him we will stand by it.' Taj's mother looked straight at the prince, slowed his progress by . . . minutes . . . seconds, and thus we were spared the hangings, the stripping away of titles and possessions, the sad, sad eyes.

I know the prince's name, but I will not mention it. This

143

gesture is meaningless in the grand scale of things, but sometimes we need to be less than grand.

We were all too grand in the most petty of ways towards Taj. Her mother saved our family, in a manner of speaking, and even if she hadn't . . . even if she hadn't . . .

Taj's mother gave birth near the entrance to the palace ground. Then died. It must have been those days of standing in the sun, waiting for the prince or the Nawab to allow her an audience, that sapped from her all energy except that needed to give her daughter life. Her family took Taj away, raised her, and kept her far, far away from the palace.

Such tales are common amongst royal families. But not ours. Taj's mother is an exception and that's what makes me think that Dadi was probably right when she said that Taj's mother, and later Taj, came to symbolize that fateful decision to turn away from the Revolt. It was a decision that saved the Dard-e-Dil family, but we were too ashamed to rejoice. From the roof of the Dard-e-Dil palace you could see trees in neighbouring states from which the Rebels were hanged. And not just the Rebels. What was the name of that Englishman who, in the wake of 1857, said he wanted to see a Muslim hanging from every tree in India? Better he remain nameless, too.

There was one tree in particular which the Dard-e-Dil royals could not bear to look at – the tree from which the Nawab's fourth cousin, ruler of a neighbouring state and participant in the Revolt, had been hanged. In Dard-e-Dil you could hear the creaking rope as his body swayed in the breeze. So the story goes. The British hanged all his heirs, too, of course, and annexed his lands. A portion of the lands was given to the Dard-e-Dils in recognition of their loyalty.

144

It was a small portion, far less than that doled out to many of the royals who stayed out of the fray. That seems confirmation enough that the British knew how close we came to switching our allegiances, and wished us to always have a subtle reminder of what happened to the lands and lives of errant princes. And, now that I think of it, couldn't they have hanged him from another tree, one less visible from miles away in a north-westerly direction?

No surprise then that we wanted no further reminders of that message intercepted and reversed. So we shunned Taj's mother and we shunned Taj. Until the unnamable prince, who was by now a bare-handed killer of tigers, became Nawab and his wives bore him no children who survived the trauma of birth. As a last resort, one of his courtiers told him of a peasant girl, only fifteen, who was already skilled in midwifery. The Nawab called for her, and when she looked him in the eye with eyes that were his eyes he knew his children would live only if she delivered them and received royal favours for doing so.

For forty-eight years Taj delivered Dard-e-Dils. Delivered her brothers and sisters, her cousins, her nephews and nieces, her great-nephews and great-nieces. Received gold and umbilical cords in return. What did she do with the cords? She took them, that's all. More to the point, in taking the cords she gave the Dard-e-Dils something her mother had never given them: a reason to remember her name. And then the three boys were born near midnight. At what times exactly? Only Taj knows, and maybe even she didn't. Of course she left the palace immediately after that. She'd delivered them, announced the timings of their births, taken their umbilical cords. Without a doubt, no question of it, she'd secured a place in the family story.

145

I looked at the picture that Rehana Apa had sent with her letter. Dadi and the three boys, laughing in the palace grounds. If they knew they were fated to bring misery to the family you wouldn't know it by looking at the photograph.

I showed Dadi the photograph that evening. She rested it on her lap and hung her head low. I waited for her to look up and when she didn't I walked over to her and placed my hands over two of the brothers so that all that remained visible was Dadi angling her body towards the boy in the centre.

'That's the most romantic picture of you and Dada I've ever seen,' I said.

'That's not your grandfather. It's Taimur.'

She wouldn't say any more about it, and no matter what I said the rest of the evening I couldn't make her laugh.

Chapter Fifteen

'Aliya, sweetoo, you must come over right away. *Futafut*. On the double take.' It was Older Starch on the phone, disrupting my evening cup of tea with Sameer.

'I would have loved to, but Sameer's over.'

Older Starch clicked her tongue. 'Bring him also. Where's the problem? Don't answer, I'll tell you. The problem is here. I have out-of-town guests coming for tea with their children who are your age. First, Raunaq and Rusty were coming to keep them company but now Raunaq has piles, poor baby. Have you ever had piles, Aliya?'

I put her on speaker phone. 'Piles? No. I didn't think Dard-e-Dils suffered from piles.'

'*Arré*, what a thing to say! Although, no, actually, you're right. Usman is the only one among us who's had them and that must be from his father's side. He's got Pathan blood, you know. But anyway, I said to Raunaq that last week there was an ad in the paper for a doctor who has a herbal cure for piles. No operation and also no need to show the doctor any part of your lower body. What's that noise?'

It was Sameer choking on his tea. I promised we'd drop

in, and hung up. Afterwards, I wondered if Older Starch was wilier than I gave her credit for. Because if I hadn't been so amused by her comments I would never have agreed to entertain her guests. But with my head full of images of Older Starch, boasting that she comes from a royal family which once owned vast tracts of land and never suffered from haemorrhoids, I walked right into her trap. And walked into it alone, because Sameer took off for a game of squash at the Club, declaring that he'd have to see more than enough of the Starched Aunts once festivities for Kishwar's wedding to the Ali Shah son got under way.

'Well, I'm avoiding the wedding,' I said. 'Kishwar said some things about Mariam Apa—'

'Everyone said some things about Mariam Apa.'

'Okay, more to the point, I'm not getting involved in the Aunts' ploys to get me married off.'

'Weddings breed weddings,' Sameer laughed, and twirled his racket in farewell.

'Aliya!' The Starcheds rose to greet me, minutes later, as I entered Older's drawing room. 'Have you met the Ali Shahs?'

Starched Aunts–1. Aliya–0.

Mind you, the four-wheel drives parked outside with their tinted windows and armed bodyguards should have tipped me off.

My aunts introduced me to the Ali Shah parents and daughters, then turned in triumph to the two boys. 'This is Khurrum, Kishoo's fiancé. You know Kishoo, Aliya. She couldn't be here, unfortunately.'

Younger Starch whispered, 'Stays at home when the sun's out. Wants to look fair on her wedding night.'

'And this is Murtaza. Just graduated from an Ivy League.

Aliya was also in America, Murti. You two have a lot to talk about.' And with that, both the Starched Aunts pushed me down on the sofa beside Murtaza.

Murtaza and Khurrum's sisters caught my eye and turned away, giggling. Their father, engaged in a discussion with Older Starch's husband about the dangers of allowing the masses to have access to Internet porn, gestured to his wife in a manner clearly meant to indicate that she was responsible for seeing to it that her daughters behave themselves. Younger Starch pulled a little bottle out of her handbag and, after instructing the Ali Shah boys to admire the painting on the wall, hastily rubbed concealer over the pimple just above my eyebrow.

Oh, please Scotty, beam me up. I'd rather face Klingons than this.

'So what did you major in at college?' Murtaza said.

'English,' I replied, quite confident that he would be unable to follow up on that.

'Really?' Khurrum leant forward. 'That was my minor.'

Older Starch distracted him with a plate of sandwiches, and Younger Starch said, 'Murtaza studied World Politics.'

'Whirled Polly Ticks.' Khurrum made a spiralling motion with his finger.

'The revolving parrot is really a bomb!' I laughed back.

'Khurrum, please go and call Kishwar. I need to know who will be at dinner tonight.' Now Mother Ali Shah was getting in on the act. Attack from all quarters.

Khurrum raised his shoulders helplessly and disappeared from the room with a mobile phone.

'Always Murtaza was standing up to his professors. Always!' His mother beamed at me and nodded.

'Really?' said a Starch. 'American professors?'

149

Murtaza nodded. 'They're all idiots there. When they talk about Pakistan, which they almost never do, they say such stupid things. One of them said our biggest problem is feudalism. Other than the usual rubbish about paying taxes, he said we treat the peasants badly. I made him look like such an idiot in front of the whole class.'

'What did you say? Aliya, did you hear? He took on his professor.'

I smiled benignly at my aunt and hid behind a *samosa*.

'I told him he should come to Pakistan. See how my family looks after the people on our lands. We've built medical facilities; every year we bring in someone from the cities to talk to the women about birth control; if anyone has a dispute they come to us and we resolve the situation without bribery or favouritism. And they are so grateful they want to kiss our feet. But we tell them they don't have to do that. Then I said, "Professor, sir, has anyone ever tried to kiss your feet?" That really shut him up.'

'Tell them what you said about cities,' his mother urged.

'*Hanh*. I also said the poor people on our lands are much better off than poor people in the city, who have to rely on the government for justice and medical care and things like that.'

This was too much for me. 'But you are the government! The National Assembly is teeming with landowners. Both on the government and the opposition benches. And incidentally, in all your talk of the largesse you provide to these benighted souls, you never mentioned education.' Masood so often said he wanted to learn to read and write English, and I never even offered to teach him. Worse, the few scraps of English I threw in his direction were worthless words such as 'thyme'.

150

Murtaza shook his head at me. 'You citywallahs. You don't understand. I thought at least you, because of your family background . . . For centuries your family ruled over its people with the same attitude as we have. What happened to you?'

'Evolution.'

I would have won that point except that, just as I spoke, one of the Ali Shah girls whispered, quite audibly, to her sister, 'Her cousin married the cook.'

How can I justify the shame I felt at that moment?

'I should be going,' I said, putting down my teacup quite calmly. 'Only stopped in for a few minutes on my way to see Dadi. She'll start worrying if I'm late. Nice to meet you all. No, no, no need to see me out.'

Khurrum was laughing on the phone, near the front door. 'Going?' he said. 'No, not you, Kishwar. Hang on.' He lowered the phone away from his ear. 'But we haven't even discussed *Othello* and cultural relativism.'

I put a hand on his arm. 'Nice to know we've got people like you in the National Assembly.'

He raised an eyebrow. 'Well, your vote's frighteningly easy to come by. Are there more like you? Can you all register to vote in my district?'

'Only if you treat me like any other voter and bribe me.'

'I promise you a goat for a vote. See you at the wedding?'

I made some non-committal motion with my hand and opened the door. A hawk-nosed man was striding up the driveway and we nodded to each other as I exited and he entered.

'Jahangir Bhai!' I heard Khurrum say.

The Underpants Man? I turned round but the door had closed.

I got into my car and rested my head against the steering wheel.

What did he think of the whole Mariam–Masood affair? In four years we'd heard, either directly or second-hand, innuendoes and gossip and vicious conjecture aimed at Mariam, but none of it originated from Jahangir and, consequently, he'd acquired the status of a demi-god in our house.

He'd been unfailingly gracious right from the start, over four years ago, when Auntie Tano called him up to say that Aba and Mariam Apa were planning a trip to the town adjoining his lands to have a look at a mosque. 'A mosque?' Aba mouthed in horror as Auntie Tano chirped down the phone to Jahangir.

'For architectural purposes,' Auntie Tano added. 'A client of Nasser's wants the tiles of the outside wall replicated in his courtyard. So Nasser's coming to have a look, and Mariam is going to sketch the tiles for the workmen in Karachi. They're staying overnight. Do you know of any hotels . . . ?'

'Don't be absurd,' Jahangir said. 'Tell them to stay with me. I'll have my driver pick them up at the train station.'

It was that simple.

By the standard of the Ali Shahs, Jahangir was just a small landowner without the trappings of feudal power, but Aba was struck from the first by the deference of his servants. 'It made me think that Masood must be a misfit here,' Aba told me afterwards. 'Oh, he was never anything but polite, but you always knew that he knew he could leave and get a job anywhere else if we crossed certain lines. Of course, maybe he couldn't because of Mariam, but we never knew that.'

They arrived on Jahangir's lands in the early evening, and before sunset Aba had forgotten his reservations about Jahangir, a man he'd been on nodding terms with for twenty years, but had never spoken to until that day.

'He looked at Mariam when he talked. Didn't act as though her silence meant she wasn't part of the conversation. And he could interpret her gestures, her facial expressions, remarkably well. I thought, I really thought, maybe. But then dinner was served.'

When Aba told the story we all, all of us who'd ever eaten a meal prepared by Masood, put aside our reaction to the elopement to imagine, just for a moment, how it would feel to be in the presence of Masood's food again. Aba, too, closed his eyes and inhaled deeply, said, 'Chicken *vindaloo*,' and we all sighed.

'Of course, you know my cook,' Jahangir said. 'I would say I regret taking him away from you, but you'd know that's a lie.'

Mariam Apa did not fall upon the food as Aba had expected, given how long she'd been without eating. She brushed a hint of the *vindaloo*'s sauce on to her lower lip, and tucked the lip inside her mouth. She held it there for a few seconds, and then smiled. After that she ate with her customary delicacy, but her eyes were bright as she savoured each morsel, and when she finished her first helping she gasped at the incremental burn of the spices on her tongue.

Masood did not appear during the meal; he did not double as bearer here, but stayed confined to the kitchen. At the end of the meal, however, Jahangir said, 'You'll stay for lunch tomorrow, won't you? You can see the mosque in the morning and then come back. We'll have Masood cook whatever you want.' He turned to the bearer and told him to call Masood. 'Stay all weekend, in fact. Longer! I had forgotten that it was possible to enjoy company so much. '

Aba was already imagining the wedding, and hoping it wouldn't be a dragged-out series of ceremonies over two weeks.

'Nasser Sahib,' he heard behind him, and there stood Masood. Aba stood up and shook his hand warmly, thereby missing the expression on Mariam Apa's face as she saw Masood for the first time since he'd left.

Masood turned to Mariam. 'What will you have tomorrow?' he said. Mariam cupped her palms and pointed them towards Masood. *It's in your hands.*

The next morning when Aba went to see why Mariam was sleeping so late her suitcase was gone and a photostat of a wedding licence was on her bed, the print smudged here and there. People said, 'She just left a copy of the *nikah-nama* without any sign of goodbye or sorry or take care,' but I knew the smudges were the only gesture of farewell that would allow me to forgive her for leaving. After all, how could I be angry when confronted with her tears?

Aba had no choice but to show his host the *nikahnama*, and Jahangir said, 'If you think it best I'll send my men to find them. It won't be a problem.'

'Thank you,' Aba said. 'Thank you for making that optional. No, please, I have no right to make this demand, but please don't do that, not now, not ever.'

'Bibi?'

I lifted my head from the steering wheel, and ran my palm along my forehead, trying to smooth away the latticed pattern imprinted on my skin.

'Bibi, is everything all right?'

'Yes. Yes. Thank you, I'm fine.'

The man peering in at me smiled. He had been sitting with the group of servants – drivers, bodyguards, Older Starch's mali and chowkidar – when I walked out of the Starched gate.

'You don't remember me, Aliya Bibi. I almost didn't recognize you either. You were very young when I last saw you.'

'I'm sorry,' I said. 'Are you one of my aunts' servants?'

He shook his head. 'I saw you sometimes when I lived in the city before. I'm Jahangir Sahib's driver.' When I still looked confused he added, quite gently, 'My brother used to work for you.'

Things I wanted to do: push his hair off his face; shave off his beard; straighten his shoulders; hear his laugh. Anything to find a resemblance to the man Mariam had left all of us for. Or if not that, at least to talk to him, to hear how Masood seemed during those days after he left Karachi, what he said about Mariam, what he said about all those things that he must have said things about but about which I never asked. Things like what he dreamt about, and why he never married, and how come he left his village and whether he was happy.

Instead I said, 'Did Masood really have to return to the village when your father died?'

'No.' His brother looked at me as though I'd asked him about a mystery that he couldn't quite solve. 'I was there to look after the family. Masood was gone so long we thought he'd never return. He was too much a Karachiwallah.'

I looked at that man and I knew that I could talk to him for ten minutes or ten hours and he would never mention Mariam, never allude to the fact that our families were

155

connected now and maybe he had nieces who were my nieces too, though we would never, no, not even if we knew where they were, we would never sit together, he and I, at a table watching those nieces blow out candles on a cake. How could we, when even now I could not stay and talk because the other servants were watching and maybe visitors who knew who I was and knew who he was would be arriving. What's more, I couldn't go and squat on the ground with him and he couldn't sit with me in my car, both of us in the front seats like equals, and the longer we stayed as we were, he bending his back to catch my words, the more obvious it would be to both of us that we couldn't sit together, not in my car, not on the ground, and if not there or there then certainly not across the table from each other in a room filled with balloons and streamers.

I had time, I felt, for one question. 'What was he really like?'

His brother stepped back. 'I was going to ask you that.'

I nodded and started the car engine. 'I pray he's well. If you ever have any contact with him . . .'

'I don't think I will. He had a passport. He took it with him.'

Chapter Sixteen

I said goodbye to Masood's brother and drove straight to Dadi's house. She would be leaving for Paris in a matter of days, but I couldn't let her go without asking her about Taimur. Where might he have gone when he left Dard-e-Dil? Where, more to the point, might Mariam have grown up? Which is to say, Where might she have returned to when she eloped? In my mind I couldn't even narrow it down to a single hemisphere. Did she refrain from speech because speech betrays accent, and accent betrays everything? But, then, why speak of food?

I had to have answers about Taimur. I had to have answers, because how could it be that he had left home and there his story ended as far as we were concerned? How could he disappear so completely? How could someone in the family disappear so completely? If Taimur could, then maybe his daughter could, also. Her physical absence I had learnt to accept. But not to know, not even to start to guess, where she was and what she was doing, to be unable to close my eyes and see her in a context that made me smile, that was the real wound.

When I had said to Celeste, 'Can you draw her older and

happy?' I was really saying that my imagination lets me down. When I picture Mariam she is always unhappy. Sometimes she's a recluse, seeing no one but Masood, jealous of the time he spends with his friends. She is bitter that he is not excluded from the company of men whose comradeship he seeks, while she cannot meet the kind of people she's accustomed to meeting because however much they like her they'll always say, 'But good God! The husband!'

Other times she's left Masood, or he's left her, and she drifts, unable to return to the world from which she's an outcast, a middle-aged woman with no college degree and no résumé. So how does she live? How does she eat?

And sometimes, apropos of nothing, when my eyes are closed I see her walking from me. I know it's her although she looks nothing like anyone I could ever want to know – she is stooped and lank-haired and shuffling and entirely alone – and I don't call out to her because I cannot bear to incur the pain that one look at her face will cause, so instead I tell myself it isn't her and turn away.

When I told Celeste all this she said, 'So I guess that could explain the heebie-jeebie dreams.'

The dreams she referred to were mine. The heebie-jeebies were hers, in response. She said I'd jerk upright in bed maybe once, twice a month, looking like someone in a horror movie who only had seven seconds of screen time and was determined to make it memorable, even if it was only memorable for the outrageous overacting. She was generally awake when this happened – she once remarked, though she now denies it, that sleep is a bourgeois luxury – and when she tried to talk to me I wouldn't answer but she'd go on talking until I fell asleep again. The first time this happened, when we'd been in college for less than a month, she sang lullabies to me. She said it had seemed like a good idea, but after I went back to sleep she worried that it was neo-imperialistic of her to assume that 'Mary Had a Little Lamb' had any significance in my life. (I replied, 'Your neo-imperialism anticipates my post-colonialism.' Fortunately, we ceased being enamoured of such talk before long.)

I don't remember the dreams, but I'm sure Celeste is right in suggesting their connection to Mariam Apa's departure. Something happened to alter my sleep pattern after Mariam left; my old ability to fall asleep at the slightest opportunity didn't change, but often I'd wake up feeling exhausted, though there was no other evidence to suggest I hadn't slept soundly through the night. The exhaustion was far less marked when Celeste was around to talk me back to sleep, but it never went away entirely for more than a couple of months at a stretch. After a while I grew so accustomed to it that when I woke up in the morning feeling a strange heaviness of eyelid I'd just look across to Celeste and say, 'Sorry. Did I startle you?' and she always shrugged and said something like, 'You should seriously audition for the next Stephen King movie.' We stayed room-mates for all four years of college, though we could have got singles by our junior year. She said I did her a favour by not moving out and leaving her to bore herself silly, but I know that I was the one on the receiving end of a generous gesture of friendship.

I honked my horn outside Dadi's gate and the chowki-dar, who was playing Ludo with a group of servants outside a house down the street, ran to my car. 'Begum Sahib's gone out,' he said. 'But someone who says she's her sister is waiting for her in the drawing room.'

'Someone who says she's her sister? You mean you could have let some stranger into the house.'

The chowkidar spread his hands helplessly. 'But how should I know? Who am I to forbid a begum from entering the house? She got dropped off and her car left. Should I have told her to wait outside? I got fired from my last job for doing that. And your family is very large.'

He had me there. And Mohommed, Dadi's cook from Dard-e-Dil, who knew more about the family than I did, was at the bazaar. I briefly considered turning round and going home. 'Sister' undoubtedly meant 'cousin', and the last thing I wanted was a run-in with another deadly relative. But if Dadi knew I'd left an older relative sitting alone in the house she'd make some withering comment. And I was feeling sufficiently withered already.

The woman in the drawing room had her back to me when I entered. She was looking at a painting of the Dard-e-Dil palace grounds. Hard to believe that my grandparents played in these grounds as children. The long driveway and manicured lawns were a little too tidy for my taste, but I loved the scattered sculptures – particularly the fountain with its statue of a bear cupping his hands to catch the water that spurted out of a baby elephant's trunk. The palace, with its harmonious mix of straight lines and arches, stood in the background.

'From the roof we could see forever. In 1947, turn this way and you'd see Hindu mobs burning down Muslim houses; turn that way and you'd see the Muslims doing the same to the Hindus. But not in Dard-e-Dil itself. You have to give the Nawab credit for that.'

Dadi's sister, Meher, turned around and smiled at me. 'I'm getting old,' she said. 'I'm thinking favourably of that depraved aristocracy from which I was so fortunate to escape. Come here and hug me.'

I put my arms around her and she said, 'Why does my sister persist in cluttering her walls with these mementoes of bygone decadence? What do you think she'd say if we took all the paintings down while she was away?'

'She'd tell us to put them back up, and not crookedly.'

I pulled back and looked at Meher Dadi and laughed. She was wearing a sari with a sleeveless blouse, and her silver hair was impeccably styled. 'If this is getting old, bring on those birthday cakes. I thought you weren't getting in until tomorrow.'

'Changed my mind. Arrived this morning. I called Sameer last night from Athens airport to tell him I was on my way. My poor grandson! He had to wake up at some terrible hour this morning to pick me up, but what can I do? I so enjoy the element of surprise.' She sat down, her hands resting on the arms of the chair as though it were a throne.

'How's Apollo?'

She looked amused. 'For the sake of propriety we're all supposed to pretend that he's just my banker who has, over the years, become a friend. He's fine.'

'Will he ever come to Karachi?'

'Don't be silly. Why should my banker come to Karachi?'

'Have you ever thought about marrying him?'

Her eyebrows rose sharply. 'Well, we're suddenly very upfront. Have you been spending time with Samia?' She made a dismissive gesture. 'I don't think his wife would approve of the match. Are you shocked?'

'Yes.' Deeply, deeply shocked.

'Good. You should be. I don't sanction taking marriage

lightly. She's Catholic. Doesn't believe in divorce. Other than that she's not too bad. He was in a little accident last year. Nothing serious. But when the police notified her she called me. I thought that very decent. Why don't you ever visit me in Greece?'

'I suppose I'll have to, just so I can meet this mystery man. Does he look like a Greek god?'

'A fat, bald octogenarian. I'm feeling very prudish now, so let's change the subject.'

'Prudish? You've asked me to come and stay in the house where the two of you live together.'

'We do not. He lives with an old friend next door. Well, when any of my relatives come to stay he does. Now change the subject.'

I tried to imagine any of my friends having this kind of conversation with a great-aunt. Impossible. Usually it was people of Meher Dadi's generation talking about marriage and people my age trying to change the subject.

'There's something I want to show you.' I ran into Dadi's room and brought out the picture, newly framed, from Baji's flat. 'I met Baji in London. She gave me this photograph. I thought Dadi should have it. I never know where I'll find it when I go into her room. One day it's by her bedside table, the next day on her dresser, the day after that it's hidden away in a drawer.'

Meher Dadi took the picture in both hands and looked at it for only a moment before putting it face down on the coffee table. 'I can't look at it. It breaks my heart. Even now.' She looked up at me. 'Why is that? I can look without sadness at pictures of all the dead I've wept for – my parents, my husband, my childhood friends – but this picture, oh Aliya, I wish you hadn't shown it to me.'

'Dadi said the man in the centre is Taimur. Not Akbar.'

Meher Dadi's face went blank. 'Your Dadi and I were close to all three of the brothers.'

I knew that blank expression. I'd worn it often enough myself. 'There's something you're not telling me.'

'And you should respect that.' Dadi swept into the room in her best imperious manner. 'Meher, the painting of the palace is crooked. Why can't you ever . . .' The end of the sentence was lost in Meher's hair as the sisters held each other and swayed back and forth, Meher's arms around Dadi's neck. For all their wrinkles and hanging flesh they looked unspeakably lovely. When they drew apart Dadi wiped a tear off her sister's cheek; the action would have been merely efficient if it hadn't taken that extra split-second to accomplish.

'You arrive early just so you can catch me looking less than my best,' Dadi sniffed. 'I'm going to freshen up. Aliya will entertain you.'

Meher Dadi rolled her eyes. 'Oh Apa, I'm not some beau coming to call on you.'

Dadi ignored that comment. Just before she left the room she said, 'Tell Aliya about Partition.'

'Which details?'

'The ones she doesn't know.'

She was trying to ensure I didn't ask any more questions about Taimur. He had been gone for nine years by the time Partition took place and, despite my fascination with all family history, I really wasn't interested in 1947 at that particular instant. But I couldn't very well tell Meher Dadi that; not with what Partition had meant to her generation.

'What do you know about the not-quites and nineteen forty-seven?'

163

Only that of all the twin stories, Akbar and Sulaiman's was the one I never told to entertain crowds. Not for the same reason that I never told Mariam Apa's story; no, Akbar and Sulaiman left no great mark on my psyche. Their story was just, well, boring. Judge for yourself: the two brothers (Taimur now long gone) disagreed politically. Akbar was a Leaguer, Sulaiman was a Congress man. One believed that Nehru and the Congress were dangerously power-hungry; the other believed the same of Jinnah and the League. The brothers fought; the fighting turned bitter. The whole family was drawn into the battle and forced to take sides – all other causes of division and unity among the Dard-e-Dils were forgotten, and all that remained were the Pakistan camp and the united-India camp. When Partition actually took place, one country coming to life on 14 August, the other on 15 August, the Dard-e-Dils sighed, said, 'Born on opposite sides of midnight like Akbar and Sulaiman,' and took that as a sign that the family rift was inevitable. It was the curse of the not-quites raining down on the Dard-e-Dils yet again, except this time, instead of losing land, wealth or architectural plans, they were losing each other.

(Later, during the bloodshed of 1971, when East Pakistan became Bangladesh, there were those in my family who said it was inevitable. Because there had been three brothers. If Akbar and Sulaiman were Pakistan and India, then of course there had to be a third country to represent Taimur. The stupidity of that statement is unparalleled, but it seems sagacious compared to the other kinds of stupidity that did the rounds of West Pakistan in those days. Let me take that back. Stupidity is too tame a word to describe justifications of genocide and rape. Dadi always claimed that 1971 killed Akbar. Not the war, the talk. His heart couldn't take that hatred. One of the last things he said was, 'But if the three of us couldn't work things out what hope is there for anyone? We are lost, utterly lost.' This deserves more than an aside, but I've lived too long with silence about those dreadful days, and I lack the heart and stomach to speak of things I don't even want to believe possible.)

To return to Meher Dadi and her reaction to my version of Akbar and Sulaiman's fight: she laughed.

'Look at them,' she said. She held up the photograph, palm covering Dadi's face so I was forced to focus on the three boys. 'Akbar, Taimur, Sulaiman.' She pointed to each in turn. Yes, that was Taimur in the middle, but he wasn't keeping the other two apart as I had first thought. Akbar's arm lay atop Sulaiman's arm, across Taimur's shoulder. Akbar's fingers pulled Sulaiman's ear lobe; Sulaiman's palm cupped Akbar's neck. 'You think Nehru or Jinnah could have ripped these boys apart? They'd have left the country together, moved to Timbuktoo, if they thought national politics threatened to make enemies of them.'

'What are you saying?'

'Aliya, you have to understand love.'

Oh, that again.

'Aliya, when did your grandfather leave Dard-e-Dil for Karachi?'

'Summer, nineteen forty-six.'

She nodded. 'Hasn't that ever struck you as strange?'

Before she even finished the sentence I realized how strange, how very strange the timing was. In the summer of 1946 no one knew for sure that Pakistan would become a reality. So how could Akbar's reason for coming to Karachi have been his desire to be a Pakistani?

Meher Dadi turned slightly and pointed up at the painting of the Dard-e-Dil palace again. 'He made his decision there, on the first of July, nineteen forty-six.'

The family, she said, had gathered on that date for the Nawab's birthday but, coming so close after Congress's rejection of the Cabinet Mission Plan, the evening was anything but celebratory at the start. Sulaiman and his wife had just returned from a European holiday and when dinner was served, the promise of wine and food turning the evening festive at last, he and Akbar broke away from the rest of the crowd and forwent the delicacies of the royal kitchen to sit on a verandah and talk. The three months Sulaiman had been away was the longest period the brothers had ever been apart, and Meher Dadi recalled how, even during the initial stages of the party, Akbar was more cheerful than he had been for weeks. Dadi watched the brothers walk towards the verandah and said, 'Thank God.' She asked Sulaiman's wife, 'Is your husband also impossible to live with when his brother isn't around?' Sulaiman's wife – a beautiful but insipid woman whom Sulaiman had married in haste without remembering the repentance part of the axiom – probably responded but Meher Dadi swears she can't remember a word the woman ever said. Nor does she remember what took her to the room which led out to the verandah where the brothers sat, but she can't forget what she heard when she got there.

At first it seemed like just another conversation about politics, although how anyone could think any discussion of politics was 'just another conversation' in 1946, I don't know. In fact, I'm sure that right from the beginning there

166

must have been something about the conversation which marked it as unusual. Why else would Meher Dadi have stayed to eavesdrop?

Imagine a summer night with crickets chirping and a cool breeze carrying away the oppressive heat of the sunlight hours. In the background, the tinkle of glass and laughter and the spurt of water from fountains. But something else was in the air – an edge of desperation to the revelries. Someone that evening had reached down to a flower bed and let a handful of rich loam trickle through his fingers and, though he was merely looking for a fallen pearl button, the word 'symbolic' raced through the gathering. Seemingly oblivious to this, two brothers, identical, reclined on garden chairs, the glow of cigarettes held between their gesturing fingers prompting fireflies to swoop in for a closer look.

'How can you say you believe both in secularism and in this Pakistan idea?' Sulaiman picked up an ashtray and held it on his knee, within Akbar's reach.

'I believe in secularism. But I don't believe in Congress. If they aren't willing to compromise now, why should they do so when the British leave? Oh, Sully, the divisions exist. Blame it on who you will – the British, the politicians, the Hindus, the Muslims, whoever. Fact is, they exist today to an extent they never have before. And relationships are not motor cars; they can't be reversed. Not between individuals; not between groups. Certainly not between Congress and the League. If the English had left after World War One things might have been different. But now it's too late for the dream, Sulaiman.'

'If this Pakistan comes into being and you support it, then it will be too late.'

'Don't you see that history has left us behind?' He passed his cigarette to Sulaiman, who always liked the last drag best. 'The other not-quites shaped history; we are shaped by it. We have no power except over our own lives.'

'And each other's, Akbar.' Sulaiman stood up and Meher Dadi ducked back into the shadows of the room to avoid being seen. She always regretted doing that, she said. Maybe if she'd stepped out, stopped the conversation, everything would have been different.

'How can you even consider leaving your home?' Sulaiman said with a gesture meant to encompass all of Dard-e-Dil. 'Because that's what you're thinking about, isn't it? It's not just in theory that you're "for" Pakistan. You actually want to go there, don't you? We both know that however the borders are decided – I can't believe I'm talking about this as though it will really happen – but if it does, there's no chance that Dard-e-Dil will fall in Pakistan. So if you choose Pakistan you have to forfeit home. How can you do that? I don't understand how anyone can do that, let alone my brothers. First Taimur, now you.'

Akbar sighed. 'When Pakistan happens – and it will happen, Sulaiman . . . I thought for a while that the Cabinet Mission Plan might work, but since Nehru has chosen not to accept . . . Oh, but never mind that for the moment. Yes, when Pakistan happens we'll all have to choose whether to stay here or go there, and I believe I'll go. But I'll only be going next door.' He laughed. 'I mean, it's hardly as though I'm planning never to see the rest of my family again. Most of the Dard-e-Dils will stay here, I know that. But I wish you'd think about coming with me. Think of it, Sulaiman: a new country with all the potential in the world.' He gestured around him, just as Sulaiman

168

had done seconds earlier. 'Let's admit it, this life is over. And for all its decadence and claustrophobia we'll weep for it. But we'll scold our children if they do the same. Maybe that's why Taimur left when he did. He didn't want to watch his world die.'

'Oh, good God.' Sulaiman smacked a palm against his forehead and stood up to pace the verandah. 'That's the real reason you're planning on leaving for Pakistan, isn't it? You think you'll find Taimur there. Why? Because Liaquat's the only politician he ever said a kind word about? Because of those times he said he wanted an option other than England or Dard-e-Dil? Akbar, you idiot.'

Can we believe Meher Dadi's account of what happened next? How clear a view did she have while trying to hide out of the brothers' sight? She claims that even as Sulaiman seemed to insult Akbar his hand reached out to brush an insect off Akbar's shoulder. Akbar did not see Sulaiman, but he felt – or saw – the insect, and his own hand reached back to flick it off. He flicked Sulaiman's hand away instead, without realizing that it was the very tips of Sulaiman's fingers he had touched. He must have thought he'd made contact with the insect, because he didn't turn round and hold Sulaiman's hand in apology as he would otherwise have done, but said instead, 'Get that damn thing off me.' Sulaiman's face turned to stone and he cursed Akbar, 'Go to hell,' and then Akbar's face, too, became granite.

'One of us has moved on with his life since Taimur left. One of us isn't going to spend the rest of his life amidst the crumbling decay of what was once grand just because he's sure that's the place his brother will return to. I'm not the idiot here, Sulaiman. Taimur isn't coming back. So stop tailoring your politics to fit his return and admit the truth.

You've been miserable since you married that poor woman, and rather than facing the present you concoct visions of future happiness that anyone else can recognize as a pathetic substitute for living. India, free and united and blissfully democratic. Taimur home. Your marriage . . . Well, I don't know how great a leap of the imagination transforms that into joy. Sometimes you're such a child.'

Meher Dadi rushed out to stop the impossible from happening, but it was too late. Sulaiman caught Akbar by the collar. 'You're right. You've moved on. I haven't heard you mention Taimur's name in over a year. And you'll move on again. Move on from me. Move on from your home. Is there nothing, no one you're tied to except yourself?' Sulaiman pushed Akbar away as though his touch was contaminating. 'When Taimur wrote about kites that have their strings snipped he must have anticipated a moment like this. So pack your bags, brother. Go. Who knows? Maybe Taimur really will come back. Maybe he's only waiting for you to leave.'

'Oh, please.' Akbar made a dismissive gesture and turned to go back inside.

'He came back four years ago. Akbar, he came back.'

Everything happened in slow motion. The expression on Akbar's face changing from disbelief to bafflement to anger; the explosion of fireworks in the sky behind the brothers; Akbar's fist slamming into Sulaiman's jaw.

Sulaiman cupped his chin and tried to sit up. 'It's true. When Mama was dying he came back. Taimur came back. I was in her room when he slipped in. Just after dinner. He stayed all night talking about the past, making her smile, making me laugh. In the morning he left.'

'When Abida and I were in Delhi?'

Sulaiman shook his head. 'The two of you were in the room next door.'

'And you didn't call me?'

'Taimur said if I did that he'd leave.'

'Liar! You damned liar.' Akbar picked Sulaiman off the ground and hit him again.

Sulaiman made a horrible sound. It took Meher Dadi a second to realize he was laughing. 'Is that an emotion, Akbar? Sorry. Did I bruise your ego?'

'You're lying. He didn't come back. You're lying.'

'Really? Remember how everyone thought Mama was delirious in those last days because she kept talking about seeing Taimur in her bedroom?' Akbar had his head in his hands now, but Sulaiman, spitting blood, pressed on. 'Please, please, Akbar, do me a favour and go to Pakistan the day it becomes a reality. Go on, leave Dard-e-Dil. Taimur will be back in a flash when he hears you've gone.'

Akbar stood up. 'Well, accept this gesture of brotherly love, then. I'll leave now and stay away altogether. For ever.'

The next day he flew to Karachi to accept a long-standing offer to join a British company. He never went back to Dard-e-Dil.

Chapter Seventeen

I left Dadi's house before my grandmother emerged from her room. Meher Dadi seemed to understand. 'You can't leap from that story into idle chit-chat,' she said. 'Go home. Sit out in the garden where the crickets chirp, and listen to the weeping of ghosts. They deserve a little attention now and then.'

I did just that. It was my favourite time of day; trees and houses and electricity poles silhouetted against the sky which was not so much dark as absent of light. The after-glow of sunset, an in-between time. I lay on the grass, kicked off my shoes and held my hands up, fingers apart, to allow the breeze to caress as much of my body as possible. The rustle of leaves was a benediction. Karachi's nights remind you that you can love a place, and for me that's always been a reason to rejoice. But that night I thought of Akbar flying into Karachi for the first time. How alien it must have been to him. How lost he must have been in that first moment when he disembarked and thought, My children will call this home. They will know sunsets over the ocean and the taste of crab so fresh it's barely dead and they will hear blessings in the breeze from the sea. But they will not know Sulaiman and they will not know Taimur. And in not knowing those two, they will not know me.

He was twenty-six.

History betrayed Akbar and Sulaiman. At any other time the elders of the family would have chastised them for their foolishness, told them they weren't boys any more, forced them to shake hands. But it was 1946 and all sorts of foolishness was in the air.

When the brothers walked back to the dining room, several feet apart, the assembled company took one look at Meher's tears and Sulaiman's jaw and a cacophony of questions arose.

Sulaiman spoke first. 'My brother has just convinced me that Pakistan is a good idea. We can send the dregs of Dard-e-Dil there, and he'll be the first.'

The atmosphere in that room was already tense, the good cheer brought on by dinner unable to sustain itself through dessert. If Akbar and Sulaiman hadn't been so intent on their own rage earlier they would have heard the raised voices, and from the sudden hush that followed they would have known that the Nawab, with all the courtesy and regality at his disposal, had requested that there be no more talk of politics. But the peace that prevailed was uneasy, and it took only one sentence from Sulaiman to destroy it. Before the evening was over the terms 'polite disagreement' and 'neutral party' had disappeared from the Dard-e-Dil lexicon. Akbar aside, all the other Dard-e-Dils present at the palace that evening would continue to co-exist within a radius of a few square miles until the following year, when Pakistan came to life, but it was a strange, strained year with few moments of family solidarity.

(The Nawab? Everyone gathered at the dinner called him Binky. How effective could he have been in bringing them to order?)

Perhaps it was inevitable, the falling out. In a family like the Dard-e-Dils – so proud and so stubborn – it's hard to imagine people shrugging their shoulders and calling the choice between India and Pakistan just a matter of different opinions. And yet, instead of blaming the family characteristics, we blame Akbar and Sulaiman.

When Samia told me not to mention my grandparents to Baji, it was because the general consensus – on both sides of the border, though I wasn't aware of that until Samia explained it to me – was that ties between the Indian and Pakistani sides of the family would eventually have been renewed if it hadn't been for Akbar and Sulaiman, each declaring that he did not want to hear his brother's name again, each constantly reminding the rest of the family of all the harsh words, the insults, the curses that had been hurled across the Nawab's table. The only one who could have brought the brothers together was Dadi, or so it is claimed, but she never tried. Worse, when Akbar once – while picking candles out of a birthday cake and looking sadly at the pock-marked frosting – wondered what his brother was doing, Dadi accused him of being spineless.

How to reconcile this story with my own memory of Dadi crying, 'We were girls together.' I think I know the answer. They weren't happy together, my grandparents. Ami once told me the reason Aba so seldom raises his voice to anyone is that he grew up in a house filled with shouting. So, if Dadi railed against Akbar for mentioning Sulaiman, maybe it was just because she was looking for an excuse to rail against Akbar.

But is it possible that in twenty-five years there was never a moment when they were simultaneously nostalgic for everything they'd left behind, for every voice they could no longer hear? The truth may be that it was easier to make one swift break and swear never to look back. The truth may be that Dadi loved Akbar too much to allow him to begin to think of everything he'd lost.

But what of everything she had lost?

I stood up and walked over to Mariam Apa's hibiscus. After Mariam left, the mali asked Ami what should be done about the hibiscus. Ami told him to look after it as Mariam had, and never, never to snip off the branch which curved in front of the dining-room window. I sometimes think Ami was the one who missed Mariam most of all. She wasn't haunted by her absence, or angered by her departure, or disturbed by all she had failed to see. She just missed her. If Mariam were to come back, Ami would be the only one who'd say, 'I'm glad you're here,' and consider the conversation ended. But suppose Mariam were to come back with Masood? That could never happen, so I don't even speculate.

Speculate, I demanded of myself. Go on, speculate.

But I couldn't.

I ran my fingers along the hibiscus plant, scoring the bark with my fingernails. When Mariam was around it hadn't mattered, but now I felt so terribly the need to have her explained. I had thought Taimur could lead me to her, if I only asked the right questions about him, but he grew more and more elusive. To leave your home and never go back – to commit yourself completely to making another place home – that I could understand. Dadi and Akbar's story doesn't baffle me, though it sometimes saddens me. But to

175

leave home, alone, and then to return just once, for one night, that I cannot comprehend. Somehow he must have followed the lives of his family. How else would he have known his mother was sick? How else would Mariam have known that, other than Dadi, who was in Paris at the time, the closest relative she had to turn to was Aba? Her closest relative in Pakistan, that is. Why Pakistan and not India? Was she in Pakistan already? Had Taimur ended up in Pakistan, as Sulaiman claimed Akbar believed he would? Or was Pakistan simply closer than India to wherever Taimur and Mariam lived? Did that mean she came from Iran? Afghanistan?

Turkey?

When Samia first went to college in London she fell in with a strange arty set who spent their Friday nights watching foreign films and ordering out for meals which, in their ethnic origins, complemented the movies. The group fell apart over an argument about whether hamburgers were suitable accompaniments to a German film, but by then Samia had developed a taste for subtitles. She came back to Karachi over her Easter holiday and demanded that Sameer and I scour the video stores for foreign films. She wasn't amused when we returned with a pile of Hollywood flicks.

So Sameer and I set off again and returned with a Turkish film, which the man at the video store told us we could keep since he had so little use for it that he really couldn't understand what it was doing in his shop to begin with. I don't remember what the movie was about beyond the fact that it involved chickens, a three-legged dog and a man named Murat. We would never have sat through the whole thing if Sameer and I hadn't been too frightened of Samia's wrath to suggest turning it off, and if Samia hadn't been too proud to admit she'd rather watch low-brow Hollywood fare. But halfway through the movie Mariam Apa entered the TV room and laughed at the subtitle, 'You want to rent a room?' Then she laughed at, 'Is that the sun?' and almost fell off her chair at, 'You look very pretty.'

Three months later Samia sent Sameer a postcard:

Guess what Sam 2! Remember the Turkish movie? Well, I mentioned it to my Turkish friend, Omër, and he says it's a great comedy. Very subtle humour! He knows chunks of it by heart – translated some dialogue for me and it really was funny, though it didn't ring any bells at all as far as my memory of the subtitles was concerned. Guess we got a lousy translation. Must go – there are strawberries.

Love, Sam 1.

P.S. How come Mariam understood the humour?

In the days that followed the arrival of the postcard I tried casually mentioning Ataturk and Istanbul and Turkish delight around Mariam Apa, but she didn't show even a flicker of interest. Still, I never quite forgot about it.

Why would Taimur have gone to Turkey?

Back again to Taimur, that inexplicable man.

It's true that there were relatives aplenty in the family who had been part of the Khilafat Movement just before the triplets were born, and throughout Taimur's childhood those relatives spoke often of that political movement which tried to show the British that Muslims around the world would not accept the break-up of the Ottoman Empire. One

177

of the uncles even stayed in Turkey for a few months, just before Ataturk declared Turkey a secular state, and after he returned he made a point of teaching all the children of the family the rudiments of the Turkish language. So it's not inconceivable that Turkey should have had a certain hold on Taimur's imagination. It certainly had a hold on the imaginations of most Indian Muslims of his parents' generation, and Taimur always loved to listen to his elders' stories. But even so . . . What was Taimur's story?

Mosquitoes had begun to buzz around me so I pulled my *dupatta* close like a shawl, using it to shield my bare arms from the onslaught. As a child I would tell myself things like, If I stay outdoors and brave the insects for a whole hour then tomorrow the boating plan will work out. If, subsequently, the boating plan didn't work out, it would be because I stayed outside only fifty-nine minutes, or because I cheated by lathering on calamine lotion afterwards, or because mosquitoes died in my dreams that night.

Was that childhood logic so different from my way of thinking now? If I ask the right questions the answers will come. If the answers don't come it's because I haven't asked the right questions, haven't pried out the necessary details from those who feel no pleasure in remembering, haven't recalled that one lift of an eyebrow which changes everything. But what about the silences that can't be retold in stories? What about the forgotten commas which shape us as much as the exclamation marks? Masood once said to me, 'Why is it that when people exchange recipes they so often forget to mention salt?'

I had laughed then and Masood, uncharacteristically offended that I shouldn't take him seriously, served unsalted food to the family that night.

178

'What is this?' Aba had said, staring down in horror at his plate, after just one morsel. 'What is this?'

How the absence of a single ingredient can alter the meal before you. How the absence of a detail can alter a story. How much salt had been left out in all the stories I'd ever heard from, and about, my family? How much salt did I leave out when I turned my memories of Mariam and Masood into a story? Well, I knew part of the answer to that. I left out my own reactions. Of late I'd been telling myself that eventually, when everything was resolved in my mind, I'd put myself in the story and say that at first I'd reacted terribly. Then I went far away and allowed myself time to think about it and my mind accepted the marriage. Then, one day, so did my heart. And so I went to visit Khaleel in Liaquatabad.

If only it were that simple.

I imagined Khaleel before me, laughing. 'Salt? How déclassé. I'd have thought you'd season your metaphors with nothing less than saffron.'

Masood loved saffron, but when he spoke about food in terms of devotion he referred back to that déclassé seasoning. 'I believe in God because all of science can never explain the miracle of salt,' he said and I, having learnt my lesson, nodded.

What if all of storytelling couldn't explain Taimur?

I stood up so quickly I had to sit down again. Could it be that simple? Mariam Apa never spoke because speaking would mean trying to explain Taimur, and that she was unable to do. So she hid in menus – hid in that wondrous yet confined world of lunch and dinner and, sometimes, tea – marking out the boundaries of what she could and could not speak of. She knew, as do we all, that it is useless to say

179

you will keep quiet on one subject, because everything is interconnected. Start talking about cricket and within five minutes you might be on the subject of yaks' milk without a single non sequitur. Ask a person one question and you set yourself up to be asked a question in return. So Mariam asked no questions, revealed no clues, started no conversations which could sprawl beyond her control. Rather than keep quiet on one subject, she kept quiet on every subject but one. It's the only way of keeping a secret.

Or . . . I squeezed my head between my hands, not knowing if I wanted my thoughts to slow down or speed up. Something was shaping inside my skull . . . Had all of us always been wrong about her silence? We assumed the silence was about not speaking, but what if it was about not not-listening? Did she move mute among us in order to observe? Was she so intent on listening because there was something she needed to hear? Perhaps, just as we were waiting for her to give us the answers about Taimur, she was waiting for us to help her understand why her father walked away from the family she missed so much when she was growing up. In the end, was the failure ours for being unable to hear the questions she shouted out through silence?

Or did we finally answer those questions and, in answering them, make it impossible for her to do anything except follow Taimur's example and leave?

Chapter Eighteen

Two rare and remarkable things: messages from both Samia and Celeste in my in-box when I logged on to my e-mail. I knew that Samia would have something to say about tea at Baji's with Khaleel so I clicked on Celeste's message first.

Hey, Babe.

How's my favourite decadent Pakistani doing? Thought of you yesterday (like that's a rare event!) while watching an old Audrey Hepburn movie with my brother – the former metal-head has become an aficionado of fifties movies. Go figure. The movie? You guessed it – *Sabrina*! I've always enjoyed it, despite its refusal to acknowledge the rigid, though unspoken, class structure in the US, but yesterday I couldn't concentrate on it. Kept thinking of you and Mariam and . . . I want to write 'Missouri' but I know that's not his name. Mussood?

So, anyway, I'm still waiting to get an epiphany e-mail from you. You know what I mean. Our likeable but flawed heroine walks out from her élite neighbourhood, and, spurred on by an e-mail from her American friend (remember, in these stories someone Euro-American has to be responsible for showing our élitist Third Worlder the light), she notices the poverty in other parts of the city for the first time – No! She feels empathy for the first time – and she turns her back on her life of privilege and dedicates her days to helping the needy. Roll credits.

Seriously, though, I know things can't be easy. What little news we get from your part of the world is pretty frightening. Tell me it's just the US media up to their old tricks. I miss you, girl. When do you return stateside?

Love,

Your favourite I-claim-to-oppose-decadence-but-live-in-a-system-steeped-in-it American.

I dashed off a reply:

C – In the kind of movie you're talking about our heroine wouldn't be inspired by a Euro-American; she would *be* a Euro-American. Possibly shown the light by some mystical but ineffectual Eastern type.

More later.

Love,

A.

Sameer came through the door, holding two glasses of Coke in his hands and two packets of chilli chips between his teeth. 'Hey!' he said, and the chilli chips fell on to the desk beside me. 'No saliva on them, I swear. Miracle of miracles . . . Is that actually a message from my sister?'

I didn't want anyone, not even Sameer, to see me reading a message about Khaleel, so I clicked from the in-box back to Celeste's message, and turned to the chilli chips. I crushed the packet between my palms and shook it vigorously to ensure an even distribution of masala. I once asked Masood if he could make chilli chips that tasted like the ones in the packet. He bit into the chilli-red potato stick I proffered him, and looked pained. 'Would you have asked Ghalib to write a letter to the telephone company for you?'

I pushed my laptop away. 'I've just developed a theory, Reemas.'

'Well, spill all, Brer Fox.'

'No, moron. It's your name backwards. Reemas.'

'Oh, Reemas. Not Remus of *Uncle* fame. Nor Remus, even, of Romulus fame. Moron yourself.' He kicked my chair, and I tried to imagine coming back to live in Karachi if Sameer wasn't here. It's all very well to love a place, but in the end what matters most is the people who live there. Why did Taimur leave Dard-e-Dil?

'Your theory, professor?'

'Snobbery is based on fear.'

'Already it sounds highly unoriginal.' He tipped a handful of chips into his mouth and followed it with a sip of Coke to accentuate the taste of the masala.

'No, no, not fear of a revolution or anything like that. Fear of squalor. Fear of being entirely powerless, entirely overlooked. It's not that we *can't* empathize with those on the lower rungs of society; the problem is that we *can*. We can imagine what it feels like to be so deprived, and it's our fear that we could, or our children could, end up like that which makes us keep our distance from the have-nots. Because at a distance we don't have to think about it.'

'Tell me you just came up with that and haven't had time to think it through.'

'Why?'

'First, are you saying there's no distinction between class and wealth? Haven't you heard your Dadi, or even your parents, or my parents, talk about the nouveau riche? Are we lower down the class ladder than the Mushtaq family next door, who pull out their teeth just so they can have them replaced by solid gold?'

'We don't know that they pull out their teeth.'

'Yeah, right. Their family suffers from a rare disease called tooth dropsy.'

'Forget about the teeth. Let's get back to my theory. I think our family's attitude towards the nouveau riche is another symptom of fear. We're uncomfortable around them because they remind us that class is fluid; the Mush-taq parents may be considered nouveau riche, but their kids are being sent to finishing school to acquire polish and within a generation they'll marry into respectable but no-longer-rich families, and they'll start turning up their own noses at the nouveau riche. This reminds us that status is not permanent; as the Mushtaqs rise, someone else will fall, and that someone might be us.'

Sameer pulled my laptop towards him and read Celeste's message. 'I see.'

'What?'

'You're feeling guilty about not devoting your life to helping the needy, and it salves your conscience to say your snobbery is related to your great empathy. Oh, *baychari* Aliya. Too sensitive to hang out with the poor! That's a Starched statement if ever!'

He was right, but so was I. 'What would you do if you saw Masood tomorrow?' How odd that I'd never thought to ask him this before.

Sameer shrugged. 'Don't know. Say hello, I suppose. Tell

184

him my palate misses him. If you're asking if I'd invite him home for tea, no I wouldn't. And if I did, he'd refuse.'

'But suppose . . . Remember he used to say he wished he could read English? What if Mariam Apa taught him? What if he's read, I don't know . . .'

'Frantz Fanon?' Sameer made a dismissive gesture. 'Are you saying it's all about education? The great leveller. You think if you read John Ashbery all differences cease to matter. Come on, Aliya. You're smarter than that.'

I felt my face flush at the mention of Ashbery. 'That's not fair, Sameer.'

'To hell with fair. You spend half an hour with this Khaleel – sorry, Cal! – he alludes to your favourite poets, and now you can't handle the fact that your biases are conflicting with your hormones, so you try to convince yourself that you're not a snob, you're just empathetic. You don't discriminate; you just have more in common with people who are educated. And you'll rewrite everything in the past which conflicts with this theory, including the way you feel about Mariam and Masood.'

I thought of Khaleel drinking tea out of a saucer. How desperately I still wanted to believe that he only did it to test me. All the poetry in the world couldn't change that. 'Okay, go away.'

'Aliya, Aloo, cuz. Listen to me. It doesn't work. I tried it. With a girl from work. She wasn't lower down on the social ladder or anything, she was just from a really different type of family. Like to like makes the most sense. Look, if it makes you feel better, tell yourself you're pulling away because of difference, not because of snobbery. Tell the truth: can you see yourself getting married to this guy? Can you see yourself coming to Karachi for the holidays and staying with his family in Liaquatabad? Don't tell me the thought doesn't appal you.'

The thought appalled me. 'Who's talking about getting married?'

'You've got to think long-term. If it's obvious from the start that it won't work out, cut your losses. Why start something that can never progress?'

'Mariam did.'

'Do you think she's happy?'

'Do you think he is? Why don't we ever ask that?'

'You know why we never ask that.'

Why did he go back to his birthplace? After his father died. Why did he go back? Was he sick of the pretence? Was it his version of an ultimatum? I'd never thought of their relationship as something with squabbles, and jealousies and demands. It was as though I could only begin to understand the relationship – why couldn't I just say 'affair'? – by making it some mythical, two-dimensional thing, larger and also so much smaller than life.

How did he hear of his father's death? How did he tell Mariam of it? When did he decide to leave?

My parents had a dinner party at our house the night before Masood left. Masood burnt the naans and had to cycle out for more, delaying dinner by a few minutes. It's a strange detail to remember, but I remember it particularly because I had only just learnt to drive and I offered to drive him round the corner to the *naanwallah*, but Masood said no.

'Don't you trust my driving, Masood?' I laughed.

'It won't look right. You chauffeuring me around.'

'What rubbish. I'll get the keys. Don't leave.'

But he did. Mariam Apa was standing in the driveway when I walked out, keyring in hand, and yelled for Masood.

186

She shook her head at me and spun her index fingers to mime bicycle wheels.

'Why is he being so silly, Apa? I drove the mali to the bus stop last week.' Then I thought of adding, Besides, Masood's virtually family, but stopped myself. No, I knew that wasn't quite true, but why did he have to go and act as though he and I were servant and mistress, rather than . . .

Rather than what? Mariam Apa's raised eyebrows asked me.

Rather than two people who often ate dinner together when my parents and Mariam Apa were out for the evening, particularly on cool evenings, when it was a pleasure to be outside the kitchen door, cross-legged under the stars.

Mariam Apa enacted dialling a phone number.

Yes, it had been a while since the news that my family was going out for the evening hadn't prompted me to pick up the phone and call Sameer or one of my school friends to make dinner plans. But I didn't appreciate Mariam pointing that out to me.

Four years later I allowed myself to consider the possibility that I was entirely peripheral to that night's story. Let's suppose – as suppositions go this is none too far-fetched – that Masood heard of his father's death that night, and not the morning after. Evidence? He burnt the *naans*. Masood never burnt anything. So let's suppose he heard of his father's death – it was the night of a dinner, everyone was congregated in the drawing room, out of earshot of the phone – everyone except for Masood. So the phone in the kitchen rang, and Masood answered, and minutes later Mariam walked into the kitchen. I'm not making this last part up. She was in the kitchen, I know, because she's the one who told me the *naans* were burnt. I was walking to my room, was in between the drawing room and my room, when Mariam came out of the kitchen. If only I could remember, but I can't, if something prompted me to ask, 'What's wrong?' or if she just held out a burnt bit of *naan* to me.

Mariam loved Masood and Masood loved Mariam and Masood loved his father and his father died and Masood hung up the phone and Mariam walked into the kitchen and the house was full of people and Mariam knew that among those people were people who might walk into the kitchen, maybe to see what Masood was cooking, maybe to see where Mariam had gone, maybe to ask for more ice. And Masood knew that all he wanted right then was to weep in Mariam's arms.

Is that when the *naans* burnt? Or was that later, seconds later, when Mariam finally put a hand on his arm, but kept her face turned slightly towards the door, alert for footsteps, and Masood said, 'This can't go on. I'll go mad. We'll both go mad.'

I can't fault Mariam for listening for all those footsteps, all those footsteps including mine. But there was a time when I thought that if Masood meant something to me I would fault her for what she did to him all those years. But, really, what did she do except love him, and love us also? Did I fault him? Yes, for months. Yes, for everything. Until one day I was able to say to myself, What did he do except love her and love her?

Sameer brushed a crumb off my cheek. 'You know you'll never see her again.'

I stood up and walked over to the glass doors which led out to the garden. Pushed aside the curtains and pressed my

188

head against the glass. The chairs on the terrace were covered in dust.

Karachi was full of corners, and I had grown up turning every corner with the hope in my heart that she would be there. How could I continue to live my life between such corners? How could I not?

Other people never reminded me of Mariam, but that's not to say I was never reminded of her. In moments when I least expected it everyday objects would become doorways to memory. A shoe buckle, a keyring, a mango seed bleached by the sun; running water, railway tracks, cobblestones and cochineal; cacti, cat's-eyes, Cocteau and kites; chipped plates, race tracks, swimming pools, diving boards, bluebottles, jellyfish, bougainvillea, stones; crickets and bats and cricket bats.

I know. Cocteau is not an everyday object, but she loved *Orphée*.

What if she were dead? How would I know? Is it better this way, this not knowing? I wondered, tracing circles in the glass. This way she can be immortal to me, in my lifetime. I don't ever have to face the finality of her death. That thought should have brought me comfort, but it didn't. If she were dead, I'd want to know so that I could weep. The circles in the glass looped outward and became spirals. I am frozen when I think of you, Mariam. My mind goes everywhere and nowhere. Nothing in my life is untouched by your absence. I think you'd like Khaleel. I don't know if that makes me run towards him or pull away.

'Aliya, what did your father mean that day over lunch? Remember, just after you got back? I escorted Abida Nani out and when I came back he was saying, "I should have fired Masood when . . ." and then your mother told him to shut up.'

'I don't know.' I had forgotten about that entirely.

Sameer stood up. 'I'm going to find your mother. Maybe she'll tell us. You can use my absence to read that e-mail which you're so desperate for me not to see.'

He left, and I turned gratefully to my laptop.

Hi, Ailment.

Your e-mail about tea at the Starcheds' had me in hysterics! Seriously. Someone rang the bell and I couldn't answer it because I was having such a *haal* picturing Older Starch stuffing food into the older Ali Shah's mouth to stop him from charming you. But obviously you don't want to hear any of this, as your last message so subtly hinted. 'How's Baji? Have you seen her recently?' my foot. Why don't you just come right out and say Cal Butt has hoovered you off your ankles? So, everyone loves him, if that's what you want to know, but, after he left, Baji (who somehow detected your interest in him, although neither Rehana Apa nor I can recall saying anything about it) said, 'Of course, you don't marry an individual. You marry a family.' Normally I would roll my eyes at this marriage phoo-pha; I mean, flings can be great fun, and if it wasn't for you I'd fling him in a second. But you've never shown signs of being able to do that one-day-at-a-time thing and frankly Liaquatabad should stop you from thinking long-term. I've gathered enough info from him to know that his Karachi relatives' English is weak, they've never left the country, and they believe in the joint-family system (the horror, the horror; imagine living in a house teeming with your own relatives, never mind someone else's). I know he lives in America (claims he wants to get a job that'll let him travel the globe), but if you and he end up together there'll have to be family interaction in Karachi and that will be a disaster, the fallout from which will not leave you unscathed at all! Call me a snob if you want to, but what the hell do any one of us have to say to the great mass of our compatriots? We can talk about cricket and complain about the politicians, but then what? *I'm not denying that they could be wonderful people*, but that's really not the point.

There – I've done my bit. Now I'm going to give you a message from him, which he wrote on my arm in some bloody indelible ink which refused to come off until half a bar of soap later. He wrote: 'Footfalls echo in the memory/ Down the passage which we did not take/ Towards the door we never opened/ Into the rose garden. My words echo/ Thus, in your mind.'

It's all a bit too pseudo for me, but I suppose you think it's charming. (Quoting Yeats is charming, Aliya; quoting Eliot is showing off.) He's still not sure when he'll be in Karachi, but he will be there before the summer is through. I've had to thoroughly wrestle with my conscience about relaying his message to you, but Rehana Apa said she'd tie me to Nelson's column and feed prunes and bran fibre to the pigeons if I didn't do it and pronto. Now, don't expect another message from me for a while. This is all too exhausting and I have to read too many books on fiscal policies of Indian rulers in the eighteenth century.

Love to the family (excl. Starcheds),
Samia.

191

The passage we didn't take. The door we never opened. What was I thinking? Sameer was right – I'd talked to Khaleel for half an hour . . . No, actually, it was more like an hour. I've never drunk a cup of coffee so slowly. Still, just an hour. Besides, I had no intention of getting married before I finished my MA, and let's be honest, when I thought of Khaleel it wasn't wedding bells I heard but something a little more akin to slow jazz. And yet . . . Samia had said something to me the night before I left London. She said, 'I don't believe in love at first sight, and neither do you. But I know, and after today you know also, that sometimes it only takes a few minutes to recognize that a person is capable of breaking your heart.' Yes.

I had mentioned heartbreak to Mariam Apa when I was sixteen and devastated over a boy who was flirting with me just to make some bleached blonde jealous. Not dyed, bleached. I ask you!

I said to Mariam Apa, 'Well at least I found out now. Bruised ego, but no broken heart. Must avoid broken hearts.'

She shredded a piece of Masood's roast chicken, flavoured with chillis and garlic and yoghurt, and poured gravy over the shreds. She gestured to the chicken on my plate, still in one piece. *A broken heart has more surface area than a heart that is intact.* Anyone who's bilingual knows that shock of surprise when you think you've been speaking in one language and someone else points out that no, you haven't. It was like that with Mariam Apa. I was so accustomed to translating her gestures into sentences that I sometimes wondered why people looked so perplexed when I claimed to be quoting her words exactly.

She had somehow got word to Babuji to star our names

on the family tree. I was convinced of it. She had starred the names and now I would never hear the term not-quite-twins without adding myself and Mariam Apa to their list. And soon the rest of the family would add our names to the list, too, if they hadn't already. How long before word of the latest not-quites crossed the border? The news would not be met with surprise. I could think of only a handful of relatives who would refrain from saying that Mariam had already brought about the inevitable disaster by robbing us of our pride. And, to be quite honest, even that handful probably wouldn't refrain from thinking it. Was I about to compound our disgrace by mirroring her actions, with a choice far less shocking than hers, yet also more significant for its refusal to walk a path far removed? Or were we, was I, in a position to show the others that not-quites were not necessarily harbingers of doom? This, then, was Mariam's farewell gift to me: the courage to take Khaleel's hand in mine and say to my parents, say to Dadi, say to Sameer and Samia and the Starched Aunts and Great-Aunt One-Liner and Bachelor Uncle and Mousy Cousin and all the rest of them, *Just because a thing has always been so, it does not always have to be so.*

I opened my desk drawer and smiled at Celeste's painting of Mariam, greying and radiant.

Then I remembered what Samia had said. *No one, not even you, will trust any feelings you have for him.*

Sameer barged into the room. 'There was a love triangle in your house. Mariam and Masood and Hibiscus-Eating Ayah.'

Chapter Nineteen

'No, you have to go to see your grandmother instead.'

'Aba!'

'Aliya, this is not open to discussion.' Aba turned to Ami. 'I can't believe you told her.'

Ami looked up from the samples of red carpet material laid across the floor. 'Nasser, you opened the bag. The cat was going to let itself out soon enough, so I saw no harm in giving it a little prod. At least our daughter can say we weren't keeping secrets from her when she was old enough to deal with everything that has twisted our lives around for the last four years. And now this man wants not only the reddest carpet in the world but one which bird droppings will not show up against.' She returned to staring gloomily at her samples.

'Well, fine then, you've told her. So there's no need for her to go and see any ayahs and start discussing family members with them.'

'Aba, please! She hasn't told me anything except that Hibiscus-Eating Ayah left in some jealous fit because of Masood.'

'Well, there's nothing more for her to tell you. That's all

we know. In fact, let me correct that. We don't even know that; it's just conjecture.'

Ami snorted.

Aba and I glowered at each other.

'I'll go to see her after I see Dadi. Happy?'

'No. You're not going. I forbid it. Who knows what stories that woman will invent just to see your reaction.'

'That woman, Aba? Oh, so she could be trusted to look after me when I was a child, but she's not trustworthy enough to repeat a few simple facts.'

'Don't you speak to me like that, young lady.'

His words were a roar, and I grabbed on to a table to give myself strength. 'Just because you're too ashamed to discuss Mariam with anyone doesn't mean—'

'Ashamed? Ashamed! How dare you think you have a monopoly on unconditional love!' That took me aback. He had always been so tight-lipped about Mariam's marriage; I had taken his silence as censure, but perhaps it was only pain. Lord, what had I been doing these last four years? In what cocoon of self-pity had I been stifling myself?

But before I could apologize or ask him what he was feeling, my mother cut in. 'Stop it. Both of you.' I could answer back to my father any time, even in the face of his rage, but when Ami barked out a command, both Aba and I turned into mush. She claimed she had learnt how to counterfeit steely resolve in order to avoid being quashed by her mother-in-law, and it certainly worked. There's no one else with whom Dadi gets on so harmoniously. Nine times out of ten Ami allows Dadi to be domineering, but that tenth time she just raises an eyebrow and Dadi subsides. There's a great deal I need to learn from Ami.

'Aliya, go and see your Dadi. Ask her if she needs help

with packing. She'll say no, but you should ask all the same. Nasser, go out and find me some samples of bird droppings.'

'Would you like them gift-wrapped?'

'My *jaan*, the red carpet was your idea. Now stop looking ineffectual.'

Aba turned to me. 'Aliya, collect bird droppings. Go and stand motionless – Ha ha! Motionless, get it? – under the *badaam* tree for an hour. If you whistle bird-calls you may only have to be there half an hour. Wear a hat, otherwise your mother won't let you wash your hair until she's sorted out this carpet problem.'

'Men are so easily restored to good humour,' I whispered, bending down near my mother to pick up the car keys.

She nodded. 'Any lavatorial remark will do the trick.'

'Hat!' Aba yelled as I walked out.

I drove to Dadi's, thinking of Celeste's e-mail. *She walks out of her élite neighbourhood and notices the poverty in other parts of the city.* I hadn't really thought about it before, but affluence and lack sat cheek by jowl in Karachi. Between the large old houses near Mohatta Palace and the smaller, modern houses on Khayaban-e-Shujaat, which displayed their wealth in accessories rather than in size, was a shortcut that took you past streets where shiny cars and designer *shalwar-kameezes* and English-speaking voices all but disappeared, replaced by tiny storefronts, narrow streets crowded with people and cycles and the occasional goat, children selling vegetables or fixing tyres or chasing each other along the roads without pavements.

I was thinking about this with such concentration that I ran a red light. Sameer did that at least twice a day and nothing ever happened to him, but I try it just once and a traffic cop appears. The cop pulled me over and stuck his head in through the window.

'Do you need glasses?' he said.

'I don't need glasses. Ten pairs of glasses wouldn't enable me to see that light at this time of day. Look how strong the sun is. It shines on the traffic light so brightly it's blinding, and you can't see which colour is lit up. I thought the light just wasn't working as usual.'

The cop looked up at the cloudy sky.

'The clouds have just come in,' I said. 'Three seconds ago they weren't there. Look how strong the breeze is; it's making the clouds rush around.'

The cop shook his head. 'You can either go to court and pay the fine there, or you can pay it directly to me.'

'Okay, I'll go to court.'

The cop was not happy with this deviation from the script. 'Please,' he said. 'Don't talk like this. I have a family to support. The courts will take hours, there'll be paper-work and all sorts of men hanging around there who misbehave around women. Why don't you just make life easier for yourself?'

'How much is the fine?'

'Three hundred rupees.'

I bargained him down to fifty, waited for him to get change for a five-hundred note from the mango seller who had been watching this with amusement, and continued on to Dadi's feeling proud of my largesse in omitting to mention to the cop my connection to the high-ranking police officer who was Younger Starch's sister-in-law's husband.

When I got to Dadi's I heard her cook, Mohommed,

chastising her as he served her tea in her bedroom. 'Begum Sahib, that's a very bad idea. Why stay in the heat of this tandoor if you can help it? You always fall sick in the heat. Remember that summer in Dard-e-Dil when you collapsed near the fountain while Nawab Sahib was talking to you?'

'That was over fifty years ago, Mohommed. Were you even born then?'

'Born? Was I born? Who do you think ran to tell Akbar Sahib?'

'I'm just joking, Mohommed. Old age has made you very crabby. Besides, the heat of Dard-e-Dil was something else.'

'Yes,' he conceded. 'Yes, it was.' He saw me and made a gesture of relief. 'Aliya Bibi. You try and talk sense into her. Tell her if she falls sick I'm not going to run around for doctors and medicines, and I'm absolutely not going to cook bland soup. I'll bring you some tea.' And with that he left the room.

'What would you do without him?' I bent to kiss Dadi's cheek.

'Remember when I suggested he retire?' Dadi smiled wickedly. 'He was so irate he threatened to quit. Come and sit closer to me.'

I sat cross-legged on the bed beside her, directly across from a framed photograph of Dadi and her female cousins in their childhood, all decked out in *gharara*, with *tikas* of precious and semi-precious stones hanging over their foreheads. Three strands of pearls going over and around the girls' heads held each tear-shaped *tika* in place. I used to assume the photograph was taken during some momentous occasion, like Eid or a wedding, but Dadi had told me, no, that's just how they used to dress every day. It struck me for the first time that she had far more photographs of life in Dard-e-Dil than she did of life in Karachi.

'No wonder you collapsed in the heat, dressed like that.' I gestured to the photograph. 'What was Mohommed going on about?'

'I've changed my booking for Paris. I'm leaving in September.'

'Seriously?'

'Hmm. It makes no sense to leave while you and Meher are here. Particularly since your violent tendencies seem to have been curbed.' She laughed and took my hand in hers, and I clasped my fingers around hers. 'Besides, I can't keep running away from the monsoon rains.'

'Why do you? Run away, I mean.'

Dadi nodded her head slowly. 'The hierarchy of love. Should I tell you about Taimur?'

I swallowed. 'Please.'

Mohommed walked in with the tea, and Dadi started talking about her tailor. When he left she told me to check that he wasn't listening outside the door. He wasn't.

'I loved Taimur.'

Her voice was flat, and for a moment I thought I hadn't heard correctly. Then she smiled, exhaled, and rested her head against the headboard. 'I loved Taimur. I've never said that aloud before. I loved Taimur.' She started to giggle, but stopped to shake her head in wonder. 'We were eighteen. So young. What does anyone know at eighteen? But I loved him all the same.'

I didn't know what to say. I felt . . . What did I feel? Something similar to the feeling you get at the end of a movie when you can't quite believe the final twist but, as soon as it happens, you can't imagine any other ending. The

199

difference was, when you watch a movie, no matter how good it is, you're never sure if it'll stay with you for ever.

I needed to say something, so I said, 'Why him?'

'Because him. Oh, Aliya.'

What had I said to make her look at me with such sorrow?

'What was he like, Dadi?'

'Like nothing else. Like my soul. Like his daughter.'

My spine prickled. I had never heard her speak in this voice before. I had a fleeting image of Taimur leaving Dard-e-Dil with this voice of Abida's nestled in his breast pocket. 'So did you . . . I mean, what did you . . . What happened?'

'He didn't love me.' She picked up the photograph by her bedside and looked at it closely. 'He didn't love me. I've never said that aloud either. I didn't think saying it would give me this urge to cry.'

'He said he didn't love you?' My eyes darted to the photograph of Dadi and the triplets. How could you, Taimur?

'Aliya, he left. Just weeks after this picture was taken, he left.' I took the photograph from her. When I first saw the picture on Baji's wall I looked at the girl's smile and thought, Was Dadi ever that young? Now I thought, Was I ever that young? Will I ever be that young?

'And before that, Dods?'

'Before that? I misread his affection, his generous compliments. I thought there was an unspoken understanding that we'd wait for him to come back from Oxford. The unspoken is a dangerous thing to rely on, my darling. Do you know the meaning of *Naz*?'

'Pride, or something like that. Having airs.'

'That misses the essence of it. *Naz* is the pride, the

assurance, that arises from knowing you are loved. From knowing that no matter what you do you will always be loved. In this picture there is such *Naz* written across my face.'

But you were right to have such *Naz*. How could anyone not love you when you smiled like this? I wanted to say that, but didn't know how to. 'Why did he leave?'

'There was another woman.'

'Who?'

'I don't know. No one from our social set, or we would have known. Must have been someone in town. That's what brought on that smokescreen letter of his with its talk of becoming a servant. She was probably of that class, which is why he thought of it. Some truth always seeps into the most elaborate lies.'

'No, wait. If you don't know *who* she was, how do you know *that* she was?'

'There was a ring.' Dadi directed me to look closely at the oil-painting of my great-grandparents, the yak enthusiast and his wife. He was dapper in his three-piece suit, holding a walking cane; she, rather more demure in her beautifully brocaded *gharara*, her hand weighed down by a ring so large I was sure if she ever took it off, her finger would remain angled down.

'That's not jade set in zircons, is it?'

'Don't be absurd. Emerald in diamonds. Her father-in-law gave it to her on her wedding day, saying she must not get too attached to it because when her eldest son married it would have to be passed down to his wife. That was before the days of high divorce rates – nowadays I'm sure people wait for their grandchildren to be born before handing down the most precious family jewels.'

201

'So why don't you have the ring? Akbar was the oldest of the triplets.'

'Well, of course, no one really knows that. Taj was the only one who was really sure of the birth order, and she disappeared without passing on the information. I think my mother-in-law just guessed that Akbar was the eldest. So, acknowledging the fact that any of the three boys could be the eldest, their grandfather decided that the ring should go to the bride of whichever brother married first. When Taimur left, he took the ring with him.'

No wonder she used to look at Mariam so strangely sometimes when she thought no one else was watching. She was searching for clues to the identity of that other woman. But Mariam looked so much like Taimur you'd almost believe she was Athena to his Zeus, springing fully formed from his forehead with no one around to whom she could attach the title of 'mother'.

'So you never loved Akbar?' I felt a sudden surge of protectiveness towards my grandfather.

'Of course I loved Akbar. What questions you ask. And you should refer to him as "Dada".'

I was silent, waiting for more.

'When Akbar came back from Oxford, and I heard his parents were arriving at my house with a *rishtah*, I was thrilled. Told my parents to accept the proposal with alacrity, and damn etiquette.' She lay back, smiling wistfully. I waited for her to continue, but she was in a long-ago world.

'And all this is related to the monsoons how?' I demanded.

'Taimur left during the first of the monsoon rains. All through our married lives, Akbar and I barely spoke to each other when the rains began. Not through anger. We just

202

knew each other's need to grieve and remember. Yes, Akbar knew I loved Taimur first. Maybe we should have grieved together, but we didn't.

'Then Akbar had his stroke, and before the ambulance arrived we heard the crack of thunder and the rain poured down. That, too, was the first of the monsoon showers. His last words were, "Oh, Abida, what a wretched time for me to leave you." Except his words were slurred and at first I thought he had said, "What a wretched time for me to love you." I've avoided the monsoons since. Because I don't want to know the hierarchy of my love. When the rains begin I don't want to know which of those two brothers I'll weep for first.'

When she said that she did start to weep, for both of them I think; and I wept also, at my own stupidity. For four years I'd thought it was pure snobbery that had made Dadi say, 'That whore!' For four years I'd nurtured an image of Dadi based on that notion of her overriding snobbery, and now, with Dadi so old (suddenly she looked so old), I saw that I had lost four years of her life because there had been such snobbery in my reaction to that elopement. I had recoiled with such horror to think that my cousin had run away with the cook, that I hadn't considered that anyone else could be better than me. I saw now that Dadi's reaction to Mariam's elopement was directed not at Mariam, but at her mother – that near-mythical woman who had known what it was to be loved by Taimur. Dadi's reaction had arisen from love, but I had wanted so desperately to be the self-righteous one that I forgot everything Mariam Apa ever taught me about listening to the silences that bracket every utterance.

'Dadi, I'm sorry.' I rested my head against her shoulder,

and when we'd both finally stopped crying I brushed tear tracks off both our faces and said, 'Salt.'

'What?'

I shook my head. 'Just thinking of something Masood said.'

'You might want to think of calling him Masood Bhai. He is family now, after all.'

I laughed aloud at her ability to surprise me, and then I thanked God for giving me the chance to know her again. Again? No, for the first time. 'We can talk about Mariam Apa. If you want to. Whenever you want to.'

Dadi smiled. 'Talk? That's not always necessary, you know.' She pushed my hair off my face. 'Let it go, my darling. Some people leave our lives; it happens. People leave. Let it go.'

I wasn't about to let it go.

Chapter Twenty

'Aliya!' Younger Starch greeted me at her front door. 'What an unexpected somersault of joy you've made my heart just do. Full triple lutz in my rib cage, I swear, at the sight of you. And what a lovely *jora* you're wearing – such a nice change from all these other young girls today who always want to be in the height of fashion. I say a few inches here and there around your hemline isn't worth the expense of a whole new wardrobe. Unless you're like Kishoo, who has to look good all the time because she has a certain image, you know. And why haven't we seen you at the *dholkis*? I think the Ali Shah boy is definitely interested.'

'Oh, well, actually I know it's time for you to go for your bridge game and I don't want to hold you up. I was just stopping by to ask if you were free for lunch tomorrow.' I knew she wasn't, but the leap from discussing Taimur with Dadi to fending off matchmaking talk from a Starch was one I couldn't make without falling into the gaping precipice of incivility, so it seemed best to terminate the conversation as quickly as possible.

'Oh, I would have loved to, but Sunday brunch at the Club is a must. Must, must, must. Oh, now I'm so sad.'

'Well, another time, then. But, since I'm here, I might as well say hello to Hibiscus-Eating Ayah.'

'Who?'

'Bua.'

'Oh, Bua! Such names you have for people. I swear, sometimes I think you must have some private nickname for me. Of course, go and see her, but if she starts talking too much just say goodbye and walk out or she'll go on and on and on and will not stop. What am I telling you this for? You know all there is to know about her. Okay, sweetie, must run. 'Bye.'

She kissed the air around my cheeks and walked out. I heard her screeching for the driver outside as I walked towards her younger children's bedroom.

Hibiscus-Eating Ayah had been my ayah, about fifteen years ago. She had come to work for us after her husband died, leaving her children to be brought up by her mother. She would go home to see them once a week, and on very rare occasions they'd come to visit her – two wide-eyed girls near my age who I recall playing with in the garden the first time we met. It was winter then. The next time I saw them it was summer and too hot to play outside, so I smiled hello and disappeared into my room. Technically speaking, it was also their mother's room, inasmuch as there was a little mattress under the bed which she would pull out and sleep on at night, and there was a corner in my closet where she kept her belongings bundled up, but when you're seven you know better than to pretend technicalities matter. I remember I asked Ami if I could invite them inside, but the more I think about it the more convinced I am that the memory is merely of something I considered doing. Even at that age, I knew about boundaries. No, let's be honest.

They gave the impression of being unwashed, and I didn't want them to get fingerprints on my new, giant-sized, snow-white stuffed bunny. (And if I had invited them in? How could that have ended any way but badly? Would it have been the first time they really thought about all they couldn't have?)

Hibiscus-Eating Ayah, known then simply as 'Bua', was a great improvement on her predecessor – a wizened woman who convinced me that my family would suffer not a whit if I regularly took a small amount of money from my father's wallet and gave it to her for her supply of *niswaar*, that ghastly, green, tobacco-based concoction which she would spit out in my basin without properly swilling out the spatter afterwards. Her endeavours to lead me into a life of guilt-based crime did not lead to her dismissal, but her penchant for *niswaar* did. She spat in the wrong direction, and though Aba's suede shoes bore no permanent mark he saw that as no reason to excuse her uncouthness. Truth is, we all disliked her and were just waiting for a reason to sack her.

Hibiscus-Eating Ayah's good-natured youthfulness was such a pleasant contrast to *Niswaar*-Spitting Ayah that I would stay up at night, past my bedtime, whispering to her about the house I'd own one day when I was married. We'd draw up floor plans for the house, which varied from week to week in every detail but one: a little room for her, between my room and my children's room, so that she could be on hand for whoever needed her to sing them to sleep.

But the plans went awry the day she ate the hibiscus.

I was in my room when I heard sounds of pandemonium in the garden, outside the dining room. On going to investigate I saw Mariam Apa, ashen, staring at Bua in disbelief, while Masood yelled. At first I didn't know which of the two women he was yelling at, just that he was demanding, 'What were you thinking? What have you done? What sort of bestiality is this?' The thought that he could be addressing Mariam Apa in this manner made the blood rush to my head, until I realized, that's impossible. He'd get fired for that. I moved closer to the dining-room window to look out, and saw that the red flowers of Mariam Apa's hibiscus bush were lying on the grass, ripped apart. Moving closer still, I saw teeth marks in petals, saw red on Bua's teeth when she opened her mouth to speak.

'Look at her,' she said, and pointed at Mariam. 'Look at that look on her face. She shows more emotion over these flowers than over anything else. Why can't you see that? She's a mad woman, deranged.'

'Aliya!' Just as things got interesting Ami appeared, on cue, and whisked me away. That day, Bua earned a nickname and lost a job. And gained another, because Younger Starch, driving to our house, saw Hibiscus-Eating Ayah leaving and hired her on the spot. No one quite understood why Younger Starch did that until a few months later, when she announced she was pregnant. She said, 'I told him I'm not having children until I know I have the right kind of help for those horrible first months of a child's life, but once I found Bua I said, "Hubby, let's go."'

I thought I would never forgive Hibiscus-Eating Ayah for the things she said about Mariam Apa, but Mariam was in such a good mood in the days following the insults that I concluded she hadn't minded them at all, and I was free to continue to feel affection for my old ayah. In the fifteen years since, my affection had never died, but it had become something I never thought about unless I saw her face to face.

I opened the door to the children's bedroom.

'*Arré*, Aliya!' Hibiscus-Eating Ayah was folding my young cousins' clothes, but when she saw me she dropped a T-shirt on to the bed and came over to hug me and whisper prayers over my head. 'I knew you wouldn't let me leave without coming to say goodbye.'

'Goodbye? Why?'

'Didn't anyone tell you? I'm leaving. Going to work for the Shaikh family who live near the KESC building. Three children, ages five to nine, and none of them as sweet as you were at that age.'

'But, you mean, my aunt's decided she doesn't need an ayah any more? How can that be? Imdi's only eight. How can she do this to you?'

'Aren't you listening? I'm leaving. She doesn't want me to go, but she doesn't want to pay me as much as the Shaikhs are offering either.'

'You're leaving only because of money? Bua, you've raised these children. All four, since the day they were born.'

'*Leh!*' she said, pointing at me as though I were a side-show freak and she was directing the assembled gawkers' attention to me. 'Only because of money! I have two granddaughters. Their stepfather is a waster; he just wants to get them married off when they reach puberty, and my daughter – you know Khadija – has always been spineless. She said, "What can I say to him? He doesn't want to bear the expense." So I said, "Then I'll bear the expense. I'll send them to school." The eldest is so smart, and there's a school near where they live where they teach English and they even have computers. Ye-es. You think I'm joking? Some rich man donated all these computers to them. Only money! You think I'm going to let my grandchildren grow up to be servants?'

'I'm sorry, I didn't . . .'

She waved me quiet. 'Oh, I'm only this upset because I feel bad about leaving here. You said it yourself. I raised these children.'

Something she had said earlier had caught my attention. 'You said stepfather? What happened to Khadija's first husband? Divorce?'

'Two years ago it happened. No one told you? He was killed in police custody. Where he used to live – it's a poor part of town, not like this – at least one person per family is killed in police custody. Allah, take pity on us.'

'On all of us,' I said. On my way to school, during my A levels, I used to see Khadija's husband playing cricket on the streets. He'd raise his bat in greeting as my car went by. When my American friends said arranged marriages were a horrific notion I always thought of the way Khadija leant against her young husband's shoulder when I saw them together visiting her mother at Younger Starch's. He was, he would have been, Sameer's age.

I felt too sick to ask Hibiscus-Eating Ayah anything else. What could she tell me, in any case? 'I have to go. Come and visit me. The Shaikhs don't live so far away.'

'Yes,' she said. 'And it's been a long time since there was a reason to stay away from your house.'

She looked squarely at me and I saw I was not the only one with questions.

'We haven't heard from either of them since they left.'

210

She nodded. 'I didn't think she'd ever do it. That's what made me angry all those years ago. Not that he stopped noticing me as soon as she walked into the kitchen, but that she knew it and yet she wasn't willing to stop walking in or to tell him to stop looking. The third thing, the thing she finally did, *that* I didn't think she'd ever do. But, after the shock when I first heard of it, I wasn't that surprised. The way Masood had of looking at her . . . How could you ever give up being looked at like that?'

Why did none of us see what Hibiscus-Eating Ayah saw? The question nagged me for days. And then Meher Dadi dropped a chance remark to Sameer, about ghosts. 'I've seen them. Of course I've seen them. Not often, but every now and then. You say that, because I believe they exist, I allow my mind to play tricks and create them, but, dear boy, perhaps you don't see them because you're unwilling to acknowledge the possibility that they might exist.'

Of course.

But what made Mariam Apa so different? What made her able to acknowledge possibilities more unlikely than ghosts? Did Taimur really become a servant – while we're admitting possibilities, why not admit that? Was Mariam's mother far beneath the Dard-e-Dils on the social ladder, as Dadi believed? Or might there be a possibility unrelated to her parents?

The only clue we had to Mariam Apa's life before Karachi was the letter which had arrived at our house, twenty-two years ago, just minutes before she did. If only Ami had saved the envelope we might have known where it came from. *I only want to say take care of her because even though she may come back here if you don't and that will make me happy I do not want her to be sad and so please make her*

211

happy. And also this way I can dream but when she is here I can only wait for what is never.

Someone had loved Mariam Apa before Karachi. Some-one who might not have been literate – the letter, Aba insisted, sounded like an oral message transcribed. But Mariam Apa had not loved this man, had not even allowed him to think that maybe one day she would. What made him so convinced that he was waiting 'for what is never'? Who was this man? He was from Dard-e-Dil or the regions around it, else why would he have started the letter with the formal greeting and respectful address: *Huzoor! Aadaab!* Unless Taimur taught him that . . .

Perhaps he was Taimur's servant.

'Servant?' Sameer said, when I propounded this theory to him a few evenings later. He had picked me up on his way home from the bank and we'd driven the five minutes from my house to Clifton beach to sit on the sea wall and eat roasted corn sprinkled with red-chilli powder and lemon juice, and to watch the grey, wind-whipped waves of the monsoon season leap at the seagulls in the distance. 'Look around you.' Sameer pointed to the crowds around the sea wall. A large section of Karachi had been hit by a power failure and the beach was the best place to escape from the heat. Whole families were out; vans that should have held no more than nine people were disgorging groups of fifteen or sixteen on to the cement pavement where, in addition to the *bhutawallah* whom Sameer and I had come to patronize, there were cold-drink sellers and *chaatwallahs* and a man with a tray of sweets hanging around his neck, who chanted, 'Cheeng-gum, chaaklait, bubbly-gum.' Other than the families, there were men strolling hand in hand, young couples sitting close together but not touching, and a woman in sneakers and a *shalwar-kameez*, walking at a great pace which she broke off every couple of minutes to untangle the wires of her walkman's headset. Between my jeans and the black burkha of the woman climbing gingerly down the rocks to the sand beneath, between Sameer's pin-striped shirt with French cuffs and the bright pink *kameez* of the man selling kites, there was a whole range of styles and colours and materials.

'You need to join the working world. Escape from your cocoon of Us and Them and the gaping hole between. How do you know he was a servant? He could have been a clerk. A tailor. A shopkeeper. An anything.'

'But not a social equal.' I took the letter out of my back pocket and passed it to Sameer.

He read it and handed it back. 'No, not a social equal. What great conclusion have you reached from that?'

A young boy came round selling plastic combs and spools of elastic. Sameer said we wanted neither but he'd give the boy ten rupees for getting us Cokes from the drinkwallah. I changed the order to one Coke and one Apple Sidra.

'We know this man was in love with Mariam. We know, we can at least surmise, she gave him no encouragement.'

'So far you're on solid ground, but I sense a swamp approaching.'

'What if it was his social status that stood in the way? What if, because of his social status, Mariam never even considered him a possibility?'

'Possible. *Shaabaash*, *chotoo*.' Sameer took the drinks from the young boy and handed him a ten-rupee note. A beggar saw Sameer's wallet and came over to us, palm outstretched. Sameer waved him away.

'But then, as she was planning to leave for Karachi, the

fact that she was leaving allowed this man to say something to her. Maybe something said in hope. Maybe something said as a reprimand. At any rate, it was something that made Mariam see—'

'Allah bless your union,' the beggar said, circling back after an unsuccessful foray to the group beside us.

'Something that made Mariam see everything she had never seen, every possibility she had never even considered considering.'

'I'll pray that you pass your exams,' the beggar said.

'And so she arrived in Karachi ready to consider the possibility of loving a cook?' Sameer said.

'More than ready. Determined to prove that she was capable of doing so. She always had the strangest stubborn streak. Remember Dr Tahir and the sari?'

'In the name of Allah . . .'

'So her silence was subversion.' For once Sameer was paying attention and not laughing. 'We look at this guy's letter and we decide his social status. You think Mariam's silence was a protest against the prejudice built into language? That's why even when she did speak it wasn't to the élite. She only spoke to Masood to order meals and even then – Did you ever notice this? – she spoke in questions not in imperatives. She'd say, *"Bhujia? Koftas? Pulao?"* Basically, she was undercutting the whole employer–servant paradigm.'

I thought of all I couldn't say to Masood's brother. 'Maybe. Yes, maybe. Why not?'

'And the ultimate test of her ability to look beyond class was the act of eloping?'

'Let's not get carried away.' I looked suspiciously at Sameer. Was he trying to out-Aliya me with these leaps?

214

But he looked quite serious. 'By that point she loved him, I'm sure. But only because she first acknowledged that it was possible to do so. Do you think that's part of the reason society was so outraged? Because by eloping with Masood she made eloping with a servant possible?'

'May Allah give you many many sons.'

'Well, I heard of more than one servant being fired straight after the elopement. For looking. For daydreaming. Did you know daydreaming is to be discouraged among servants? I read that somewhere. And Bachelor Uncle sacked his driver because he caught his neighbour's daughter staring at the driver's bare chest one day.' Sameer handed the empty bottles to the beggar and told him he could collect the bottle deposit from the drinkwallah. The beggar made an expression of disgust. What good was a couple of rupees to him?

'I can get you a job,' Sameer said, standing up and brushing down his trousers.

'This is my job,' the beggar said, and walked away.

'Works every time,' Sameer laughed, unlocking the car door for me. As we drove away from the bright redness of the setting sun he said, 'Is that what's going on with this guy, Khaleel? You want to prove something to yourself just as Mariam did?'

Chapter Twenty-One

It had nothing to do with the weather, but Mohommed still insisted on saying, 'I told her so,' when Dadi slipped and hit her head and had to be taken to the hospital. The doctor – Great-Aunt One-Liner's son – said she was fine, no damage done, but no harm, either, in staying in hospital overnight.

I offered to be the one to stay with her, and my parents agreed, but Meher Dadi said her sister had nursed her through measles when they were children so the least she could do in return was sit in the hospital room until Dadi fell asleep. Technically, only one of us should have been allowed to stay after visiting hours, but the nurses and orderlies were no match for the stubbornness of Dadi and her sister. After much wrangling, the nurse on duty finally pretended to believe Dadi's claim that I had left and gone home, even though I yelped quite loudly when the nurse stepped on my hand as I lay in my hiding place under the bed.

'And knock before you enter,' Meher Dadi said to the nurse. 'Sometimes at night I dance around naked and I don't want anyone barging in on me when I'm in that state. Not the way my breasts look now. What were once melons are now half-empty bladders.'

Older Starch was more brazen in her manner of ignoring hospital rules. 'Hello, hello, Abida Khala. What a terrible thing this is.' She sailed in with arms outstretched. 'Couldn't make it for visiting hours so I told the nurse outside of my connection to several trustees of the hospital and here I am with Maliha.' Her daughter kissed Dadi and Meher Dadi and shot in my direction a look that conveyed all the embarrassment a twelve-year-old can feel at the hands of a parent.

'There are visiting hours in the morning,' Dadi said.

'That's all the way tomorrow. Can't let you fall asleep thinking I didn't look in on you. Besides, Maliha has to be taken for waxing in the morning and it's her first time so I'm going along to hold her hand.'

'It'll hurt, won't it, Aliya Apa?' Maliha said.

Older Starch turned to her. 'Hurt? What's hurt? Do any of us live without it? But, Maliha, you've heard the story of Sameer Bhai and the lizard in the bathroom. It was the same colour as speed and it leapt on to his leg. Real acrobat it was. Just one *chalaang* from the floor and on to his shin. Shorts he was wearing, shorts! You think he didn't try to kick it off? Of course he tried. But his legs are so hairy that the lizard gripped on with its claws and climbed, one claw at a time, climb climb climb, up his shin, over his knee, up to his thigh and we don't even want to think about what would have happened next if that reptile hadn't hit a bald spot around a scar and lost its grip. Aliya, Aunts, I ask you: would this trauma have occurred if he had waxed his legs?'

I don't know what we would have said if Great-Aunt One-Liner's son, alerted by the nurses, hadn't walked in and ordered Older Starch and her daughter out of the room. He pretended I was just a pile of clothes, even though Older Starch said, 'But, Aliya.'

'Every story has a moral,' Meher Dadi said when the door closed, and then she and Dadi clutched each other and laughed so hard they knocked heads.

I was quiet through the evening, allowing them to talk as only sisters can. The talk meandered through nearly eight decades of memories, their word associations too far removed from logic to make much sense to me and I thought, For all the talking we've ever done together there's still so much I'll never know. I knew I was capturing a memory as I watched them, both lying on the bed now, so oblivious to my presence it was as though I were not yet born. They spoke of the living with nostalgia, and of the dead with mirth, and I wondered at my earlier inability to see how remarkable were the women of their generation, who spoke so rarely with regret, though they had seen so much turn to dust.

At one point I thought they were both asleep, until Dadi said, 'Remember what the old boy said on the eleventh?' and I knew 'the old boy' was Mohommed Ali Jinnah, the Quaid-e-Azam, the Great Leader, whom even my generation with all our cynicism could refer to by that title without irony. And 'the eleventh' must have been 11 August 1947, three days before Independence.

'Of course I remember,' Meher Dadi said, and she quoted, as though the words were still fresh, 'You are free. You are free to go to your temples. You are free to go to your mosques or to any other place of worship in this State of Pakistan. You may belong to any religion or caste or creed – that has nothing to do with the business of the State. We are starting in the days when there is no discrimination – no distinction between one community and another, no discrimination between one caste or creed and another. We are starting with this fundamental principle that we are all citizens and equal citizens of one State.'

Dadi nodded, and when she spoke I knew she had remembered me again. 'Perhaps we did not pay enough attention to that part about "any caste". We thought that was merely a religious term that didn't apply to us. Perhaps we did not pay enough attention at a time when our attention was worth something.'

It was the first time the word 'liberal' came to mind regarding Dadi. Her grandmother had lived and died in purdah, unseen by men who were not of the family, her life a life unconcerned with the world outside the palace, her principle interest the matter of marriage. And then, just two generations later, there was her granddaughter: Abida who went to college, Abida who rode on donkey-carts to the refugee camps in 1947 to help those who needed it, Abida who told me I had to learn to be independent because she didn't want me to become one of those women who relied on their husbands for everything. How her grandmother must have despaired of her! How the young Abida must have chafed against the rules and regulations her grandmother wanted her to follow. When she sighed sometimes and said she wished I was more like her she meant not that I should share her particular attitudes but that, like her, I should step away from those attitudes of my grandmother which badly needed stepping away from.

Dadi finally went to sleep a little after ten, and Meher Dadi came to sit by me on the window seat.

'I'm glad the two of you have resolved your differences,' she said. 'She can be a harridan, but there's no one more remarkable in the world.'

'Oh, I think it's down to a penalty shoot-out between the two of you.'

She hugged me fiercely. 'I miss my family. You all drive me mad, but coming back to Karachi is like stepping into the sea again after months on land. How easily you float, how peaceful is the sense of being borne along, and how familiar the sound of the water lapping against your limbs.'

'Do you know any Pakistanis in Greece?'

'Oh yes. There are *desis* in every corner of the globe. There's even a chap from Dard-e-Dil who comes to visit me. Haven't I told you about him?'

'No.'

Meher Dadi laughed. 'First time I saw him I thought, Oh God! Funny looking, bearded chap, clearly not Mediterranean, who cycled up my path and knocked on the door just months after I'd left Karachi. He said he was a mechanic, had lived in Turkey all his life, but his parents were from India. He married a local who was half Greek, half Turkish, so they'd hop across the border every so often. I'll never forget this; he said to me a few years ago, "My father moved here at the time of the Khilafat Movement. First World War, that was. So we missed Partition, but somehow it was my destiny to live between two neighbouring countries who are enemies." The first time we met I asked him where in India his parents were from and he said, "Same as your parents. Dard-e-Dil." I wasn't surprised he knew. I'd already met a couple of Pakistanis there, so I knew word would spread through the community. But it was a joy to meet someone who . . . Well, it's an ego thing, isn't it? Even though he'd never lived in Dard-e-Dil, I was his royal family. And not just in some distant way. His father found his first job in Istanbul via that Dard-e-Dil relative of ours who went to Turkey and learnt the language. So we were, in a very real sense, the mechanic's father's patrons.' She laughed again. 'I told him we were living in a democratic age, but it took several visits before he and I were comfortable with him coming into my drawing room and sitting down for a cup of tea.'

I could almost hear bells going off in my head. Turkey again, and now it appeared there was actually someone there who might be able to find out if Taimur had ever lived there. 'He comes often to visit you?'

'Oh, no. Once, maybe twice a year. For the first few years I knew hardly anything about him. He just wanted me to tell him tales of Dard-e-Dil, and I was so pleased to have someone around for whom all those names had meaning that I rattled off all sorts of indiscreet things. When Samia came to visit she was amazed at how much he knew about her. And he's so involved in our lives, because of those stories. I remember when I told him Akbar had died – I thought he was going to cry. And Mariam he used to be quite fascinated by. Who wouldn't be? Although he hasn't asked anything about her since the elopement. I think he thinks I'm embarrassed by it.' She shrugged. 'I'm not, you know. Just in case you were wondering.'

'He sounds like someone whose company you value.' I was holding myself in, almost unable to breathe, although I wouldn't have been able to articulate why exactly that was.

'Oh, yes. He has all sorts of tales about Dard-e-Dil himself. His parents kept in touch with their relatives there, and every so often he'll mention some lovely detail he found in his father's letters. And he and Apollo get on wonderfully. As do his wife and I. Now when he visits he

brings her along. Sometimes the children and the grandchildren, but I'm afraid they regard me as a foreign relic.'

'Do you cook vats of your *murgh mussalum* to give him a
taste of Dard-e-Dil?'

'As a matter of fact, yes. But the last time he came to see
me, just a few months ago, he brought over, oh my mouth
waters at the thought of it, *shami* kebabs that were posi-
tively Masoodian.'

'Impossible.'

'I'm not joking. He said they were from a new restaurant
in Istanbul that is driving everyone mad! Apollo tasted
them and suggested we move to Turkey.'

I was trying very hard not to clutch at straws and pull
them together as though they were jigsaw pieces which
would form a clear picture if I just got the edges right. I was
trying very hard.

'What's the name of the restaurant?'

Meher Dadi shrugged and stood up. 'Don't know. Suppose I could find out.'

'Please.'

She looked at me sharply. 'Why?'

'Please.' I thought my heart might explode.

'All right. If you insist.'

I handed her Dadi's mobile phone.

'Now? And on a mobile? That'll cost absurd amounts of
money.'

'Bonnets. Bees. What can one do? I'll reimburse Dadi.'

She checked her watch and calculated the time difference, took the phone and dialled. 'Apollo?' she said, and
reeled off strange syllables. For some reason I'd always
imagined they spoke English to each other.

Why is it that when people speak in a language you can't

222

understand they think all meaning is lost on you? If she'd been speaking in English she'd have lowered her voice, kept it steady, but in Greek she allowed all emotions to write themselves across her face and in her tone. That she missed him, that Dadi's fall had given her a fright, that she and Dadi had spent the evening reminiscing with tears and with laughter, that I had some strange notion in my head which required him to find out the name of a restaurant – all this I heard without understanding a word.

She said goodbye, repeated how much she missed him, and handed the phone to me.

'He'll make enquiries. But in return he wants you to promise to come and visit.'

'Definitely.'

She kissed me on the cheek and left me alone with Dadi. I tried not to think absurd thoughts. It didn't work. I enumerated all the reasons why I shouldn't pole-vault to the conclusion which suggested itself to me, but that entailed thinking about the conclusion, and my heart couldn't bear it. I walked around, hummed, tried to re-member as many songs from the eighties as possible, took out pencil and paper to help me work out which movie I knew more lines from: *The Wizard of Oz* or *Casablanca*. Oz won hands down, even after I excluded all the musical numbers.

And just as I was about to give up and allow myself to see that jigsaw picture, the door opened.

An old, slightly stooped man walked in. His hair was white, but thick; his face was a mass of wrinkles, though his jowls were only beginning to droop. His *sherwani* was exquisitely cut and, together with the silver-handled walk-ing stick in his hand, conferred on him an air of great dignity.

223

'Abida.' He hadn't even seen me.

Dadi, who had slept soundly through her sister's chatter, woke up with a start.

Her hand went to her mouth to stifle a scream.

'Akbar?'

The man shook his head.

'Taimur, Taimur. You're not dead, you're not.'

The man shook his head again and walked forward into the moonlight. 'I was always third on your list, Abbie.'

'Sulaiman . . .'

Chapter Twenty-Two

In Book VIII of *The Odyssey* a bard at the court of King Alcinous entertains the assembly with tales of the crafty Odysseus, hero of the Trojan war, beloved of the grey-eyed goddess, wanderer in search of a way home. Before the bard has finished his tale a stranger weeps and is asked to identify himself. He says, 'Behold Odysseus!'

Imagine how the bard must have felt to see before him that legendary figure whose name was more familiar on his tongue than the names of his own children. Imagine that, and you might begin to understand how I felt when I saw Sulaiman. I had always assumed that he was, like Taimur and Akbar, a man from another age, mythical, our lives not destined to overlap. His presence, just feet from me, had to be a trick or an apparition. How could he be alive when his brothers had been dead so long?

'Look at you.' His voice was strangely familiar; I had heard something like it many times when Aba imitated his own father's voice with all its velvety softness. He propped his cane against a chair and sat down on Dadi's bed. 'Look at you. I thought I never would.'

Dadi's hands trembled across his face. She touched a

white scar at the corner of his mouth. That was where Akbar had punched him so many years ago. She clenched her hands and sat back. 'Why now?'

'Because we're dying. We can't rely on tomorrows.'

Dadi patted her hair. 'You could have waited for one more tomorrow. I look quite good for my age, you know, when I have a little time to get dressed and put on some make-up.'

Sulaiman laughed. I liked his laugh; it hinted at a vast capacity for delight. 'The vanity of Abida. Still unchecked.'

'The same can't be said of the *Naz* of Abida.'

'No one has ever had more right to *Naz* than you.'

Dadi patted his hands. 'Where shall we begin? Not with apologies.'

'No, never with that. With an answer to your question. Why now? Because I was just in London, where my charming great-niece, Rehana, introduced me to my even more charming great-niece, Samia, and both of them then proceeded to give me an absolute earful for my stubbornness, called up a travel agent, and gave me your address. They had everything organized, from connections at the visa office to a car driven by Meher's grandson waiting for me at Karachi airport. Poor Mohommed nearly fainted when he saw me.'

Dadi waved her hands. 'Those details can wait. Tell me about you, Sulaiman. Tell me about, oh, everything. You have children? Grandchildren?'

Sulaiman touched her knee. 'Abida, did he hate me to the end?'

'So you know he died.'

'Yes. I heard about it just weeks after it happened. Someone who knew someone who knew someone in

226

Karachi told me. Tried to find Taimur after that, but nothing. Then I heard that his daughter was here and that Taimur, too, was dead.'

'Sulaiman, that someone in Karachi was me. I saw to it that you were notified. I was sure you would come. I was sure at the very least you would write.'

'I was sure *you* would write. Besides, it was nineteen seventy-one. There was a war on. And after that, as I said, you keep waiting for tomorrow. Did Akbar hate me to the end?'

'Your name, and Taimur's, were the last words on his lips.'

I think he knew she was lying. He looked at her as if to say that Akbar's last words couldn't possibly have been about anyone other than her.

'Abida, there's something I should have told you long ago. Something about Taimur.'

What he told her was this: when Abida and Meher's parents returned to Dard-e-Dil in 1938, after a year of living in Delhi, Akbar and Taimur and Sulaiman took one look at their childhood playmate, the erstwhile tomboy Abida, and did a triple take. The other girl-cousins had become women at the ages of fifteen or sixteen (in Baji's case, closer to fourteen), but Abida had bided her time, waiting for a moment when her transformation could be extraordinary. And it was. The wonder of it, Sulaiman said, was not that Taimur and Akbar had fallen in love with her, but that he hadn't. Perhaps, he said, he had, but he kept it buried because right from the start he saw that if she were to make a choice between the three of them she'd have no difficulty in reducing the list to two.

('You always had that edge of insecurity,' Dadi said,

when he mentioned that. 'You were the one who held yourself away, starting the day we got back from Delhi. I wasn't even sure you liked me any more.')

That Taimur was in love with Abida was easy for anyone to see. He turned cartwheels in the garden, sang *ghazals* of longing, offered to be twelfth man in cricket matches so that he could sit beside her among the spectators. But Akbar's love was a more brooding thing, though that may simply have been because, except on that day he hit Sulaiman and then hit him again, he could always foresee consequences.

Sulaiman came upon Akbar one day, slumped at the wheel of their father's Daimler, on the road between Dadi's house and the palace. Sulaiman dismounted his horse and got into the passenger seat.

'Rotten luck,' Akbar said. 'I suppose I should be happy for him.' He handed Sulaiman a piece of paper. 'Found this on the path. Abida's handwriting.'

She'd written Taimur's name all across the page, in Urdu.

'So that's that,' Akbar said. 'Oh, well. Better this way. No long drawn-out rivalry. Not as though this is a surprise. How could anyone choose anyone over that brother of ours?'

'Sorry,' was all Sulaiman could think of to say.

Akbar closed his eyes and leant back in the seat. 'Abida.'

Sulaiman got out, walked around to the driver's side, pushed his brother over to the passenger seat, and drove him home, the horse cantering after them.

The next day he saw Taimur, sitting on an old garden swing, looking forlorn.

'What?' Sulaiman said.

Taimur looked up. 'I overheard Meher talking to HH.'

'Oh, yes? Hard to imagine Meher and Binky having anything to say to each other. Were they discussing affairs of state?'

'Affairs of the heart. She thinks Akbar's so down today because he's in love. With Abida. Is he?'

Taimur's obliviousness to his brother's feelings shocked Sulaiman. 'What if he is?'

Taimur kicked the ground. 'If he is and I haven't seen it then maybe there are other things I haven't seen. Maybe she's in love with him.'

Sulaiman knew right then that the whole matter had to be straightened out as quickly as possible. 'She's not. She is in love, but not with Akbar. And Akbar knows it. She's in love with someone else. Wait here, I'll bring you written proof. In her own hand.' And off he went to find the paper which Akbar had crumpled up and tossed in the back of the car the day before.

It was Sulaiman's need for the dramatic gesture which did it. He couldn't just say, 'She loves you, Taimur.' He had to go and find the paper, had to give Taimur those moments of suspense, had to see Taimur's face when the suspense was over. But how can we blame Sulaiman for not anticipating what would happen next? Who could have? Taimur saw Sulaiman rush off, saw him run into Abida on his way to the car, saw her put an arm on Sulaiman's sleeve, and leapt to a conclusion: Abida had written Sulaiman a love letter.

'That's why he left,' Sulaiman told Dadi as the moon angled its rays on to her bed, creating the illusion that she and Sulaiman were still young and raven-haired, the moonlight alone responsible for the silvered quality of their manes. 'He was gone before I returned. He thought you loved me.'

'But, the other woman?' Dadi gasped.

'What other woman?'

'The one he took the ring for. The one who was the reason for that letter he wrote when he left. There had to be truth in the letter, there had to.'

'More truth than we cared to acknowledge. He wrote that because he was angry with Akbar and me. With me because he thought you loved me. With Akbar because Akbar loved you but seemed to have found a way to live without being loved by you, a thing Taimur knew he couldn't do. So he wrote in anger, but also in truth. There was truth to what he said about Akbar and me. And also – Abida, he was eighteen – he knew that letter was the one way of angering the whole family sufficiently to keep us from searching for him.'

'But Sulaiman, the ring.'

Sulaiman reached into his pocket. 'I went to London thinking I'd sell this.' I knew what was in that little velvet box even before he opened it. Dadi sighed, a woman past surprises now that this had happened. She touched the tip of a finger to the emerald. 'Explain this to me, Sulaiman.'

Taimur took the ring with him because he was eighteen and broken-hearted, and that combination often leads to a desire for symbolic gestures. He took the ring so that Sulaiman would never place it on Abida's finger. Sulaiman knew all this because Taimur had told him so.

'So he really did come back?' Dadi said. I had pressed myself against the wall by now, each muscle constricted into a mass of tension. Each muscle, especially the heart.

Sulaiman pressed her hand in apology and nodded. It was

just after Abida and Akbar were married. Sulaiman was in his mother's room, watching her sleep, trying not to notice how like a claw her hand had become, and Taimur opened the window and hopped in. Even in the dark Sulaiman knew it was him. He was taller and broader and the English suits he had favoured were replaced by a long *achkan* over *churidar* pyjamas, but his smile was still pure Taimur.

'It's your idiot brother, Sully,' he said. He said it in English.

Sulaiman held him and thought, Everything will be all right now.

'Can't let a girl get between us, can we?' Taimur said, when he finally pulled away.

Sulaiman had long ago guessed why Taimur had left; for a moment he hesitated, and then he told Taimur the truth. Taimur tried to shrug, opened his mouth, closed it again. 'She loved me?' he said at length. Sulaiman nodded. 'Does she still?'

'She married Akbar.'

'Oh,' Taimur said. 'I see.'

He went over to his sleeping mother and held her hand. A long time went by.

Summer had ended and the breeze was cool enough for some members of the family to sleep with their windows closed. Sulaiman was about to shut the window which Taimur had flung open, when he heard the window in the room next door creak open.

'Look at that moon, Akbar,' Abida exulted.

Taimur got up and walked over to the window. If he leant out, just a little, she would see him. He didn't lean out. He pushed the window closed and rested his head against the wall. 'God help me,' he said. 'I can't stay. I thought I could. But I can't.'

231

'Taimur?' It was their mother waking up.

He stayed by her side all night, telling her all the memories he had of her from his childhood. She seemed to derive greater comfort from that than from any of the medicines, or prayers, or tales of miracle cures with which she'd been regaled in the preceding months. But he barely looked at his brother, and Sulaiman knew that as Taimur sat there his rage was mounting against his brother for allowing him to misinterpret his words so completely. At one point Sulaiman tried to leave, but Taimur was up and barring his way to the door before he was halfway across the room. 'If you leave to call Akbar I'll be gone before you knock on his door.'

But in the early morning, when their mother finally fell asleep, Taimur turned to Sulaiman with an expression of sorrow. 'It's no one's fault,' he said. 'And Akbar's a far finer chap than I. Don't tell him I was here; it'll break his heart. And never a word to Abida about any of this.'

'Where will you go? Where have you been?'

'Far away. It doesn't matter. I'm well, that's all you need to know. Goodbye, Sully.'

Sulaiman would have done anything to make Taimur stay, so he tried the most unforgivable thing he could think of. 'She might still love you,' he said.

Taimur smiled. 'Yes, I think she might. Maybe I'd stay if we weren't not-quites; maybe if we hadn't grown up believing ourselves capable of bringing about something terrible. Maybe. But, then again, maybe not. Because I, and you, and she, we all love Akbar. Here.' He pressed a velvet box into Sulaiman's hands. 'I have no right to this. One day you might even know what to do with it. I certainly don't. Tell Mama I love her.'

'You already did that.'

Smiling, Taimur left.

When Sulaiman finished talking I was close to tears, but Dadi did something entirely unexpected. She laughed.

'Sulaiman, that's sheer melodrama. My life! Such passion, such tragic miscommunication, such revelations in the aftermath of the main action. It's too absurd.' She took the ring from Sulaiman and weighed it in her hand. 'It would have broken my finger.'

'No regrets?'

'To be loved by two such brothers. That's a rare gift. You've given me back my *Naz*.'

'Make that three such brothers,' Sulaiman said, and kissed her hand. 'Just to increase the melodrama.'

Dadi laughed again, and then she turned to me. 'Aliya, did the thought that flashed through my mind flash through yours?'

'Which thought is that?' I felt strangely shy in the presence of my great-uncle, who had only just seen me.

'Mariam's mother might well have been high-born.'

'No, Dadi. I didn't think that at all.'

'Good. That's a start.'

Sulaiman stood up. 'I wonder who she was. The wife. Whoever she was, she was much later. Samia told me Taimur's daughter – Mariam – is much younger than your children and mine. He must have waited a long time before he was ready to love someone else.'

'Or maybe he and his wife were so happy together, just the two of them, that it was many years before they felt they could allow anyone else into their lives. Why not that, Sulaiman? Let's love Taimur enough to believe that. Aliya, look!'

I turned to look out of the window, but the thudding sound against the glass had already told me what she was staring at.

'Take me to the balcony, Sully.' He lifted her up in his arms, that man nearing eighty, and I opened the glass door to let them out. The sound of the rain beating down was almost deafening, but though I couldn't hear I could see her telling him to put her down.

Sulaiman slid the door between us closed so that the rain wouldn't whip into the room, and then it really was as though they were two characters in a movie and I was watching them with the sound turned off. What an evening, what an evening! Taimur left because he loved Abida, and stayed away because he loved Akbar. He went to Turkey. Yes, he did. He went to Turkey and looked up his uncle's Turkish friend – the Dard-e-Dil uncle who went to Turkey talked often of his Turkish friends. Through these friends he found employment, occupation. Perhaps he taught Urdu somewhere. Or English. Or Persian. Then he met the mechanic from Dard-e-Dil, and together they talked of their ancestral home. One day the mechanic told him that Meher was in Greece, and Taimur knew at last he had found a way to receive word of all the Dard-e-Dils without any of them receiving word of him. And how did Mariam and Masood's story fit into this? And how did mine?

I looked out on to the balcony again. She'd waited almost sixty years for this story, Dadi had. How different would her life have been if she had heard it earlier? These stories, this salt . . . How could we ever exert ourselves to the simplest physical action when all our lives were so dependent on this seemingly passive act of listening?

I stepped out on to the balcony. Dadi raised her hands to the skies, her nightgown clinging to her frame, and inhaled the heady scent of parched mud gulping water. As I watched her I knew that the monsoon rains would wash away streets, blow down electricity wires, create stagnant pools of water prime for mosquito orgies, but for those few minutes there seemed no price too high for the sight of rainwater eddying bougainvillea flowers around Abida's bare feet.

'Sulaiman!' she cried out above the noise. 'I'm so glad I've had my life.'

Chapter Twenty-Three

Of course I was happy that Sulaiman was in Karachi. To watch him with Dadi and Meher was like watching a dance in which a group of three would become two against one, and then three again, and then a different two against one, but always back to three again. Sulaiman and Abida teased Meher about being the youngest, the one who always wanted to act older than her age ('What on earth were you doing talking to Binky about Akbar's broken heart?' Dadi said, but she laughed as she said it); Sulaiman and Meher teased Abida about her regal airs ('Remember when Abida got stuck up that tree with the cradling branches, and instead of admitting she was stuck she said, "I am not in the habit of descending." How old were you, Abbie? Eight?'); and Meher and Abida teased Sulaiman about the folly of men ('Well, of course that ended in divorce. You only married her because she did that thing with her lips, Sulaiman. That sensuous, snarling thing. Remember when Ama, with an air of pious innocence, asked her whether her mouth had those muscle spasms often?').

How could I not be happy?

But every day that he was there I'd hear some mention of

Taimur and remember: I had understood Taimur's story, but I was no closer to understanding Mariam's. Perhaps all the explanations I had thought of were true. Perhaps none of them were. But if I were to retell her story, with what would I fill the gaps between all I knew and all there was to know?

That may have been what I was thinking about that July evening when I lay in my garden, mosquito coils around me, watching a candle flame bobbing past the windows of the house as Ami searched frantically for something – Ami always seemed to feel the need to search frantically for something when we were swallowed up by the darkness brought on by a power failure.

'I've brought you a surprise,' Sameer said, turning the corner of the garden and coming into view. 'I think I should start a limo service between the airport and town.' So saying, he disappeared into Mariam's old room through the French doors and promptly tripped over something. I heard the thud as he fell. Ami came running. 'Oh good, you've found the box. But why are you lying down, Sammy?'

In that moment a bunch of thin, green, stringlike things came flying towards me and fell, several feet from where I lay. I rolled over to them.

Stems.

'Khaleel?'

He stepped forward into the garden. 'If the mountain won't go to Liaquatabad,' he said, and squatted beside me.

I turned on to my side to look at him and he lowered his knees to the ground. 'Hey,' he said, and I wanted to cup my hand against his larynx and feel the muscles move beneath my palm as he spoke.

'Hey yourself.' There was a tiny cut at the base of his

237

index finger, giving me all the excuse I needed to touch. You know what it felt like, the touch. Don't you? At the very least you've imagined it.

'I have something for you in Sameer's car.' I wanted to tell him it could wait, whatever it was. But he was gone already.

I touched the grass on which he'd been sitting. He was here. He was actually here and there was no doubt in my mind now . . . no, not my mind . . . there was no doubt now in any part of me that he could break my heart. What a blessing. All the active-passive listening I'd ever done in my life had brought me to this moment, to this darkness in which I awaited light, knowing it was time for me to don my costume, make my entrance and speak the words. Which words I didn't yet know, but they were, they would become, part of someone else's story, one generation, or two, or three down the line.

The lights flared back on and I went inside. Sameer was in my parents' room, the door ajar.

'But do we know anything about him? What's his family?'

Sameer ignored Aba's second question. 'We know Samia likes him. And Rehana Apa, whose opinion you'd trust completely if you knew her. He's been to Baji's for tea. She invited him to return. What more do you need to know?'

I entered the room. 'He's staying with his family in Liaquatabad.'

Aba's eyes rose sharply at this, and even Ami looked unhappy.

'And he's brought over dinner, so you can't say I have to whisk him away before we've eaten,' Sameer added.

'Dinner? Why? Does he think we're not capable of feeding our guests?'

238

'Nasser, now stop being annoying. It's a thoughtful gesture, although, of course, he could just be trying to get into our good books. I didn't really mean that, Aliya. Where is he?'

'Gone to get something from the car.'

'Probably the food,' Sameer said. 'I'll help him. Can I just microwave it and tell Wasim we're eating right away? I'm starving.'

Sameer was so good with exits.

'This is the boy from the plane, is it?' Ami asked.

'What boy from the plane?' Aba looked wounded.

'Girltalk, Nasser. You didn't mention the Liaquatabad part, Aliya. Why not?'

'Why do you think?' I blew out the candle which was flickering, forgotten, in the blaze of the lamplight around the room. We had reached an impasse.

Or perhaps not. 'You know you're in Karachi now.' That was Aba, of course. It had taken him several seconds to think up this line. 'There are certain rules you have to live by. Just as a mark of respect to others.'

I knew that. I knew that I had never admired people who claimed to be non-conformist but were really just self-absorbed. I knew that it was all I could do at that moment to stay in my parents' company with Khaleel at a short sprint's distance.

'I hope he hasn't brought burgers for dinner.' Ami didn't meet my eye as she said this.

'Food's on,' Sameer said, poking his head in. 'And this is Khaleel.' Khaleel shook hands with my father, nodded at Ami, smiled. I could see them thinking it was clear that I'd fallen for his good looks alone.

'Are you having power failures in Liaquatabad, too?'

'I don't know, sir. I came straight from the air—' He bit off the last syllable and looked at me to see if he'd committed a faux pas.

Why hadn't Sameer just picked me up and driven us to a restaurant?

'That smell,' Ami said.

Now what? Don't tell me he wasn't using deodorant.

'Good God!' Aba said.

I stepped out into the dining area, and then it hit me, too. A smell that was not so much a smell as a miracle. Different strands of smells coming together like an orchestral symphony. Aba moved to one side, and my eyes helped my nose to pick up each nuance of detail. There on the table: *biryani, timatar cut, bihari kebabs, aloo panjabi, raita*. But these names don't tell you enough. They need a prefix: Masoodian.

I grabbed on to Khaleel's arm.

'Quite a journey your cousins sent me on. Said they'd arrange my ticket, and next thing I knew I was travelling via Istanbul. Some guy met me at the airport – said he knew your great-aunt – and handed me this package of food. If Sameer hadn't come to the airport in Karachi, with a list of his connections poised to leap off his tongue in a swallow dive, those customs guys would have confiscated the package for sure. You could see their mouths watering at the thought of it.'

'Do you know . . .' I could barely form the words. 'Where it came from?'

'A restaurant. Your great-aunt's friend translated the name for me. The Garrulous Gourmet.'

Somehow we made it to the table, and sat down. What can I say about the food? That nothing had ever tasted better. That words reveal their inadequacy every time I try to describe it. That sometimes it seemed we were all eating faster than was possible and other times so slowly it defied all the laws of motion. That the grains of rice in the *biryani* were swollen but separate; that the saffron had been sprinkled with a hand that knew the thin line between stinting and showing-off; that the chicken was so succulent you had to cry out loud. I could tell you about the *aloo panjabi* with its potatoes that reminded us why a nation could live on potatoes and die without them; I could mention its spices, so perfectly balanced you could almost see the mustard seed leaning on the fenugreek, the cumin poised on the dried chillies. If that's not enough let me try to evoke the *bihari kebabs*, the meat so tender it defied all attempts to make it linger in our mouths, and yet it lingered on our tastebuds before graciously making way for all the other tastes worthy of attention. And, while I can still think of it without falling to my knees in thanks, allow me to mention the *timatar cut*, which takes the familiar tomato and transports it into a world inhabited by ginger, garlic, chillies, green and red, *karri pattas*, and the sourness of tamarind. To eat that meal was to eat centuries of artistry, refined in kitchens across the subcontinent. The flavours we tasted were not just the flavours in the food, but also the flavours the food reminded us of and the flavours the food remembered.

But saying all of this is not enough. When I tasted that food I saw Mariam in a kitchen, a vast glorious kitchen, brushing saffron off her husband's neck and dusting it on to her own lips. I saw Mariam listing names of vegetables – *mooli, loki, bhindi, shaljam, gajjar, mattar, phool gobi* – as though the list were a *ghazal*, while Masood kneaded

241

mangos to pulp in a bowl which suddenly had four hands, not two, intertwining and pressing. When I tasted that food I saw Mariam older and happy.

Khaleel said something to make Aba laugh and I saw Ami lean forward to Khaleel and speak, speak without stopping until she had to stop because Aba threatened to eat the last piece of chicken on her plate since she didn't seem interested in it. Khaleel looked at me and I wanted everyone else to disappear. But in some sense they had disappeared while he was looking at me in that way he had of looking at me.

When the meal was finally over – the plates not licked clean, not entirely, because that would have meant that the cook miscalculated quantities, but nearly so, so very nearly so – Khaleel picked up the last grain of rice on his plate and, with everyone else distracted by satiation, he placed the wonder of it all on my tongue.

'I'm stopping in Istanbul again on my way back to America,' he said softly. 'Right before the semester begins. You're flying out around that time, too, aren't you?'

Ami turned to ask him something and I was left thinking of all that his question implied. Was it merely coincidence, the timing of all that had happened? Or would I never have asked the questions I asked if I hadn't met Khaleel? How can we ever know why one thing happens and not another? Perhaps, I thought, watching the curve of his neck as he laughed, perhaps when we tell our stories our stories tell on us; they reveal what is and what is not explicable in our lives. In all those years Mariam lived with us I never asked that she be explained to me. That she was who she was was enough. The answers I'd been searching for so desperately since then all stemmed back to one question. The question of why she loved Masood. I had reasons now, I had explanations for every thing she'd ever not said, for everything she'd done. Her mother's social status; a desire to subvert hierarchies; a search for answers about why Taimur left; her final conversation with the man whom she had never considered loving (who might even have been Meher Dadi's friend from Turkey, or his son). All these were answers and together they might even form a whole. Some of them might even be more than conjecture. But none of this tells me why she loved Masood. Khaleel rested a hand on the back on my chair, his palm pressing against the small of my back in the spaces formed by the latticed design of the wood. No, none of this answered the unanswerable question.

The real question, the one that only I could answer, was this: Was I willing to take that first step? To take Khaleel with me into a room full of relatives and say, 'Mariam and I are not-quite-twins. This man, I don't know what will happen between us, but I think he's worth the risk of heartbreak. He's worth it not because of Masood, not because of Taimur, not because of Taj or Dadi or anyone, but because. Just because. Why do you call us not-quite-twins as though we are something incomplete? More than twins, say that. Or better still, say fallible, like you; capable of error, like you; given to passion, like you.' This was a speech that I'd prepared, rehearsed in front of the mirror. Could I ever make it when even the best of the Dard-e-Dils, even my parents, had quailed when he walked in?

My mother said something I didn't catch and Khaleel replied, 'When our hearts live, we are more than ourselves.'

I stood up and walked over to the window. My parents took this as some sort of signal. They told Khaleel there was no need to clear the table, Wasim would do that, then said goodbye and retreated to their room. Sameer had disappeared somewhere. Wasim took a stack of plates and vanished into the kitchen. There was such an air of familiarity about the silence in the room. I looked out at Mariam's hibiscus branch. The glass between it and me was both a window and a mirror. I reached out to run my fingers through the air, parallel to the branch. Khaleel bent down to pick up a plate. My fingers traced the curve of his spine.

A NOTE ON THE AUTHOR

KAMILA SHAMSIE was born in 1973 in Pakistan. Her first
novel, *In the City by the Sea*, was published in 1998 and
shortlisted for the John Llewelyn Rhys/*Mail on Sunday*
Prize. In 1999 Kamila also received the Prime Minister's Award
for Literature in Pakistan. She lives in London and Karachi
and is completing her third novel.